AN AFFAIR TO REMEMBER

AN AFFAIR TO REMEMBER

the GREATEST LOVE STORIES *of all time*

MEGAN GRESSOR & KERRY COOK

FAIR WINDS
PRESS
GLOUCESTER, MASSACHUSETTS

For Sophie and Dad

Acknowledgements

Thanks are due to the following for permission to reproduce photographs in this book:
Getty Images: pages 28, 29, 65, 70, 71, 77, 90, 104, 105, 117, 136, 137, 151, 168, 190, 206, 207, 213, 265.
National Archives of Australia: page 179.
National Library of Australia: page 42.
TRANZ International Image Library: pages 12, 22, 23, 34, 35, 46, 54, 64, 82, 91, 96, 110, 111, 116, 124, 125, 130, 131, 143, 157, 160, 161, 182, 199, 217, 224, 230, 236, 244, 251, 255, 268, 278, 285, 288, 294.
photolibrary.com: cover rose image

Text © Megan Gressor and Kerry Cook 2004
Megan Gressor and Kerry Cook assert the moral right to be identified as the authors of this work.

First published in New Zealand in 2004 by Exisle Publishing

First published in the USA in 2005 by
Fair Winds Press
33 Commercial Street
Gloucester, MA 01930

08 07 06 05 04   1 2 3 4 5

ISBN 1-59233-128-9

Library of Congress Cataloging-in-Publication Data available

Text design and production by BookNZ
Cover design by Vivien Valk, 1bluedog design
Printed and bound in China through ColorCraft Ltd, Hong Kong

CONTENTS

INTRODUCTION

If all the world loves a lover, as the saying goes, then it loves a love story even more. Boy-meets-girl is one of humanity's favourite and enduring narratives, from the tales of courtly love that beguiled medieval nobility to the modern-day preoccupation with the affairs of the rich and famous.

Generations have thrilled to the tale of Romeo and Juliet, Abelard and Héloise, Scarlett and Rhett. It seems that we just can't get enough romance – especially romances that involve drama, conflict, heroism and sacrifice as well as undying love. And when the affair in question is real, not fictional, it's all the more powerful.

So what's the appeal? Well, there is the biological imperative; or, in the words of 'As time goes by', the theme to the greatest cinematic romance of all, *Casablanca*: 'Woman needs man/And man must have his mate/That no one can deny.' We are hotwired to seek that special someone with whom to share life's great adventure. But there's more to it than just hormones.

The notion that it's worth taking a chance on love – to stake everything on the cards coming up hearts – appeals to the gambler within us; all the more so as modern life grows ever more predictable and humdrum. There's something intoxicating about the idea of being swept away by a grand passion that brooks no denial; to risk losing all for the man or woman of your dreams. For one and one do not make two, as G.K. Chesterton once wrote: they make two thousand times two; two *million* times two.

While it's still the same old story, every love affair has its unique dynamic, which is what makes them so endlessly fascinating. *An Affair to Remember* is a compilation of 43 of the most memorable romances of all time.

Included in it are grand affairs of history — epic tales such as the passion of England's naval hero Lord Nelson for Emma Hamilton; the doomed Mary, Queen of Scots, for the scheming Lord Bothwell; or the Sun King Louis XIV for Madame de Montespan, that seductress whose dabbling in the black arts plunged France's *ancien régime* into turmoil.

When the lovers are of royal descent, it only magnifies the story's glamour. Here are several right royal romances, from Charles II's adoration of the enchanting orange seller Nell Gwynn, to the infatuation of Ludwig of Bavaria for the adventuress Lola Montez, to Edward VIII's passion for the American divorcée Wallis Simpson, for whom he sacrificed his crown.

If power is the ultimate aphrodisiac, as Henry Kissinger once said (well, he would, wouldn't he?), then political unions must be among the most erotic of the lot. Certainly the affairs of notables such as Irish nationalist hero Charles Stewart Parnell and Kitty O'Shea, the married woman for whom he imperilled his career; Britain's wartime Prime Minister Winston Churchill and his darling Clementine, who inspired him during the darkest days of the Blitz; and former Russian political prisoner Anatoly Shcharansky and his bride Avital, who fought tirelessly for his freedom, have a particular resonance ... perhaps because the partners were embroiled in affairs of state as well as the heart.

And if music is the food of love, then affairs of the arts must be among the most lyrical of all, perhaps because artists have a heightened appreciation of beauty. The love of writer George Sand for composer Frédéric Chopin, the obsession of singer Elvis Presley for his dream teen queen Priscilla Beaulieu and the infatuation of Beatle John Lennon for artist Yoko Ono make for especially sensual reading.

There is something utterly irresistible about the love lives of celebrities – especially film stars whose private lives often eclipse anything portrayed on screen. Think of Bogart and Bacall, Gable and Lombard, Tracy and Hepburn. These are just some of the couples whose sexual chemistry was obvious on and off screen. And if such stars have lost as well as loved – Ingrid Bergman, for instance, whose illicit passion for Italian director Roberto Rossellini effectively ended her career – then it only makes their liaisons the more alluring.

You'll find all these love stories and more in this book. Some took place centuries ago, others are as contemporary as the union of soccer legend David Beckham and his bride Victoria, aka Posh Spice. Some ended in heartbreak, others in happy-ever-after. Some were charming, others controversial. Some flamed as brightly, and briefly, as candles. Others endured for a lifetime. But each of them was an affair to remember.

Megan Gressor
Kerry Cook

HISTORIC
LOVERS

MARIE ANTOINETTE AND COUNT AXEL FERSON

October 16 1793: The wheels of the mud-spattered wooden tumbrel creaked as it slowly pressed forward through the crowds lining the narrow streets of Paris. Ragged citizens sporting tricolour cockades screamed insults and flung rotting vegetables at the tumbrel's occupant, a haggard woman with her arms bound behind her and a simple white cap covering her cropped grey hair. A howl of hatred burst from a thousand throats as the tumbrel drew up to the scaffold on which stood the guillotine, the French Revolution's most feared instrument of execution.

On a balcony overlooking the hellish scene, artist Jacques Louis David caught his breath, snatched up a stick of charcoal and began feverishly sketching on a scrap of paper. Nothing he had produced as a former court painter and official artist of the French Revolution surpassed the pathos and vitality of the rough drawing he quickly finished as the guillotine's blade flashed down, striking off the prisoner's head.

Marie Antoinette, a loving wife whose one great affair ended in tragedy.

In his notes David entitled his sketch of the woman on her way to execution 'The Widow Capet'. But she was better known, both then and now, as Marie Antoinette, last queen of France.

History has been unkind to Marie Antoinette. 'Let them eat cake,' she is supposed to have retorted when told her starving subjects had no bread. But it was actually an earlier French queen, Maria Theresa, consort of the Sun King Louis XIV, who made this inflammatory remark, before Marie Antoinette was even born.

She was said to have been vain, extravagant, frivolous and so promiscuous that her legions of lovers even included her own son, the young dauphin. The truth was that Marie Antoinette, the child bride of the impotent boy king Louis XVI, had but a single extramarital affair, with the handsome Swedish diplomat Count Axel Ferson, the love of her life. This romance was to be her undoing, ending in her losing not only her crown but also her head.

Marie Antoinette's tragedy was that she was born at the wrong time into the wrong social position, and married the wrong man. Loving, loyal and kind-hearted, she would have made an excellent bourgeois wife and mother. But she became enmeshed in the court intrigues and national unrest leading up to the French Revolution, and paid for it with her heart and her life. She may not have lived like a queen but she died like one, facing the guillotine with extraordinary grace and style; as was said of another beheaded monarch, nothing in her life became her so much as the leaving of it.

Antoinette (she was never called by her first name during her lifetime) was a political pawn from the day she was born, 2 November 1755. She was the ninth of the Austrian Empress Maria Theresa's sixteen children. Desperate to secure her beleaguered country's borders at any cost, the iron-willed empress married her brood off to any of the royal families of Europe who were likely to aid Austria in its long-running war of nerves with its predatory neighbour, Prussia. She had always earmarked Antoinette to be the bride of the young dauphin of France but, preoccupied with state affairs, didn't realise that the girl was growing up wild.

Antoinette could scarcely read and write by her thirteenth birthday, and spoke no French at all. But that was no barrier to the marriage preparations: at the age of fourteen, the pretty young hoyden was bundled off to France to marry a boy she had not even met. She was never to see her mother or her native land again. On a sandbank in the middle of the Rhine River that bordered the two countries, Antoinette was unceremoniously stripped of her Austrian clothes and dressed in French finery symbolising her new nationality. She couldn't hold back the tears as every childhood trinket and keepsake was taken from her forever.

But the dismay she felt then was nothing to her consternation when she met her husband-to-be. Gangling, intensely shy and physically awkward, young Louis was, like his bride, born in the wrong time and place. Well-intentioned but dull, he was bored by politics, preferring to tinker away at the forge of his own specially outfitted blacksmith's shop.

Due to a minor physical abnormality, Louis was unable to consummate the marriage. His diary entry for their wedding night reads simply '*Rien*' (nothing). And nothing continued to happen every night for the next seven years of their life together. Overcome with embarrassment, poor Louis could not bring himself to explain his problem to the bewildered Antoinette. But in his own way he sincerely loved her, for with her fresh complexion, sparkling eyes and exquisite figure (the design of the classic champagne glass is said to have been inspired by the shape of her breasts) she was not hard to love.

And despite her frustration, Antoinette became very fond of the bumbling, inept Louis, for he was a decent, conscientious fellow who worried a great deal about the injustices of the medieval system of government he inherited when his grandfather Louis XV succumbed to smallpox in May 1774.

When Louis and Antoinette learned they were now the rulers of France, though still only in their teens, they collapsed, crying: 'God help and protect us, for we are too young to rule!' They were too young, but God failed to protect them from their naivety and inexperience.

The new king attempted cautious reforms of the unwieldy *ancien régime*, but was hampered at every turn by entrenched class privilege, obstructive parliaments and bloody-minded provincial jurisdictions. Added to this was the international intrigue with which Antoinette in particular had to contend. Her every action was spied upon, her letters tampered with, her correspondence with her mother, the Empress, coming under special scrutiny. She was never allowed to forget she was a foreigner, and as France descended into a morass of financial mismanagement she found herself a universal scapegoat.

Antoinette's stocks rose temporarily when she gave birth to a daughter, Madame Royale, in 1778, then later to other children. Louis had finally been talked into an operation to correct his impotence by his brother-in-law, now the Emperor Joseph II of Austria, and he was overjoyed at being a father at last. But because his problem had been an open secret for so long, rumours soon spread that the children were not his – but had been fathered by Count Axel Ferson.

This Swedish nobleman had fallen in love with Antoinette at their first meeting at a costume ball, when she was still a newlywed. The blond, blue-eyed Ferson, who was then touring the continent to complete his education, wrote in his diary, 'The Dauphine is the most charming princess I have ever seen.' He didn't see her again for three years, while he continued his travels and learned the soldier's trade. On his return to France he set tongues wagging with his devoted attention to the young queen.

They were seen everywhere together, riding, playing tennis, dancing, chatting.

Poor Louis, aware of his shortcomings as a husband, turned a blind eye to the love that was blossoming between Antoinette and the dashing young Swede. Others were less forbearing, however, and Ferson realised the scandal was threatening to engulf Antoinette. He chivalrously removed himself from the scene by joining General LaFayette's expeditionary force assisting the American colonists in their fight for independence from Britain. The Swedish ambassador to the French court noted approvingly that 'by absenting himself [Ferson] will avoid danger of all kinds, but it evidently required firmness beyond his years to resist such attraction.

'During the last days of his stay the queen could not take her eyes off him, and as she looked they were filled with tears ...'

This time Ferson was away for five years. Relinquishing Antoinette nearly broke his heart, for as he wrote to his sister, 'I cannot belong to the woman to whom I should like to belong, so I will not belong to anyone.' Finally he could bear his exile no longer. He returned to Antoinette's side, to protect her from the dangers that were now openly threatening to destroy her. He was at her side when a revolutionary mob, fresh from having stormed the Bastille, besieged the Palace of Versailles to demand that the royal family return as virtual prisoners to the ancient royal palace, the Tuileries, in Paris.

In the long, anxious months that followed, Ferson found ways of slipping in and out of the Tuileries to support and console Antoinette. Foolishly, he acted as intermediary in her desperate pleas to foreign governments to intervene on the royal family's behalf. Any hint of outside interference only inflamed the mob's rage, but Ferson was reckless in his campaign to free his beloved queen. He masterminded the royal family's intended escape to Montmédy, in France's east, where troops still loyal to the crown were stationed. They fled in disguise, with Ferson posing as the family's coachman, but got no further than Varennes, where a suspicious official recognised Louis from his portrait on a bank note. He and Antoinette were hustled back to the Tuileries, while Ferson was banished to Brussels, where the queen later wrote to him, urging him to forget about her: 'Do not write to me; it would endanger you, and above all do not come back here under any pretext. We are closely watched day and night … Adieu … I shall no longer be able to write to you.'

But Ferson refused to give up, bombarding Antoinette with love letters written in invisible ink. But the more he tried to help, the worse matters became. It was Ferson who, from Brussels, persuaded foreign military authorities to issue a proclamation threatening Paris with fire and sword if Antoinette and her family were harmed. This meddling roused the revolutionaries to such fury that they stormed the Tuileries, massacring the Swiss guards and several members of the royal entourage, and dragging Antoinette, Louis and the children off to a dismal, ancient fortress called the Temple. There they were separated, Antoinette being closely confined in a damp narrow cell, under constant surveillance. Yet somehow, even then, she managed to smuggle letters to Ferson, imploring him to forget her for the sake of his own safety. He gallantly refused, treasuring a curious ring she enclosed with one of her letters as a token of her love. Ferson wore this ring, which was set with an unidentifiable stone, on the third finger of his left hand for the rest of his life.

But despite – or perhaps because of – Axel's efforts on her behalf, matters went from bad to worse for Antoinette. Louis, deposed from his throne, was now known only as 'Citizen Capet', an old family name. But the mob still wasn't satisfied, and on 21 January 1793 he was sent to the guillotine for treason.

Antoinette was then moved to an even grimmer prison, the dreaded Conciergeries. She spent nine months there, always sleeping fully dressed in widow's weeds, every moment expecting to be summoned to the guillotine herself. She had not long to wait. In October that year it was Antoinette's turn to mount the scaffold.

No trace remained of the fresh-faced Austrian girl who had come to France over twenty years earlier. The horrors of the past months had turned her hair grey, and she was pale and drawn. Yet she was scarcely 38 years old.

When Ferson received word of her death, he poured out his agony in a letter to his sister, writing bitterly:

> *She for whom I lived, since I have never ceased to love her; she for whom I would have sacrificed everything; she whom I loved so dearly and for whom I would have given my life a thousand times – is no more. I do not know how to go on living. My dear, how I long to have died at her side, and for her …*

Ferson may not have been able to die with Antoinette, but he died like her, at the hands of a revolutionary mob in Stockholm some seventeen years later. Sweden was then in the grip of a political crisis, a distant echo of the French Revolution, and Ferson, now Grand Marshal of the Swedish Army, was an obvious target for the discontented. He was set upon and dragged from his gilded coach, in which he had been riding in an official procession. He fought desperately for his life, laying about him with his sword, but soon fell under a hail of cobblestones.

He was stripped of his military regalia and decorations, and the story goes that the finger on which he wore the queen's ring was cut off and thrown into a river. The man responsible was said to have suffered such remorse that he dragged the river until he found the ring, later placing it in Ferson's coffin. But it was considered bad luck to bury it, and so it was given to his family. It remains with them to this day, a reminder of the forbidden love that flowered between a doomed queen and her unhappy, devoted courtier.

NAPOLEON AND JOSEPHINE

She was born a Creole on the Caribbean island of Martinique and christened Marie-Rose-Josèphe Tascher de la Pagerie, but the world remembers her as the Empress Josephine. She travelled to France to marry the Vicomte Alexandre de Beauharnais in 1779, the same year that a ten-year-old boy sailed from Corsica to France to attend the French Military Academy at Brienne. His name was Napoleon Bonaparte. One day the fate of all Europe would depend upon the love of Napoleon for his Josephine.

Josephine's marriage to Beauharnais was not happy, and it ended when he went to the guillotine in 1794, a victim of the French Revolution's hatred of aristocrats. Josephine survived only by her talent for attaching herself to powerful men: first General Hoche and later Paul François Baras, one of the leaders of the Revolution. Charming, voluptuous and seductive, she was a woman no man could resist for long.

She met Napoleon in 1795 when he was called to Paris to help defend the Republican Government from attack by Royalist national guards. Within 24 hours the intense young artillery officer had routed the Royalists, and was immediately hailed as the saviour of the revolution. Plenty of pretty Parisiennes were ready to prove their gratitude to the young Corsican hero but he was a shy fellow, as timid in love as he was brave in battle – until he met Josephine Beauharnais.

Napoleon was only 26 then, but he already knew his destiny: to rule a united Europe. He had no time to waste, not even on lovemaking. He dashed off passionate love letters to Josephine between battles, and snatched moments from military conferences to rush to her apartment to embrace her in front of her startled friends. Obsessed with his dreams of greatness, he could never relax – he continually paced up and down, he had a nervous tic, he suffered from sudden violent rages and terrible indigestion. His only release from tension was when he was with Josephine. With her bewitching dark eyes, her mature beauty and her Creole languor, she was the perfect foil for his restlessness. Explaining her appeal later to a friend, he said, 'She had that certain something that was irresistible. She was a woman to her very finger tips.'

And by now he didn't wish to resist her – he was determined that she should share his destiny. Late one night in March 1796, on the eve of his departure to take over the command of the French Army fighting the Austrians in Italy, Napoleon dragged Josephine into a mayoral office and virtually forced the sleepy mayor to marry them. Josephine was six years older than Napoleon, but he gallantly added two years to his age and subtracted four from hers on the marriage certificate so that officially, at any rate, they were the same age.

Napoleon's passion for Josephine exceeded his passion for France.

Their marriage got off to a bad start. On their wedding night, Josephine's pet dog Fortune refused to vacate his usual sleeping place on her bed. Napoleon insisted and the jealous dog bit him on the ankle, leaving lasting scars. But Napoleon survived, and within 48 hours of their marriage he left for Italy. He bombarded Josephine with love letters, often two or three a day, begging her to join him on the campaign, telling her of his devotion to her.

Not one day has passed that I have not loved you, not one night that I have not clasped you in my arms. I curse the call of glory and ambition which has wrenched me from you who are my life, my soul. In the midst of military affairs, at the head of my troops, in my inspections of the camps, my adored Josephine holds undisputed sway over my heart, possesses my mind, engrosses my thoughts ...

The French have a saying about affairs of the heart: that there is one who loves, and one who allows himself to be loved, in every relationship. This expression might have been coined for Napoleon and Josephine. From the moment he met her he was obsessed by her, while Josephine, her passion slower to surface, merely tolerated his devotion. It wasn't really until he had crowned her Empress of France that she realised what an extraordinary man she had married, and then her love for him matched his for her.

Josephine de Beauharnais. Napoleon divorced her but their love endured to the end.

But for now she did not wish to join him in Italy, wanting to stay in Paris to entertain her lover, Hyppolyte Charles, a young Adjutant-General in the army. Somehow Napoleon sensed she was being unfaithful to him, and it gnawed at his heart. 'You have lovers of whom the whole world may know – and for all that, I will only love you ten times more!' he wrote sadly. 'Is this not madness, fever, delirium?'

But if his marriage was not going as smoothly as he could have wished, his career was right on course. After his army had defeated the Austrians in Italy, honours were heaped upon him. He was created Commander-in-Chief of the Army in the Orient, appointed First Consul of the Republic for life, made Emperor of France. His troops had subjugated Europe, and his dream of complete power was fast becoming reality.

But with the cruel irony of history, the higher Napoleon rose, the more precarious became Josephine's position. Napoleon had his empire; now he wanted a dynasty to rule it forever. But Josephine could not oblige. Month after month, year after year, she failed to conceive. In vain she protested that she had had two children by her first husband; now it seemed that she had become barren and Napoleon's spiteful relatives, who detested Josephine, urged him to get rid of her and find someone who could bear him a son. After much heart-searching, Napoleon regretfully decided that he must divorce Josephine for 'reasons of state'. He had to have an heir.

This decision was a bitter blow to Josephine, but she of all people understood that the ravening ambition that drove Napoleon could not be denied. She behaved superbly at the official announcement of the Imperial divorce. 'Devoid now of all hope of bearing children who could satisfy the requirement of his dynastic interests and the welfare of France, I proudly offer him the greatest proof of attachment and devotion ever given a husband on this earth,' she told the assembled court. And that proof was to release him to marry another woman who could give him an heir.

Three months after the divorce, Napoleon married the 18-year-old Austrian Archduchess Marie-Louise, who presented him with a son within the year. At last he had a successor, and he promptly gave the baby the title 'King of Rome'. Overjoyed on his behalf, Josephine, now in virtual exile in her mansion of La Malmaison, generously sent her congratulations, but the new empress feared Josephine's influence over her husband and did her best to keep them apart. But Napoleon was by no means finished with his first wife. He created her Duchess of Navarre, settled an enormous pension on her, and corresponded with her for the rest of his life.

When his fortunes were overwhelmingly reversed and he was packed off to Elba by his enemies in 1814, it was Josephine, not Marie-Louise, who wished to share his exile. 'I am certain that he expects me now,' she told her friends excitedly. But it was not to be. Within a few weeks of Napoleon's abdication as Emperor of France, Josephine contracted diphtheria. She died on 29 May 1814, with Napoleon's name on her lips. Napoleon's grief at this news was intense. When he returned to Paris after his escape from Elba in February 1815 he locked himself in the room at La Malmaison in which she had died. When he finally emerged he was in tears. 'Good woman, good Josephine,' he sobbed. 'She truly loved me!'

He was looking at a portrait of her at the moment of his own death in 1821 on the island of St Helena, in exile once more. 'France ...' he is said to have gasped as he died. '... The army ... And at the head of the army – Josephine!' In death, as in life, he had named his three abiding passions, but the greatest of the three was his Empress Josephine.

Lord Nelson
and Lady Hamilton

Rear Admiral Horatio Nelson stood transfixed on the deck of his ship the *Vanguard*. Advancing towards him, over the calm waters of Naples harbour, was a flotilla of flower-decked barges on which stood an orchestra playing *Rule Britannia*. In the lead barge was a strikingly lovely woman clad in a gown embroidered with anchors entwined with his own initials. Her glorious dark hair streamed down her back as she swiftly ascended the *Vanguard*'s ladder to where Nelson stood waiting.

She paused dramatically and the orchestra, as if on cue, fell silent. Then Emma, Lady Hamilton, burst into tears. 'Oh God, is it possible?' she cried, staring adoringly at Nelson. Then she collapsed at his feet in an ecstatic swoon.

What man could resist such a reception? Certainly not Horatio Nelson – from that moment on he was wildly, passionately infatuated with Emma Hamilton, one of history's most enterprising adventuresses. Never mind that he was already married to Frances Nisbet, or that Emma herself was married to Sir William Hamilton, the British envoy to the Court of Naples. Never mind that Emma's background was rather less than ladylike. Nelson, the naval hero who had never known defeat, had been utterly routed – by a woman.

Theatricality was second nature to Emma Lyon. Born in 1765 to a poor Cheshire blacksmith, she blossomed into a dazzling young woman who would stop at nothing to escape the poverty of her childhood. By the age of eighteen she was presiding over London quack John Graham's dubious medical establishment, 'The Temple of Health'. It offered all manner of 'cures' to the credulous, from milk baths to a 'magnetic throne', but its chief attraction was Emma – standing on a pedestal, attired in a few wisps of transparent muslin, she posed as the 'Goddess of Health'. Her admirers were many, and it was not long before she was under the 'protection' of the aristocratic Charles Greville, the son of an earl and aspiring parliamentarian.

Entranced by Emma's combination of earthy good humour and startling beauty, Greville engaged special tutors to educate her in all the social graces. Within three years the Cheshire farm girl had disappeared forever and a polished, witty woman of the world had taken her place. Her beauty was immortalised by the painters Joshua Reynolds and Romney, and soon all the fashionable society ladies were copying the 'Emma' look.

But Greville's ambition outweighed his love for Emma. When gambling debts compromised his career, he literally sold her to his uncle, Sir William Hamilton, who took her with him to his diplomatic post in Naples.

Lady Hamilton. Nelson thought her 'beautiful beyond belief.'

At first outraged by Greville's perfidy, Emma decided to make the best of things. By 1791 she had married the doting old Hamilton, and she then coolly proceeded to take the corrupt Court of Naples by storm. Her love of drama continued unabated, and she became all the rage with her famous *Attitudes* – a series of theatrical impressions of classical characters. She became the close friend and confidante of Queen Maria, sister of France's murdered Marie Antoinette. Maria's detestation of Revolutionary France was legendary. Emma, an ardent patriot, knew that war was fast approaching between England and France, and she knew that the British Mediterranean Fleet urgently needed Neapolitan bases. She used her influence on Queen Maria to allow the visit of an English squadron to Naples in 1793. And the Commander of the squadron was … Horatio Nelson.

At their first meeting Nelson seemed more taken with Emma than she with him. He found her: 'A young woman of amiable manner … beautiful beyond belief.' But that was as far as it went – then.

Five years later, when Nelson returned to Naples as the hero of the Battle of the Nile, a decisive victory over the French, Emma began to realise just what manner of man he was. His naval feats had made him England's darling, and Emma decided that he deserved a hero's welcome back to Naples. That was when she staged her elaborate reception committee and fell at his feet.

Lord Nelson. His ménage à trois *with Lady Hamilton and her husband scandalised London society.*

Until that moment, Nelson's whole life had been the navy. He had had little time for dalliance in a career that had seen almost continuous active service and cost him his right arm and eye. But now, fascinated by Emma, he lingered in Naples for a year.

Their idyll was interrupted when revolutionary French troops invaded Italy and sacked Naples. The Neapolitan court fled to Sicily, but Nelson offered the Hamiltons refuge aboard his flagship *Foudroyant*. The trio set up a bizarre shipboard *ménage à trois* as they cruised the Mediterranean. Hamilton loved Emma, but he hero-worshipped Nelson, and he was only too happy to play the part of the amiable cuckold.

London was humming with the scandal when the trio returned there in 1800, but Nelson was so enthralled with Emma that he no longer cared about his reputation. He separated from his wife Frances and moved in with the Hamiltons at their estate at Merton, outside London. A year later, Emma bore him a daughter, Horatia. Nelson was a devoted father, and his love for Emma increased a thousandfold. Lord Hamilton seemed to share the lovers' joy. He stood by his wife and friend as the social outrage intensified. When he died in 1803, Nelson was holding his hand while Emma smoothed his pillows.

Now there was no obstacle to Nelson marrying his 'divine Emma' – except the call of duty, the one thing that could tear him from her side. His naval career went from strength to strength. He was almost single-handedly responsible for the British victory at Copenhagen, for which he was created a viscount. In 1803 he was given command of the Mediterranean Fleet, and he spent the next two years blockading Toulon.

Emma was never far from his mind when he was away on service. He bombarded her with letters, sometimes two or three times in a single day. He was almost incoherent in his passion and need for her. 'If I could tell when to begin a letter to my dearest beloved Emma I could never tell when to stop,' he wrote. 'I want and wish to tell you all my thoughts and feelings but that is impossible, for thoughts so rush upon thoughts that I cannot tell where to begin …' In another letter he called her his 'Dear wife, good adorable friend'. He was constantly haunted with fears for her future should he fall in battle, and was determined to secure her future well-being at all costs.

Nelson was feeling more than usually fatalistic on the morning of 21 October 1805. As ever, his thoughts turned to Emma. He quickly penned a codicil to his will: 'I leave Emma, Lady Hamilton, a legacy to my King and country that they will give her an ample provision to maintain her rank in life,' he wrote. '… These are the only favours I ask my King and country, at this moment when I am going to fight their battle.'

Nelson's men totally defeated the combined French and Spanish fleets off Cape Trafalgar that day, capturing some twenty enemy ships. But at his hour of greatest victory, he was mortally wounded by a French bullet. As he lay dying on the deck of his ship the *Victory*, he whispered piteously, 'Take care of poor Lady Hamilton.'

But while a grateful nation lavished money and honours upon Nelson's family, it ignored his final wish. Emma was still seen as the tawdry temptress who had lured England's finest son from the path of virtue, and she was barred from his state funeral at St Paul's.

Emma never really recovered from Nelson's death. She stayed in bed for weeks, weeping, then went nightly to hear the famous tenor John Braham sing *The Death of Nelson* – and fainted at every performance. Shunned by the society that had once worshipped her wit and beauty, she spent her final years in impoverished obscurity on the Continent.

She died at Calais in 1815, and was buried in a plain deal coffin with her own petticoat for a shroud. On her breast lay a worn leather purse containing her most precious earthly belonging – a lock of Horatio Nelson's hair.

Pocahontas
and Captain John Smith

As the large bearded man was led toward the sacrificial stones, hundreds of half-naked Indians crowded around to watch the death of this strange white prisoner. Captain John Smith muttered a final prayer and bowed his head to destiny. He knew the redskins hated and feared the palefaces and he knew that they were going to kill him – they had no option. They were fighting to preserve their hunting grounds from the European invaders.

It was 1607 and John Smith had recently sailed from England. He was on an exploratory trip that had been set up to discover which parts of America would be best suited to British colonisation. He and the rest of his party had landed and established their base – a village called Jamestown. The British needed food and Smith was sent to explore the rivers around Jamestown. He was looking to establish some sort of trade with the Indians of the area – British manufactured goods for local produce.

Smith and his party were met by the mighty Red Indian chieftain Prince Powhatan, Emperor of Attamoughkamoula, the area afterwards known as Virginia. The great chief was extremely courteous, and invited the whites back to his village for a celebration feast.

Little did Smith know that Powhatan wanted to keep the English party captive while the Indians doubled back to attack Jamestown. Although the attack did not succeed, Smith did not realise that until much later.

Smith had eaten his fill of the celebration feast. He was tired. He wanted to make his deal with the Indians and return to Jamestown. But the Indians refused to let him go. They continued to ply him with food and drink. It was as if they were waiting for something. Smith wondered uneasily why they were crowding around him so closely. Then he knew. Three hefty braves suddenly grabbed him from behind and began pulling him towards two great stones on the floor.

Smith was thrown to the ground and his head held over the stones while two warriors raised stone tomahawks to dash out his brains. And while Smith said his silent prayer a beautiful young girl made a sudden decision. Pocahontas thought this summary execution was barbaric and totally unfair. Her father had tricked Smith and the rest of his men. His invitation to the feast had been nothing more than a sham – a device to buy time so that his men could attack Jamestown. Smith and his party were no longer needed and it was now time to dispense with them. The exquisite, 13-year-old princess shouted to Powhatan: 'He's mine, Father. Stop! This is my man.'

Captain John Smith: 'big, whiskery bear-man that is of my heart.'

Powhatan stared as his daughter threw her tiny body between Captain Smith and the raised tomahawks. Nobody moved. All eyes were on Powhatan. The old man smiled and signalled that his warriors should release Smith. Pocahontas had saved the Englishman's life. He was now officially her possession.

For Pocahontas it was a case of love at first sight. She buried her face in Smith's beard and declared that he was her 'big, whiskery bear-man that is of my heart'. It all proved too much for Smith – he was simply grateful to be alive.

Many years later, he wrote an account of his rescue in the third person. It describes how 'as many as could layed hands on him' and dragged him to the two great stones that had been brought before Powhatan. On these Smith 'layed' his head. 'And being ready with their clubs to beat out his brains, Pocahontas, the king's dearest daughter, when no entreaty could prevaile got his head in her armes and laid her own upon his to save him from death. Powhatan was content that he should live after this.'

Smith spent two months playing with the beautiful princess and then returned to Jamestown. Pocahontas was besotted with the great white adventurer, remembering his kindness, the strange stories of his homeland and, most of all, that big, muscular, hairy body – so different from those of the males of her tribe. She decided to travel to Jamestown to visit him. She dressed herself in her best white doeskin petticoat and a cloak made from the feathers of gaily coloured birds and set out to woo the man she loved.

Princess Pocahontas was just thirteen when she saved John Smith's life.

Smith was delighted to see the little Indian princess and introduced her around the colony, where she became immensely popular with the white settlers.

Despite the fact that Powhatan had released Smith, he was still looking for ways of ousting the whites from Indian territory. He prepared an ambush for Smith and a group of men who were out on another food-gathering trip, but Pocahontas got wind of the plot and quickly warned Smith. She and the men escaped before her father's warriors arrived.

Smith was amazed and touched at the young girl's bravery. He offered her anything she wanted as a reward for saving him a second time. But they both knew there was no payment great enough. Pocahontas merely asked that nobody inform her father of her part in this second rescue. This time it would cost her her life.

John Smith looked down at the proud, raven-haired princess. It was obvious that she loved him. Her lustrous brown eyes stared up at him trustingly. The great bearded man felt unworthy of her love. What had he done to deserve such affection? Smith felt proud and humble at the same time. He gently bent down towards her perfect lips and kissed them. A feeling of peace overwhelmed him. He suddenly realised that despite their different ages and cultures, the one thing he wanted most in the world was to marry this young Indian princess.

Pocahontas was now sixteen – a good age for marriage in those days. John Smith decided there was no point in waiting any longer. Tragically, however, the marriage proposal was never made. In 1610 Smith was injured in a gunpowder explosion and became so ill that the Jamestown colonists sent him back to England for medical attention. Pocahontas was told that he was dead.

The girl was stricken. Nobody had known of their marriage plans. Nobody thought to console her. There was nothing left for her to do but to return to her father's tribe and grieve for her lost love. For the next three years Pocahontas tried to forget her English lover, throwing herself into Indian tribal customs. But it didn't work. She hungered for the civilisation of the man she had loved. Smith had shown her some of the drawbacks of the Indian way of life and her unhappiness caused these flaws to be magnified. She decided to leave her tribe and go and live among the whites.

The British colonists were delighted that Pocahontas was back. In fact, they used her as a type of hostage to protect them against Indian attack. But they did not ill-use the girl, and she became more and more attached to the culture she had chosen to adopt. She learned to read and write, dress like a white woman, and was even baptised a Christian, being christened Rebecca.

In 1613, Pocahontas became the first Indian to marry a European when she wed a kindly tobacco grower named John Rolfe. It was not a love match – Pocahontas was still in love with John Smith. Nevertheless, Rolfe made Pocahontas very happy. They had a son whom they called Tomas. Rolfe was extremely proud of his new family and decided to take them home to England to show them off.

Pocahontas was instantly the toast of London. She was presented to King James, had her portrait painted, and mingled with the cream of British society. She became 'the enchanting savage' and was feted for her beauty, intelligence and regal bearing. Unhappily, the climate did not suit her as well as the society. She became ill and Rolfe decided to take his precious wife back to America.

Shortly before they were due to sail, Pocahontas learned that John Smith was alive and well, and in London. He had survived the gunpowder accident after all. He came to visit her as she lay ill. It was an emotional meeting. Pocahontas stared up into the face of the man who had inspired her to totally change her life. She would never have married Rolfe if she had known Smith was still alive. As she wept for all the lost time she cried, 'They told me you were dead!' not once but many times.

Pocahontas never returned to America. She died in England in 1617. The shock of discovering that Smith was still alive had broken her heart.

THUNDERBOLT AND YELLILONG

An Australian bushranger and a part-Aboriginal girl had one of the most poignant and tumultuous love affairs of all time. The bushranger – Thunderbolt – has become part of Australian folk legend, but the girl, Yellilong, is all but forgotten.

Thunderbolt was born Frederick Ward, at Windsor near Sydney on 16 May 1836. Yellilong was born no one knows where, but she was only about eighteen when Ward met her as a 27-year-old outlaw. Ward was a well-educated man for the times, but opportunities for work weren't great when he was 20 and he turned to cattle stealing.

He was a well-built, athletic man, with a mane of black hair and a jutting beard. But his looks and physique didn't help him when he was brought before a court and sentenced to ten years on Cockatoo Island, which was then a prison in Sydney Harbour. It was supposedly impossible to escape from Cockatoo Island because the harbour was infested with sharks. But after five years Frederick Ward preferred to risk death in the jaws of a shark to being confined any longer. One night he dived into the harbour and swam towards what is now Balmain.

Twice he was attacked by what he called 'a black marine creature of fearsome size', but somehow he managed to beat his way clear and arrive at the shore unharmed. Now his destiny was set. If he were ever recaptured he would get life imprisonment or the gallows, and it was hard to say which was worse. Frederick Ward took to the road as a highwayman – a bushranger. There was no other course.

He fell on the New England district of New South Wales with such energy that he immediately gained the name Thunderbolt. Later, as his seven-year reign as king of the roads earned him a reputation that was only to be equalled by Ben Hall and Ned Kelly, he was known as Captain Thunderbolt.

Six months after his escape from Cockatoo Island, Thunderbolt met Yellilong. She was an educated woman. As a very young child she had been found wandering apparently abandoned on a station near Armidale, and the station owner had taken her into his family and brought her up as his own. But when Yellilong was about sixteen the station owner died, the family disintegrated and Yellilong found herself alone again. She joined up with a band of Aborigines and wandered with them for two years. But she was always a lonely figure, because although the Aborigines were kind to her she was different – very different.

Her tall, slender, full-breasted body, long black straight hair and pale golden skin indicated that her ancestry might have been some exotic mixture of Nordic, Oriental and Aboriginal – but nobody knew. She belonged to no world and no people, and she enhanced her difference by insisting, probably because of her upbringing, on always wearing European clothing – a dress that covered her splendid body from neck to knee, shoes, and a scarf around her head. That was how she was dressed when Thunderbolt, mounted on a superb stolen grey stallion, rode into the Aboriginal camp.

Thunderbolt later told friends, 'I just couldn't believe it when I saw her. I knew in that moment I had found the only woman I would ever want and I had found her in the most unlikely place available.'

Yellilong apparently felt the same. Within four hours of his riding into the camp he was riding out again – with Yellilong mounted behind him. 'We made love that first night,' Thunderbolt said later, 'under the stars; and then every night and day for months in the cave where we set up home.'

Their early lovemaking was disturbed by a young warrior member of the band that had sheltered Yellilong. Despite her difference, he had apparently wanted her for a wife. He followed the couple for ten days and several times flung spears at them from behind shelter. Thunderbolt finally discouraged him by shooting him in the arm.

Yellilong soon became pregnant, and before a year was out she bore Thunderbolt twins – both boys. Thunderbolt kept them all in comfort from the proceeds of his highway robberies. Now at the head of his own band, Thunderbolt struck from Singleton to Maitland, at Quirindi and Murrundi. Anywhere there was a coach, a traveller, or a hotel to rob, Thunderbolt and his men rode. But he always went back to his beloved Yellilong and their two sons in the cave near Muswellbrook, which was the nearest thing they had to a permanent home.

Yellilong could not bear to be away from Thunderbolt while he made his long and dangerous rides seeking plunder. She insisted on leaving the children with a part-Aboriginal friend and riding with him. She was first seen riding with Thunderbolt at the head of a band of bushrangers 15 kilometres north of Singleton in January 1865. The outlaws were trying to rob the Northern Mail coach but the coach horses had bolted. The outlaws followed with pistols blazing. One of the passengers, John Bushel, said later, 'I saw the woman riding near the leader of the band. She was wearing men's clothes and firing a pistol, but it was obvious she was a woman from her fulsome figure and long flowing hair.'

The coach escaped, but Yellilong appeared time and time again riding with Thunderbolt and his band of bushrangers. Then Yellilong fell pregnant again and for some months at least had to remain at home in her cave hideaway. During this time there was a long break in Thunderbolt's career. Apparently Yellilong was so heartbroken at the thought of being left behind that the great Thunderbolt agreed to wait quietly at home and do no more bushranging until the child was born.

It was born in September 1867 – a girl. Thunderbolt and Yellilong were back on the road together within a month. Not much more than two months later – just before Christmas – Yellilong was dead.

She had suffered a flesh wound in one of the bushrangers' many running battles, and although it was not a severe wound it became infected. Not for the outlaw Yellilong the luxury of a

Thunderbolt's death reunited him with his lover and fellow outlaw, Yellilong.

town doctor. She developed a high fever and, a fortnight later, died in the arms of Thunderbolt in the cave near Muswellbrook with her three children beside her. Thunderbolt buried her himself outside the cave that had been their home. He placed his three children with friends and left money for their upbringing. Then he threw himself into bushranging with such demoniac energy that some said he was seeking death – because that was the only way he could rejoin Yellilong.

He found it in May 1870 riding along the road to Uralla when he encountered Trooper Constable Walker. Thunderbolt turned and fled but the trooper ran him down in the Rocky River. Pistols in hand, the two men faced each other. Walker, who was to gain great fame as the man who brought Thunderbolt's seven-year reign to an end, said in his report: 'Thunderbolt waited a long time before firing at me – and then his shot went very wide.'

It was thought by his friends that Thunderbolt did not want to win that fight. And he didn't win it. Walker's return shot did not go wide. Mortally wounded, Thunderbolt lingered long enough to be taken in a cart to Uralla where he died uttering a word that sounded to those who watched very much like 'Yellilong'.

Bess and Harry Houdini

Handcuffing your husband, placing him in a weighted box and casting him into deep water may seem an odd way of demonstrating your love and support – especially if you do it day after day, year after year. But Beatrice Houdini was no ordinary wife – she was the helpmate and stage assistant to her husband Harry, the most famous escape artist of all time.

Spectators caught their breath as the seemingly indestructible Houdini freed himself from a straitjacket while hanging suspended by his heels 70 feet above the ground, or emerged smiling from an hour's immersion underwater in a sealed coffin with no breathing apparatus. Such feats could only be done with the help of God or the devil, they thought.

Only Harry and Beatrice knew just how much of his extraordinary success he owed to her …

Houdini, whose real name was Ehrich Weiss, was born in Appleton, Wisconsin, on 6 April 1874, the son of a Hungarian rabbi. A short, agile lad with a shock of dark hair and an endearing smile, young Ehrich always excelled at gymnastics. He started his own professional trapeze act and toured with his brother while still in his teens, changing his name to Harry Houdini in honour of the legendary French magician Robert Houdin.

Like all good American boys, Houdini had two 'sweethearts' – his mother and his wife, Beatrice. He met Bessie, as he called her, in 1893. She was a diminutive brunette high school senior with a pretty, heart-shaped face dominated by huge brown eyes. It was love at first sight for the young tumbler and the schoolgirl, but there was one problem – her domineering mother. She wanted to keep her little girl to herself, and forbade Bess and Harry to meet.

Love may or may not laugh at locksmiths, but Houdini certainly did. One day he calmly smuggled Beatrice out of her locked room, virtually under her mother's nose, and eloped with her. They were married the same day at Coney Island, and so began one of the most astounding theatrical partnerships of the early twentieth century.

Bess was almost as agile an acrobat as Harry himself. She also looked very fetching in tights, and soon replaced Harry's brother in his trapeze act. They did well in clubs and music halls with tumbling displays, magic acts and mind-reading feats, but after a while Houdini began to yearn for new worlds to conquer. He wanted to make his name in something new – escapology.

Together Harry and Bess sailed for England, where they had heard that Scotland Yard's Superintendent Melville was boasting that nobody could escape from his set of specially made

Bess and Harry Houdini, an astounding theatrical partnership.

handcuffs. Harry accepted the challenge, and Melville had him wrap his arms backwards around a metal pillar, and then manacled his wrists. 'I'll be back to free him in a couple of hours,' he told the assembled spectators, and headed for the door. He had hardly got there when a voice right behind him said: 'Wait a second and I'll come with you.' Melville spun round, astounded, to see Harry beside him, the handcuffs open on the ground. It had taken him only a split second to liberate himself. The elated

Bess rushed to his side and kissed him. The Houdinis were on their way.

Before long Harry was the talk of Europe with his feats, which became more elaborate and extraordinary every day. He emerged from a supposedly escape-proof dungeon, built by Oliver Cromwell in Leicester, in record time. He chained himself to the mouth of a cannon with a 15-minute fuse, and freed himself with nine minutes to spare. In 1903, in Moscow, he was locked into a prison van that was simply a sealed, windowless metal box on wheels. As he had been stripped and carefully examined for hidden tools or escape implements, no one believed he could get out. But a short time later he was walking the streets of Moscow in his birthday suit. The astonished authorities could only conclude that he must have swallowed a file and regurgitated it later to enable him to cut his way to freedom.

Hidden instruments did play a big part in his acts. Bess, now his frontwoman and stage assistant, would palm him a tiny pick or file under cover of a loving kiss or 'final' embrace before he commenced his death-defying act. Sometimes he would hide them in a false metal finger to conceal them from inspectors from the audience.

Houdini never revealed the full extent of his tricks, but he always denied possessing any magical prowess. He put his success down to his highly developed physical powers, saying: 'I make not one muscle but every muscle a respective worker, quick and sure in its job. Practice has made my fingers super fingers and has helped my toes do the work of fingers.' But above all, he said, he kept a cool head: 'My chief task was to cast out fear. When I am stripped and manacled, nailed securely within a packing case and thrown into the sea, or when I am buried alive under six feet of earth, it is necessary to preserve absolute serenity of spirit.'

And that serenity was largely drawn from the presence of Beatrice by his side. One of his closest brushes with death occurred on a wintry morning in Detroit in 1906, a day on which Bessie was confined to bed with a cold. Harry decided to go on with his act anyway, and it was one of his most spectacular: he dived, handcuffed, weighted and chained, through a hole cut in the iced-up Detroit River.

But he had not reckoned on the strong current and was swept helplessly downriver to find, when he had wriggled out of his chains, that he was trapped under the ice. Minutes passed, and the spectators became convinced that this time the mighty Houdini had met his match. Reporters rushed from the scene to compose his obituary and soon newsboys were bellowing the story from every street corner. Poor Bess heard the news and rushed weeping from the hotel room to buy a paper.

But when, distraught, she returned to the hotel, it was to find Harry waiting for her, unable to speak from the cold. Quickly the relieved Bess ran him a steaming bath to thaw him out. It was half an hour before he was able to tell her that he had survived by placing his lips right at the underside of the ice, where a tiny air pocket allowed him enough oxygen to swim back to the hole he had jumped through over ten minutes earlier.

Encouraged by this feat, Harry and Bess began to work on more sophisticated acts involving limited air. Enraged by a fake

Indian medium's challenge to better his record for surviving for ten minutes in an airtight coffin, Houdini perfected his breath control so that he could survive 73 minutes' immersion at the bottom of the New York Sheraton Hotel's pool in a sealed coffin that doctors declared held only 15 minutes' supply of air.

Harry was the sensation of America and Europe, and he now entered his 'miracle' phase, in which the credulous attributed his escapes to supernatural intervention. Sir Arthur Conan Doyle, the creator of Sherlock Holmes and an amateur spiritualist, declared: 'He is a great medium. He can dematerialise himself out of safes.'

Such statements appalled Harry and Bess, who both knew just how much of the Houdini 'magic' was due to concealed keys, special rings that doubled as escape implements, bent nails, tiny hooks and simple physical strength. They began to devote themselves to exposing spiritualist frauds, upsetting séances and revealing fake mediums' tricks. Harry became so zealous that he even wrote a book denouncing his boyhood idol, Robert Houdin.

These activities didn't interrupt the Houdinis' quest for more and more extraordinary escapades. Harry began planning two stunts that would leave all his others for dead: being thrown over Niagara Falls in a weighted barrel, and escaping after being frozen into a block of ice. Both these stunts featured in a film written by and starring Houdini entitled *The Man from Beyond*. The plot revolved around a man who had become frozen in Arctic ice, who was somehow revived after a century to engage in all manner of escapades, including the famous Niagara Falls scene, a stunt so realistically executed that the *Tribune* declared: 'There is no fake about this: Houdini actually does it.'

Loyal Bessie helped prepare him for the 'ice-capade' by having him lie in a special deep bathtub that she kept topped up with ice cubes, but she was beginning to worry about her husband's health. She knew just what toll had been taken by more than three decades of daring deeds. His body had absorbed a lot of punishment, and it was beginning to break down.

But Harry wouldn't listen to her protests. Ironically, it was his sense of showmanship that contributed to his premature death in October 1926. Boasting that his stomach muscles were as hard as they had ever been, he allowed a student to pummel his abdomen. As a result he felt extremely unwell that night as he went on stage, but he insisted on performing all the crowd's favourite stunts. Then he collapsed and was rushed to hospital. Doctors diagnosed acute peritonitis and he died in Bess's arms after a nine-day struggle, saying simply: 'I'm tired of fighting.'

Bess was heartbroken. Her only comfort came from a handwritten note Harry had left in his safe for her, reading: 'Yours in life, death and forever.' But he was not to be hers in death.

Despite their activities exposing mediums, the Houdinis obviously retained some spiritualist beliefs, for they had agreed that in the event of either's death, the other would be contacted from the after-world with a special form of words. This was a code they had used in their music hall mind-reading days, and the bereaved Bess was elated when a medium approached her with the correct formula. Harry must still be with her!

But it transpired that the medium had read the formula in a biography of the Houdinis, and had not heard it from Harry at all. Right until the day of her death in 1943, Bess waited for a message from her beloved husband. Finally she was forced to conclude that even the great Harry Houdini could not escape from the hereafter.

RIGHT ROYAL
ROMANCES

BOTHWELL AND
MARY, QUEEN OF SCOTS

The spectators gaped as the tall, elegant woman entered the Great Hall of Fotheringay Castle. She was dressed all in black, save for a white bridal veil under which her auburn hair glowed. They marvelled at her composure as she gracefully climbed up onto a dais in the centre of the Hall. She stood quite still as two hooded executioners stripped off her clothes, dropping them one by one on the dais until she wore only a red petticoat, the colour of blood – and of martyrdom. Then, as custom decreed, they knelt and begged her forgiveness for what they were about to do.

'I forgive you with all my heart,' she replied with a smile, 'for now I hope you will make an end to all my troubles.'

Then Mary, Queen of Scots, just 44 years old and still beautiful, laid her head upon the black-swathed block on the dais. Her lips moved in prayer as the executioner's axe descended once, twice, three times. They were still moving fifteen minutes

Mary, Queen of Scots. Her passion for Bothwell led to scandal and imprisonment.

after her head was finally severed from her body. Was she begging for God's mercy – or calling for James, Earl of Bothwell, whose passion and ambition had brought her to this shameful death?

'In my end is my beginning,' she once embroidered on a hanging for her royal dais of state – but nothing in her early life could have prepared Mary Stuart for the fate that would one day befall her.

Born in 1542, the only child of King James V of Scotland, she succeeded her father while still only an infant. Her French mother, Mary of Guise, sent her to France to be brought up in the court of Henry II and his queen, Catherine de Medici.

With her slim figure, reddish-gold hair and amber-coloured eyes, the young Mary appeared the contemporary ideal of a Renaissance princess. 'Her beauty shone like the light at midday,' wrote a poet of the time, and she was acclaimed throughout Europe. Such were her artistic accomplishments, her command of languages, her talents for dancing and riding, that all France rejoiced when she was betrothed to young François, Henry and

Catherine's son. The two royal youngsters were married in April 1558, in a union intended to unite the kingdoms of Scotland and France. Not for the first time – nor the last – Mary was being used as a political pawn.

But she was genuinely fond of François. She enjoyed a brief, glittering reign as his consort when he was crowned King of France after Henry's death in 1559, but his premature death a year later left her a widow at the age of eighteen – a widow before she was properly a wife, for the marriage was never consummated.

Mary returned to Scotland in August 1561, totally unprepared for the political situation that awaited her. Scotland had turned Protestant in her absence, and her devout Roman Catholicism earned her the distrust of many of her subjects. Eager and inexperienced, ruled by her heart rather than her head, Mary became infatuated with her cousin, Henry, Lord Darnley, 'the lustiest and best proportioned long man' she had ever seen. She was captivated by his long blond hair, by his skill with the lute, by his 'virginal look which he would lose'.

Mary didn't realise it then, but Darnley's virginity was long since lost; he was a handsome fellow, but he was weak and dissolute. Drunken and promiscuous, he was already suffering from the first ravages of syphilis.

Mary married Darnley in July 1565, and it was not long before she realised just how foolish she had been. She had antagonised both Elizabeth and the Scottish nobles with her reckless marriage, and Darnley soon showed his true colours. Weak, vicious and ambitious, he continually badgered her to make him king in his own right. His insane jealousy of anyone who had influence over her knew no bounds.

The scales finally fell from Mary's eyes the night he and a gang of nobles murdered her trusted secretary and confidant, David Rizzio, in front of her when she was six months pregnant. Now she wished with all her heart to be free of such a husband.

Help came from an unexpected quarter. James Hepburn, fourth earl of Bothwell, had long admired Mary's looks and grace. Fiercely ambitious, he believed that Mary might be induced to bestow upon him what she had steadfastly denied Darnley – the Crown Matrimonial.

Bothwell was crude, bluff and forceful – the opposite of the suave gallants of the French court with whom she had grown up – but something in Mary instinctively responded to his rough wooing. They became lovers, and for the first time Mary Stuart knew the joy of physical satisfaction. In the eight months following Rizzio's death, the passionate, impulsive young queen fell completely under Bothwell's spell.

It was a dangerous game she was playing, but she didn't realise just how dangerous it was until the small hours of 9 February 1567. That was the night that Kirk o'Field, the house on the outskirts of Edinburgh in which her husband was staying, was blown up. Darnley and a servant were found dead in the garden. They had been strangled while trying to escape the explosion.

It was clear that Bothwell had had a hand in the murder, but historians still argue over the extent of Mary's involvement. Her behaviour over the next few months was compromising, to say the least. Perhaps this was because she *was* compromised – by now she knew she was expecting Bothwell's baby. She had to act, and quickly – but how to avoid seeming to condone Darnley's murder?

Bothwell stood trial, but intimidated his accusers with a show of strength by his own private army. Then he swooped down upon Mary as she was returning from a visit to Stirling to see her and Darnley's infant son, James, and 'kidnapped' her. True, he had some 800 henchmen with him at the time, but when Mary's servants put up a fight, she insisted upon accompanying Bothwell – 'rather than be the cause of bloodshed'. He bore her away to Dunbar Castle, where he completed his plan to rule Scotland by making violent love to her. Mary seemed to find nothing to object to in this: she appeared to delight in being dominated by the virile, brutally direct Bothwell.

'Albeit we found his doings rude, yet were his words and actions gentle,' she wrote to the Bishop of Dunblane. Her subjects were horrified, and his enemies declared that he must have bewitched the queen, so completely was she in his thrall.

Bothwell led Mary back to Edinburgh, holding the bridle of her horse as if she were his captive. Nine days later, in May 1567, she married him in a hasty ceremony at Holyrood Palace, moving as if in a trance. Her scandalised subjects, outraged by the transformation of their pretty monarch into a murderer's plaything, posted a banner reading 'Wantons marry in the month of May' on the palace gates. It was a warning of what was to come. Now, whenever she appeared in public, her people cried, 'Burn the whore! Burn the adulteress!'

A bare month after the wedding, the rebellious Scottish nobles made their move. They made Mary a virtual prisoner after a pitched battle against her and Bothwell's forces at Carberry Hill, and the lovers were forced to part. Bothwell embraced her in full view of the two armies, then galloped away on his charger, hoping to raise a new army to free her. They were never to see each other again. He fled to Scandinavia, and was imprisoned in Zeeland, where he was to die, insane, in 1578.

After the battle the nobles hounded Mary to divorce Bothwell, but she refused, saying that if she renounced him she would acknowledge herself to be 'with child of a bastard, and forfeit her honour'. But her honour was already forfeit, and she never delivered the child: at the end of July, worn out with heartbreak and stress, she miscarried 'deux enfants' – twins. Exhausted by loss of blood, she allowed herself to be bullied into abdicating her throne in favour of her 13-month-old son, James. But her sorrows were not yet over.

She escaped from captivity in 1568, raised an army and after its defeat fled to England to throw herself upon Elizabeth's mercy. This was an unwise move, for the English queen had long seen her as a threat, and held her as a prisoner for many more weary years. Some of her hopelessness was reflected in a sonnet she wrote during this time:

> *What am I, alas, what purpose has my life?*
> *I nothing am, a corpse without a heart,*
> *A useless shade, a victim of sad strife,*
> *One who lives yet, and wishes to depart.*

Life held no savour for her now Bothwell was gone, but she

was still the centre of controversy. Roman Catholics saw her as their figurehead in the struggle against Protestant Elizabeth, and over the years there were many conspiracies to free Mary and place her upon the English throne. By 1587 Elizabeth had had enough. She signed a warrant for Mary's execution at Fotheringay Castle.

Mary went gladly to her death, after nearly twenty years of lonely captivity without her Bothwell.

LOUIS XIV AND
FRANÇOISE DE MONTESPAN

It was rumoured that Françoise Athenais de Montespan celebrated black masses at which babies were sacrificed in order to keep her hold over Louis XIV. The king himself looked at the beautiful young woman who had been his mistress for thirteen years and began to have doubts.

It was hard to disregard the rumours and gossip that placed his beloved Françoise right in the middle of one of the most sensational criminal cases of seventeenth-century France – a case known throughout Europe as the Poisons Affair. Could the woman who swore she loved him have plotted against him? Could the woman who had borne him seven children have cooperated in black masses with witches and wizards? Could the woman who was miraculously blessed with a peaches and cream complexion, a mop of flaming red hair and sparkling blue eyes have involved herself in one of the ugliest intrigues of the day?

Louis didn't know what to think. He was in love with

Françoise. She was his witty and brilliant hostess at Versailles. But he was the Sun King – he had been brought up to consider himself God's vice-regent on Earth. He couldn't afford the scandal of being closely associated with a woman who was being dubbed a poisoner and a necromancer. Françoise would have to go.

Françoise Athenais de Rochechouart, Marquise de Montespan, was born in 1641 of a powerful and aristocratic family. Very early in life she decided that she wanted to have power over people. She was intelligent, beautiful and very ambitious. She made a marriage of convenience to the Marquis de Montespan in 1663, a marriage that helped her become appointed lady-in-waiting to the Queen of France, Maria Theresa of Austria. She promptly fell in love with the king and began to look for ways to make him fall in love with her.

Louis was not in love with Maria Theresa – the marriage had been purely dynastic. She lived in rooms near his own, and he went out of his way to visit her daily, but she never managed to capture the young king's imagination. After Maria had given birth to three children he practically ignored her. Louis was looking for a woman of spirit and fire. Sadly, Maria Theresa had neither. Louis was a sensualist, whereas she was something of an aesthete. Her royal chronicler described her as a gentle soul, 'in fact a queen, at heart a nun'.

Louis had become used to power at a very young age. He succeeded to the French throne in 1643, when he was only four years old, and although he did not effectively rule until he was 22, he became accustomed to getting what he wanted very early in life. He was the ruler of the largest group of people in Europe (18 million, compared with Spain's six million and England's five and a half million). It soon became obvious to Louis that he could make his own rules. He could order France into war, which he did. He could cultivate the great artists and writers of the time, which he did. He could order magnificent palaces and châteaux to be built, which he did. And he could indulge his sexual appetites, which he did.

When Françoise Athenais de Montespan and Louis first met, the king was romantically involved with Louise de la Vallière, who was pretty, lovable and rather stupid. Louis was fond of his young mistress but he wanted more. He wanted a sensuous, intelligent woman who could be the great hostess that the Versailles Palace demanded. Louis had a passion for Versailles that was almost an obsession. It was the symbol of his supremacy – the glory of the architecture complemented the glory of the Sun King.

Françoise quickly realised that neither the queen nor the meek Louise de la Vallière were serious rivals – she could have the king if she wanted him. She made a play for Louis, and very shortly after she had ousted la Vallière as his official mistress. Louis showered Françoise with money, clothes and jewels. He was so besotted with his beautiful mistress that he built her a weekend love bower, the Château de Clagny, and the two of them would sneak away for illicit assignations while the rest of the court pretended not to notice.

One person had no such scruples. The Marquis de Montespan was still in love with his wife and he wanted her back. He wrote to Françoise, imploring her to return to him. She refused. Montespan wrote another letter. This time Françoise showed it to Louis, who put the matter into the hands of one of his ministers.

'Montespan is indiscreet,' he said. 'I rely on you to keep him quiet.'

But Montespan refused to be kept quiet. He arrived at the king's palace, strode up to his wife and slapped her face, then informed the watching courtiers that his wife was a harlot. Françoise laughed and asked that her husband be removed. The king was not amused. He ordered that the Marquis be sent to the Bastille as punishment for embarrassing the king's mistress. This seemed rather hard lines, as the king's mistress happened to be poor Montespan's wife. Eventually Louis relented and Montespan was released from prison, instead being banished for life to his country seat.

From then on Françoise reigned supreme. She queened it over the most glittering court in the world. She was the mistress of a man who said: 'The State? That is I,' and really meant it. Louis' every word was law and, to a lesser degree, so was Françoise's.

The king showed his pleasure in the liaison by legitimising the children of their union. Françoise was radiantly happy – she had power, wealth and the affections of the man she loved. She knew that Louis was not entirely faithful to her, but she was not unduly worried by his indiscretions. He always came back.

One day he didn't come back. Louis was in love with the beautiful Duchesse de Fontanges. Françoise began to worry. Suddenly her position at court didn't seem as secure as it had been. She discovered that many of the court ladies made a habit

Louis XIV looked for spirit and fire in a woman and found it in Françoise de Montespan.

of visiting a fortune teller called Monvoisin when they needed love potions to ensure the devotion of their swains. Monvoisin also had the reputation of being a poisoner, charlatan and necromancer. It was whispered that the fortune teller specialised in selling poison to any of the court ladies who wished to dispose of an unwelcome rival. Françoise began to visit Monvoisin in the hope that she could buy some potion or spell that would win Louis back.

Suddenly the Duchesse de Fontanges died after a mysteriously brief illness. The French court began to talk. Whereas before Françoise had been described as 'alluring and radiant, sparkling with life and animation', now people were referring to her as having 'passion without love, pride without dignity and splendour without poetry'. Popular gossip had it that Françoise had been visiting the fortune teller since she first met Louis, to buy love philtres and powders to win the king's love and to supplant his mistress la Vallière. It was further suggested that she had participated in black masses and poisoned her rival, the Duchesse de Fontanges.

Louis had no option but to order an inquiry into the affair. Monvoisin was arrested. The subsequent revelations shook the throne. Françoise and most of the court ladies were involved. There were numerous witnesses who swore they had seen these prominent women enter the fortune teller's house on many occasions.

Françoise de Montespan. When she fell out of favour, she employed a fortune teller to win back the king's love.

The inquiry lasted three years. Thirty-four people were executed, four were sentenced to hard labour in the galleys, and 34 were banished and fined. Monvoisin was publicly burned to death. Louis also decided to officially suppress large amounts of the information that was revealed in the inquiry.

Whether it was the doubt thrown up by the Poisons Affair or whether Louis had tired of Françoise is not known, but the case spelled the end of their affair. Louis drifted into an affair with a governess whom, after the queen's death, he married. Françoise was banished to the position of discarded mistress.

She stayed at court until the king's new wife decided to purge Versailles of its more unsavoury elements. Françoise was one of the first to go.

Françoise died in 1707, an unhappy and bitter woman. She had certainly had dealings with Monvoisin and had recourse to magic in order to win and keep the king's love, but the charges concerning black masses and attempted poisonings had not been proven against her. She felt that she had been exiled without a fair trial.

And her crime?

She had played the game of the Sun King and come away burned.

CHARLES II AND NELL GWYNN

That royal libertine Charles II was Queen Victoria's favourite ancestor, which just goes to show that even the most prudish ladies love a handsome, hell-raising rake.

Tall and dark, Charles was nicknamed 'Black Boy' for his swarthy, lady-killer looks. 'Surely God would not damn a man for a little irregular pleasure,' he would often say – but in his case, the pleasure was all too regular. 'Above all, be civil to women' was a precept that was drummed into him as a child, and it was advice he took very much to heart. A precocious lad who was forced to grow up too fast in a turbulent era, Charles fought his first battle at the age of eleven and sired his first bastard at sixteen. And that was just for starters – while still only a boy, he had as many as seventeen mistresses at one time.

His longing for love sprang directly from his unhappy, dangerous childhood. He was born in 1630, and hustled away to the Continent for safekeeping when his father, King Charles I, ran foul of Oliver Cromwell. When his father was later executed as a 'public enemy, tyrant and traitor', young Charles was well and truly launched into his career as the 'Beggar Prince' of Europe, sponging off continental royalty while attempting to stake his claim to the English throne.

The years of poverty and despair left their mark. Charles grew reckless and cynical, declaring that he cared for nothing but the pursuit of pleasure – the pleasure of love. But he also cared, very deeply, about wresting his crown from the Roundheads. He attempted to invade England in 1651, advancing as far south as Worcester before being routed by Cromwell's men. Further frustrating exile followed, ending only after Cromwell's death, when Charles' subjects, bored with Puritanism, invited him back to Britain. He was crowned King of England in 1660, and the austerity of the Cromwell era was soon forgotten in the excesses of the Restoration.

In 1662, the young king married the dowdy Catherine of Braganza for political reasons, but matrimony couldn't cramp his sexual style. There was no shortage of beauties willing to share the royal bed, and he had five especially favourite mistresses: the Duchesses of Cleveland, Portsmouth, Mazarin and Richmond – and Nell Gwynn, a saucy actress whom he loved the best because she made him laugh the most.

We know how 'Sweet Nell' looked from contemporary portraits – she was blessed with rounded pink limbs, dewy dark eyes, a tender mouth and cascading ringlets. She looked a cuddly armful and that is precisely what she was.

For a royal favourite, Nell sprang from very humble beginnings. She was only ten years old when Charles was crowned king, but she already had a full-time job as a barmaid in her mother's bawdy house in Covent Garden. Nell didn't fancy a career like that of the enormously fat, gin-swilling Madame Gwynn, however; she had already set her sights on the stage. By the age of thirteen she was an orange seller at the new King's Company Playhouse in Drury Lane. A year later she landed a small part in a play by Thomas Killigrew – as 'Paulina, a courtesan of the first rank'. This was a prophetically named role, for before long Nell was under the 'protection' of actor Charles Hart, and then of Lord Charles Bockhurst. He later joked that Charles II ought to have been called Charles III – because he was Nell's third Charles!

Nell first caught the king's eye in 1667, when the scheming Duke of Buckingham, seeking to displace Charles' long-time lover, Lady Castlemaine, pointed out the charms of the popular young actress. But Charles was unusually slow to respond. It wasn't until two years later that, enraptured by Nell's sparkling performance in Dryden's *Tyrannic Love*, Charles invaded her dressing room behind the stage and made impetuous love to her on the spot. Nell was soon equally enamoured of Charles, and within a year she bore him a son to add to his growing brood of bastards. Naturally she named him Charles, and before long she had another son by the king, little James.

One of the things that endeared Nell to Charles II was that, unlike most royal mistresses, she asked nothing for herself, seeming content to bask in his love. She was also completely faithful – right up to the day of her death, she never took another lover. But best of all, she had a ribald wit. Audiences loved her for her rough and ready tongue, and she was as quick with an oath as

Charles II. His affairs were legion but he doted on Nell.

with a joke. The common people adored her because she was one of their own, and never pretended to be anything else.

The doting king showered Nell with priceless trinkets, with land, money and houses. But what she wanted most of all was a name for her two sons. Passionately maternal, she demanded that Charles ennoble the boys, but he was taking his time about it. The story goes that Nell became so exasperated that one day, spying Charles walking below the window of her house in Highgate, Nell dangled her first-born over the sill, shouting: 'Unless you do something for him, here he goes!'

Quickly the shaken king replied: 'Save the Earl of Burford!'

Charles created the elder boy the Duke of St Albans, as well as Earl of Burford, and made the younger one a peer. But the proudest day of Nell's life was when a warrant was issued bestowing the royal surname of Beauclerk upon her sons. Now there was some talk of making Nell the Countess of Greenwich, but a sudden decline in the king's health put paid to that scheme.

Nobody knows the cause of Charles' final malady, but it was certainly unpleasant. Doctors attempted any number of remedies on the unlucky king: they bled him, cauterised him, dosed him with foul potions and generally abused his tortured body 'like an Indian at the stake', according to Lord Macaulay. Yet throughout his ordeal Charles retained the urbanity to apologise to his attendants for being such 'an unconscionable time dying'.

Nell Gwynn, 'that merry slut' who nevertheless remained faithful to the king.

The distraught Nell was not allowed at his bedside – that was the prerogative of the long-suffering Catherine of Braganza. Dutifully Charles begged his wife's pardon for the pain his philandering must have caused her, but his last thoughts were of 'that merry slut', Nell Gwynn. 'Let not poor Nelly starve,' he implored his brother James.

James, who succeeded Charles in 1685, honoured this final request. He made sure Nell had plenty of pocket money, but she spent it as fast as he doled it out, running up enormous bills which she would initial with her spidery, unformed signature: 'EG'. But the pleasures of extravagance soon palled, for Nell was truly heartbroken by the death of her royal lover. She only survived Charles by a bare two years, succumbing at the age of 37 to what was described as an 'apoplexy'.

She died at Pall Mall on 14 November 1687, and her funeral oration was spoken by a future Archbishop of Canterbury, who piously intoned: 'Joy shall be in Heaven over one sinner that repenteth, more than over ninety and nine just persons who need no repentance …'

It is doubtful how much rejoicing Heaven did over the cheerful trollop Nell Gwynn, for one of the things that drew Charles to her was her lack of modesty or shame. She may have been illiterate, of low birth and illegitimate, but her quick wit and infectious joy in life endeared her equally to king and commoner. Her memory lived on in Chelsea Hospital, the old soldiers' home she persuaded Charles to endow in memory of her father, whom she claimed was a Royalist captain who had lost his life in the battles against Cromwell's army. Every Sunday, in the hospital's lavishly appointed chapel, the veterans would raise their voices in grateful thanks to the Almighty for his blessings – and maybe also to their benefactress Nell Gwynn.

Czar Nicholas and Alexandra

Nicholas Romanov, former Czar and Autocrat of All the Russias, looked across the grim confines of the room at his dear wife, 'Sunny'. The terrible events of the past years had left their mark but she was still beautiful as she sat serenely in her chair – still every inch an empress.

Drawn by her husband's gaze, Alexandra looked up at him as he stood by the doorway. Nicholas smiled at her sadly then, wordlessly indicating his drab and worn apparel, gave an ironic shrug. Alexandra's eyes filled with tears as she tried to return his smile. Fate had taken Nicholas' throne from him and humiliated him by making him a prisoner. What else lay in store for her poor husband and children?

Even deep in the basement of the house where they were held captive, the Romanovs could hear cannon fire. Outside the city of Ekaterinberg, a White Army was coming to rescue its emperor, held prisoner by the local Soviet authorities. Inside the 'House of

Special Designation', Nicholas II of Russia tried the door to the basement. It was locked. Masking his apprehension, he walked across to his wife where she sat surrounded by their children – Olga, Tatiana, Maria, Anastasia and little Alexei. Alexandra took his hand and pressed it tenderly against her face, wet with tears.

Her love for Nicholas had not faded with the passing years, but had grown into a passionate devotion. Nicholas knelt by her side and embraced her broken-heartedly. She had been all that he had ever really wanted. If only they could have lived a simple, happy life together – far away from the terrible responsibilities of the throne.

Suddenly, the door swung open and a stream of brutal-looking men in uniform burst into the basement. Their faces were blank and pitiless as they faced their prisoners. Alexandra opened her mouth in horror as she saw the guns in their hands but the soldiers started firing before she could scream …

Nicholas II was born in May 1868, destined to become the last Czar of Russia. Brought up to believe in the divine right to rule, his role as emperor was tragically miscast in the turbulent play of early twentieth-century politics. He was a handsome youth who bore an uncanny resemblance to his cousin, who would become King George V of England. But Nicholas was an anachronism who never understood that the age of absolute monarchs had passed.

When Nicholas met the woman who would so dominate his life in years to come, she was called Princess Alix of Hesse-Darmstadt. One of Queen Victoria's grandchildren, Alix was a proper English gentlewoman. Her manner was cool and aloof, hiding a deeply passionate nature. Nicholas was captivated by her serious beauty. Alix was a strikingly attractive young woman, tall, with features that were cast in the classic mould. With her large, sad eyes and her auburn hair gathered high to reveal her lovely neck and shoulders, Alix was Nicholas' romantic ideal.

He fell in love with Alix and asked her to marry him. She accepted his proposal but Nicholas' father Czar Alexander III and Queen Victoria opposed the idea of their marriage. In frustration Nicholas wrote in his diary, 'My dream is to some day marry Alix.'

Then, in 1894, Nicholas' father died, and Nicholas became czar. He was now free to marry, and he and Alix were wed on 14 November 1894 at the Winter Palace in St Petersburg. Alix (now called Alexandra Fedorovna) wore a gown of silver brocade, and on her head was the diamond wedding crown of Imperial Grand Duchesses. Nicholas was dressed in the uniform of his old regiment, the Hussar Life Guards.

The ceremony was a magnificent one, but it was to be overshadowed by the coronation of the new czar and his wife. On 14 May 1896, they became Emperor Nicholas II and Empress Alexandra Fedorovna, the eighteenth Romanovs to rule Holy Russia. It was a glittering affair. Heads of state and members of the ruling families from all over Europe attended the spectacular event; tens of thousands of metal cups with Nicholas' and Alexandra's monograms were distributed free among the narod, or common people.

At the beginning of his reign, the peasantry of Russia took Nicholas to their hearts. He was their 'little father', and when

Nicholas and Alexandra drove through the streets of St Petersburg in their ceremonial procession the crowds cheered and waved. At first, all was joy in the royal couple's life. But from the start, Alexandra dominated Nicholas with her strong-willed love. Nicholas was the passive half of their relationship and allowed himself to be devoured by Alexandra's consuming passion. Their letters of the time reveal much of the great physical need they had for each other.

'I kiss you all over,' wrote Alexandra. 'I love you and long for your caresses,' replied her husband, 'Nicky'.

Four beautiful daughters – the Grand Duchesses Olga, Tatiana, Maria and Anastasia – were born in rapid succession. Then in 1904 a boy, Alexei, was born. Nicholas and Alexandra were overjoyed by the arrival of their little czarovich. Unfortunately, their happiness was short-lived. On 8 September 1904, Nicholas wrote in his diary: 'Alix and I are very disturbed at the constant bleeding in little Alexei.' Their son had haemophilia. Alexandra withdrew from court life in an attempt to cocoon her son in a safe and protective family environment. She created a cosy but unnatural world for herself in the palace apartments and tried to make Nicholas join her in her charade of domestic normality. Tragically for himself and for Russia, Nicholas did so.

A Romanov emperor simply could not retreat into an ordinary family life. Nicholas II ruled over 130 million subjects and his responsibilities were enormous. An atmosphere of unreality began to surround the throne as Russia was rocked by crisis after crisis – the Russo-Japanese War of 1904-05, the 1905

Revolution and then the First World War. Nicholas, on the advice of his wife, refused to make any compromises to the changing course of history in the early twentieth century. When he did make concessions to democracy they were always too little and too late.

Nicholas and Alexandra. One of the great royal love matches.

'I suffer over you as over a tender soft-hearted child who needs guiding,' Alexandra confessed. 'Be Peter the Great, John [Ivan] the Terrible, Emperor Paul – crush them all under you.'

But Nicholas was not of his ancestors' stuff. He was a gentle man who loved his wife and children and expected his people to love him in the same way. He never argued with his wife, however. 'Tender thanks for the severe written scolding,' Nicholas responded to her exhortations to be stern with his subjects. 'God bless you my darling, my Sunny! Your poor weak-willed little hubby, Nicky.'

As the appalling casualties of the First World War sapped the national morale, the Empress Alexandra began to rely on a dubious mystic called Grigorii Rasputin to help cure her son's haemophiliac condition. Possibly because of his hypnotic powers,

Rasputin did seem to be able to stop Alexei's bleeding. The young czarevich's condition was unknown to the public, however. All they knew was that a disreputable 'holy man' had become palace favourite while Czar Nicholas was away commanding at the front. Rumours of Rasputin's depravity spread swiftly, but Alexandra would hear no criticism against 'Our Friend'. The situation deteriorated rapidly as Alexandra, ruling in Nicholas' absence, interfered in the governing of Russia.

The population had by now turned against the czar and his empress, and when the 1917 Revolution occurred Nicholas was forced to abdicate and he and his family were made prisoners of the state. After signing away his rights as monarch, Nicholas sobbed like a child on the breast of his wife.

The Romanovs were kept prisoner at Tsarskoe Selo and then transported to Tobolsk in Siberia. Their final move to Ekaterinberg had been seen as a hopeful sign at first, but the grim reality finally emerged. On the night of 29 July 1918 Nicholas and Alexandra's tragic love affair ended when they were executed by Soviet soldiers in the basement room of the 'House of Special Designation'.

Death alone had finally killed their love for each other.

VICTORIA AND ALBERT

Victoria, Queen of the United Kingdom of Great Britain and Ireland, Empress of India, lay dying. On the wall above her head hung a portrait of a handsome, dark-haired man painted over half a century before. Her eyes, dimmed by age, flickered as she stared up at his image.

On 22 January 1901, Queen Victoria, the longest reigning monarch in English history, died peacefully in her bed. Her body was laid out in state, covered by the same veil that she had worn as a pretty young bride of 21, over six decades earlier. On her head was placed her widow's cap.

Not all the turbulent years between, nor the growth of the mightiest empire the world had known, could dim the love Victoria had borne her 'dear husband, Albert'. But for Victoria and Albert it had by no means been love at first sight. The two young cousins had first met as a result of royal matchmaking – it was considered 'suitable' for the future Queen of England to marry Prince Albert of Saxe-Coburg.

Their initial contact was friendly but not romantic. Victoria was a petite girl of seventeen who was pretty rather than conventionally beautiful. But she had such a charming smile that it transformed her face with radiance, and her voice was as sweet as a bell. It seems that at first she held no more than a sisterly affection towards her serious-minded cousin Albert.

'I may like him as a friend, and as a cousin, and as a brother, but not more. One can never answer beforehand for feelings, and I may not have the feeling towards him which is requisite for true happiness,' she wrote to her Uncle Leopold, King of Belgium.

For his part, the handsome Albert, with his black hair, blue eyes and broad shoulders, found the little princess 'incredibly stubborn'. It was not the most auspicious of beginnings.

Nearly three years were to go by before the two cousins met again. During these years Albert travelled around Europe broadening his education, and Victoria emerged from her childhood cocoon as the glittering young Queen of England. As monarch of an empire on which the sun never set, as the saying went, she found herself in an exciting new world. Her life as a child had been cloistered and protected. For companions she had her maids-in-waiting and her female relatives. Opportunities to meet people had been limited.

The idea of marrying and having to share her new status with a man now irked the newly independent queen. After all, she was only nineteen. Might she not be allowed to rule for a while on her own? She thought of her predecessor, Queen Elizabeth I. Had Elizabeth needed a king to help her rule?

Destiny lent a hand when King Leopold suggested that his

nephew, Prince Albert of Saxe-Coburg, visit Windsor Castle to pay his respects to the new queen. It was expected of the shy prince that he press his suit with Victoria. Albert knew where his duty lay, but his heart must have been full of trepidation at the thought of proposing marriage to the ruler of a great nation. Then, on the evening of 10 October 1839, Victoria's desire for independence and Albert's Teutonic reserve melted away as they came face to face for the first time in three years.

Victoria saw a tall, startlingly handsome man striding up the castle stairs to greet her. His blue eyes looked straight into hers. 'Your Majesty,' he murmured as he kissed her outstretched hand and bowed gracefully before her. She could not help noticing how broad his shoulders were under his elegant dress coat, and how his lips had lingered on her hand. Albert straightened up to look at his little cousin, the queen. Her eyes were shining. Had she, too, felt something between them?

That night Victoria wrote in her diary, 'I beheld Albert … who is beautiful.'

There was no doubt that Victoria and her German prince had fallen desperately in love with each other. In the following days they were seen together at royal banquets and strolling in the gardens of Windsor Castle, deep in conversation. But a problem existed to mar the young couple's idyll. It was virtually impossible for Albert to propose marriage to Victoria. Although he was her suitor, it was she, as a constitutional monarch, who had to choose a husband.

It cannot have been an easy task for a young woman in those

Victoria and Albert. Victoria had a nervous breakdown after his death at the age of 42.

days to have to do her own proposing. Indeed, as the days wore on and she saw more and more of Albert, it must have become almost unbearable to her as she worked up the courage to ask him to marry her. Dancing together at a ball three nights after their meeting on the castle stairs, Albert swept away all her doubts and fears in one heartfelt gesture. Victoria had given her beau a bouquet of flowers. Unable to find anywhere to place them,

Albert impulsively slashed a hole in the front of his uniform and placed the flowers over his heart. Everyone present in the ballroom was moved by the prince's gallant act. Victoria needed no further proof of his devotion. She called him to her rooms the following day and asked for his hand in marriage. No longer needing duty as a guide to his feelings towards Victoria, Albert declared that yes, of course he would marry her.

They were married on 10 February 1840, in the chapel at St James' Palace. Albert was resplendent in military uniform and Victoria was beautiful in satin and lace. Together they stood before the altar and were joined as man and wife, Prince Consort and his Queen. Then the joyful couple drove in procession past the cheering crowds to their honeymoon at Windsor.

In such a puritanical era as the one Victoria was to rule, the love she felt for Albert was passionate to say the least. Victoria needed physical affection and Albert gave it to her wholeheartedly.

At first her new husband was merely Victoria's consort and not a ruler in his own right. However, as marriage strengthened the bond between them, Albert began to exert his influence as a husband. Victoria began to rely more on Albert's judgement regarding matters of state and to devote herself to being a mother and a wife. But she could still be the imperious young monarch from time to time. Once, when having an argument with Albert, Victoria used her position as queen to silence him. Mortified, he left the room. She followed him and knocked at his door, commanding that he open the door to his queen. Albert remained silent. She kept knocking and repeating that she was the queen and that he must open his door. At last she could bear it no longer and when she knocked for the last time and he asked who was there, she cried: 'Your Victoria, Albert.' He opened the door and they fell into each other's arms.

Victoria bore nine children to Albert and the happy domestic image surrounding the throne found much approval with the British people. Theirs was an almost perfect union of body and soul. A marriage of political convenience had resulted in the love match of a lifetime. Albert and Victoria humanised the monarchy by showing the world that royalty could feel emotions like ordinary people. At their castle at Balmoral, in Scotland, they abandoned much of the pomp and ceremony that attended their lives at Windsor. Surrounded by their children, they enjoyed each other's company in a manner unique to nineteenth-century royalty.

In December 1861, after twenty years of married bliss, Albert fell ill, but would not allow himself to rest. Always the conscientious young man determined to do his duty, he wouldn't spare himself despite Victoria's pleading with him to take to his bed. Eventually he collapsed, terribly ill. The queen was distraught. Her 'dear one' was at death's door. For over a week Albert struggled to live but, on a cold winter's day, he died in Victoria's arms. He was only 42.

Victoria suffered a nervous breakdown as a result of Albert's death. For 'two dreadful first years of loneliness' she tried to adjust to life without him. Even when she finally returned to public life she wore widow's clothes. She could not forget her late husband. Every night at Windsor, Albert's clothes were laid out on the bed; every morning, fresh water was put in the basin in his room. Above her bedstead there was a head and shoulders study of him. Victoria created a shrine of his personal belongings in an attempt to keep the memory of Albert alive.

For the rest of her long life (she lived to the age of 82), Victoria always remembered. Forty years after his death, when Victoria herself finally passed away, she was buried beside her Albert in the mausoleum near Windsor.

LOLA MONTEZ
AND LUDWIG I OF BAVARIA

Ludwig I of Bavaria was waiting impatiently in his private chambers. He had requested a visit from the notorious Spanish dancer Lola Montez, and she had agreed to give him a special demonstration of the frenzied dancing that had already made her famous – or infamous – throughout Europe. But Lola was late, and the king irritably paced around the room. What did she mean by making him wait?

Suddenly the door swung open and Ludwig gasped as an astonishingly lovely woman burst in, brandishing a glittering stiletto. Was this an assassination attempt? Mesmerised, the elderly king watched as the raven-haired woman slowly raised the stiletto high above her head, only to lower it again to slash open the front of her gown – revealing, according to Lola Montez's own account, 'two heaving hills of snow'. Ludwig gaped wordlessly at this glorious apparition. Then, crying, 'Such beauty cannot be real!' he advanced purposefully. Dancing displays were the last thing on his mind now; he had other plans for Lola Montez. She was not his first love, and she was not to be his last – but she was the one for whom the entranced king gladly forfeited his crown.

Ludwig had always known that his subjects expected their monarch to be a bit of a hell-raiser, and he did his best not to disappoint them. On the day of his birth, 25 August 1786, his father Prince Maximilian of Zweibrucken was ceremoniously presented by his devoted troops with a curious christening present for the royal tot. It was a lavishly embroidered cushion that had been stuffed with hair from their own beards and moustaches, symbols of their masculinity. The message was clear: little Ludwig was expected to grow up to be an exceptionally virile man.

And he did. Ascending the Bavarian throne in October 1825, Ludwig immediately devoted himself to his twin passions – architecture and women. The buildings he erected to beautify Munich, his capital, made it the talk of Europe, but his sexual energy was even more legendary. 'Variety is the spice of life,' he would say as a justification for changing his mistresses every week. His marriage to Thérèse of Saxe-Hildburghausen didn't slow him down, even though it produced four sons and four daughters.

Ludwig never claimed to be faithful to any of his legion of lovers, but Lola Montez managed to enthral him for three tumultuous years. She was more than a match for him in the art of love. Flagrantly unconventional, she smoked cigarettes in public, horsewhipped her critics when she wasn't challenging them to duels, and if a man attracted her, she didn't hesitate to tell him so. 'I like you,' she would say. 'What do you propose to do about it?'

Some men found her too hot to handle. One exhausted lover, the novelist Alexandre Dumas, declared ungallantly, 'She has the evil eye. Those who look upon her will die!' Other notable admirers, such as the composer Liszt and Nicholas I of Russia, were more appreciative of her charms, which were considerable.

She was not really Spanish; she was born plain Maria Gilbert in Ireland in 1818. But her flashing black eyes and ebony hair made her look every inch the 'Andalusian beauty'. 'There was something provoking and voluptuous [about her] which drew you. Her skin was white, her wavy hair like the tendrils of the woodbine, her eyes tameless and wild, her mouth like a budding pomegranate,' raved one admirer, adding more circumspectly, 'Unluckily, as a dancer she had no talent.'

That hardly mattered, for her celebrated and suggestive 'Spider Dance' was nothing more or less than a striptease act. It portrayed 'the distortions of a girl bitten by a poisonous spider', according to the programme notes, and reached its climax with 'a minimum of clothing covering her shapely body as she danced with fiery passion and sensuous movements'. Outraged critics attacked her outfit – or lack of one – as 'the most indelicate costume possible', but audiences loved her, on occasion showering her with a hail of golden nuggets.

She made something of a habit of taking off her clothes, and not only on stage. Once, when confronted with a mob howling for her blood, she contemptuously bared her bosom, utterly silencing them. When creditors threatened to imprison her for non-payment of debts, she calmly removed her dress and dared them to take her with them. The rest of the time she wore chaste black, in keeping with her 'Spanish' image, complete with a mantilla and crimson rose adorning her sable hair. Soon smart women everywhere were copying the 'Lola look', even the novelist George Sand, who usually favoured male attire.

But not everyone was beguiled by her beauty. Her dancing debut on the London stage was ruined when Lord Ranelagh, a rejected suitor, denounced her as an 'Irish impostor'. Mortified, Lola fled to the Continent, singing in the streets of Brussels for her supper … but not for long. She was 'looking for a prince', she said, and she found him in Ludwig of Bavaria.

Ludwig was pushing 60 when they met, while Lola was still in her twenties, but the difference in their ages didn't worry her. 'His soul is always fresh and young,' she declared. Ludwig was equally smitten. 'I know not how, but I am bewitched,' he told his ministers. He no longer allowed her to perform in public, preferring to keep his 'Lovely Andalusian' to himself, and he lavished gifts upon her. He granted her a pension of 20,000 florins a year, and he built her a miniature palace in the Theresienstrasse that he had fitted out with golden beds, silk sheets and Sèvres bathtubs. He made her Countess of Landfeld and Baroness Rosenthal, and when his ministers protested he threatened to sack them.

Lola gave equally short shrift to her detractors. She took to carrying a whip, and was accompanied everywhere by a ferocious

Ludwig I was besotted by the exotic Lola Montez.

bulldog that was ready to rip the seat out of the pants of any impertinent subject who cheeked the uncrowned empress of Bavaria. Poor long-suffering Thérèse was quite eclipsed. 'The Queen is the Queen, but I rule,' declared Lola with superb arrogance.

Opposition to the power of the 'Spanish woman' mounted, but the besotted king simply wouldn't listen. And Lola refused to be intimidated. When a rioting mob converged upon her mansion in Munich, she grabbed a revolver and marched out to confront them in her dressing gown. After delivering a virulent tongue lashing – Lola could swear in nine languages – she fired at the rebels, and was only saved from their wrath by the timely intervention of a detachment of the royal guards led by the king. But Ludwig couldn't save her – or even himself – for much longer. Ironically, it was Lola's sympathy for the wave of liberalism then convulsing Europe, more than her profligacy, that enraged the Bavarians.

Her dabbling in politics led to a movement to banish her

that Ludwig, his throne tottering, was powerless to quash. In 1848 she was issued with a deportation order, which she recklessly ripped apart in the faces of the police. Unimpressed, they bundled her into her carriage at gunpoint and escorted her to the border. Her brief reign was over. She was not yet 30.

Lola Montez, the sultry stripper who seduced an aging king.

The resilient Lola soon picked up the threads of her career and went to dance in America and Australia, presenting her own version of events in her show *Lola Montez in Bavaria*, as well as in her lurid autobiography. As the years passed and her charms dimmed, she turned to lecturing for a living, delivering speeches on topics like 'The Art of Beauty'.

Then, suddenly repenting her sensational past, she caught religion. It quickly became a mania and she was admitted to a New York asylum, where she died at the age of 43 on 17 January 1861, an open Bible in her hand. What remained of her fortune was left to the New York Home for Fallen Women, none of whose inmates could have fallen with quite the same style as Lola Montez, the sultry stripper who seduced a king.

Ludwig's career nosedived after Lola left him. He was forced to abdicate in favour of his son, Maximilian II, in March 1848 when revolution broke out in Bavaria. The rest of his life he devoted to the pursuit of women who resembled Lola. His passion for pleasure finally killed him; when he observed that his powers were beginning to wane at the age of 82, he decided to undergo a bizarre rejuvenation operation. But the incision turned septic and he died in Nice on 29 February 1868.

Ludwig was buried in Munich next to the grave of his official consort, Thérèse, but there were many who felt he should be lying beside the love of his life, the outrageous Lola Montez.

EDWARD AND MRS SIMPSON

'Oh Thelma, the little man is going to be so lonely,' said Bessie Wallis Warfield Simpson when her friend Thelma, Lady Furness, told her of her plans to leave England for a six-week visit to America early in 1934.

'You look after him for me,' came the light reply as Thelma continued packing. But she probably wouldn't have gone anywhere had she realised just how well her friend Wallis Simpson intended 'taking care' of the man being discussed. He was Thelma's lover, David – better known to the rest of the world as the Prince of Wales and future King Edward VIII of England – and a man Mrs Simpson had had her eye on for some time. But why should Thelma suspect her friend of trying to steal her man? She was no sultry seductress – she herself admitted that her jaw was too wide, her hair too straight and her figure too slight to be considered 'beautiful, or even pretty'.

However, the petite divorcée from Baltimore, America, did have considerable wit and style, a flair for fashion and an indefinable something that had won her two husbands – Winfield

Spencer and Ernest Simpson. Neither of those marriages had ultimately worked, and Wallis knew as soon as she set eyes on her friend's royal beau that he was the one man in the world for her. 'He was the open-sesame to a new and glittering world,' she said later.

He was also a glamorous figure in his own right, a handsome and generous Prince Charming in the austere England of the Depression era. He was a little eccentric, however. He spoke with a distinct Cockney accent, astonishing in one of his noble birth, and he favoured unconventional clothing – garish plus-fours and checked stockings. His hobbies included playing the bagpipes and embroidering.

His father, the starchy King George V, frequently wondered aloud whether David was up to the responsibilities of the throne. Such paternal misgivings were a regular feature of David's unhappy childhood. George V boasted that he had been terrified of his own father, Edward VII, and saw no reason why David should not be equally terrified of him. He saw nothing odd about publicly abusing David for his supposed shortcomings until his son was well into his thirties. David's mother, the aloof Queen Mary, was cold and unloving, and left David's rearing to the sadistic and unbalanced Nanny Peters. As he grew, the young prince yearned for the love denied him by his family.

George V may have believed that his heir lacked kingly qualities, but in fact he was an extraordinarily popular Prince of Wales. For one thing, his courage was legendary: during the First World War he insisted on serving in France, flinging himself into battle wherever the fighting was fiercest. He seemed almost to court danger, and when Lord Kitchener remonstrated with him, he replied with reckless gallantry: 'What does it matter if I am shot? I have four brothers.'

He also endeared himself to the common people by his intense interest in their welfare. 'Something must be done,' he declared when he met unemployed miners during a visit to the troubled coalfields of South Wales in the mid-1930s.

Ever unconventional, he dispensed with pomp and ceremony, insisting on selecting his own friends – and lovers. He had a fondness for married women – there was Mrs Freda Dudley Ward and Thelma, Lady Furness. And then there was Wallis Simpson.

David liked Americans for their easy informality, and he was immediately drawn to Wallis (she was rarely called by her detested given name). She was neither sycophantic nor impertinent, achieving the right blend of respect and genuine interest in his royal duties. It was a potent mix for the lonely young prince.

'She promised to bring into my life something that wasn't there,' he said later. 'I was convinced that with her I'd be a more creative and more useful person.'

Others put forward less worthy reasons for his growing obsession with the twice-divorced American. 'He made himself the slave of whomever he loved,' sniffed displaced royal favourite Freda Dudley Ward. 'He was a masochist, he liked being humbled, degraded, he begged for it!' He was certainly soon a slave to his love for Wallis, but he had no idea at first just how dearly it would cost him.

The Duke and Duchess of Windsor, one of the most famous love affairs of the twentieth century.

When George V died in 1936, David – now known as Edward VIII – was determined to make Wallis his queen. Their affair was a well-kept secret from his subjects because Fleet Street felt the public could not handle its idolised new monarch being linked with a commoner and a divorcée, but David was convinced he could talk the British Parliament into accepting Wallis as his consort. To his dismay, his plans were met with uncompromising resistance from his government. Prime Minister Stanley Baldwin tried to convince him that Wallis would be an unacceptable

Queen of England, and in desperation David proposed a morganatic match. Again the answer was no, but now the young king refused to listen.

'All that matters is our happiness,' he said, telling Baldwin: 'I can't do my job without her; I am going to marry her and I will go.'

At first Baldwin did not take seriously David's threats to abdicate if he could not have his American bride on his own terms. But others saw that he was in deadly earnest.

'Make no mistake, this is one of the great loves of history,' observed Winston Churchill.

'It is no ordinary love,' conceded Queen Mary, who was appalled by her son's entanglement.

Soon it became clear that it was a love that would brook no denial. On 11 December 1936, David broadcast his moving abdication speech from Windsor Castle.

'You must believe me when I tell you that I have found it impossible to carry the heavy burden of responsibility and to discharge my duties as King as I would wish to do without the help and support of the woman I love,' he told his stunned subjects.

In the early hours of the next morning he quietly set sail for the Continent, where Wallis, in hiding from the press, awaited him. He had been king for just eleven months, and had never been crowned. His younger brother Bertie, the Duke of York, was crowned King George VI in May the following year, and David wed his Wallis a month later in a private ceremony at the Château de Cande, near Tours. Not one member of the royal family was present, and David never forgave his brother, England's new king, for the message informing him that he and his wife would now be known as the Duke and Duchess of Windsor, but that Wallis would never be called 'Her Royal Highness' – which had been David's dearest wish.

Now began their life together in exile. Wallis felt that she must make up for what David had lost: 'My husband gave up everything for me,' she said. 'My duty, as I saw it, was to evoke for him the nearest equivalent to a kingly life that I could produce without a kingdom.'

But it was a kingdom David seemed to think was well lost for love. He had no regrets. Years later he told a friend: 'I've spent the best years of my life with Wallis, and I can tell you that nothing I gave up equals what she has given me. Happiness, of course, but also meaning. I have found her to be utterly without faults, the perfect woman.' On another occasion he said, 'She gave me comfort and love and kindness ...'

The Windsors led a life of luxury and leisure, a perpetual round of luncheons, cocktail parties, dinners, galas and endless travel. But inevitably the pleasure palled, and the duke began to yearn for a useful function. Again and again he begged his brother to find him a suitable job, but he found it was not easy to be a king in exile. He was not welcome in Britain, where it was feared he would overshadow the shy Bertie, and the best position that could be found for him was the governorship of the Bahamas – as far out of harm's way as possible, whispered the uncharitable.

The royal family also made it clear that Wallis was still

considered an adventuress who had lured the king from the path of duty. She was not to be really forgiven until the duke died of cancer in May 1972. Wallis was invited to Windsor Castle for his funeral and subsequent burial in the vault of Frogmore, where he had requested to be laid to rest near his great-grandmother, Queen Victoria. She spent the night at Buckingham Palace, where she was photographed staring out a window, her face a desolate mask of grief.

Even though the royal family now made overtures to the duchess, she increasingly retreated into her own private world of sorrow. The duke's room at their last home, a château at the Bois de Boulogne outside Paris, was kept exactly as he left it. She paid off the 22 servants who had tended them both, leaving herself alone but for her devoted butler Georges and his wife Ophelia, and her lawyer, Maître Suzanne Blum. 'The nights,' she said shortly after the duke's death, 'are rather agony.'

Her health declined after a series of strokes during the 1970s. Daily bulletins of her health were sent to the British embassy in Paris and passed on to Buckingham Palace. The queen agreed that when the time came for Wallis to rejoin her husband, she could be buried alongside him at Frogmore. And, true to this promise, when Wallis died in 1986, aged 89, she was buried beside her beloved David in the Royal Burial Ground of the Windsors. The love story that divided an empire had finally reached its end.

LITERARY
LOVERS

Lord Byron and Lady Caroline Lamb

In the spring of 1812, Lady Caroline Lamb wrote in her diary that a devastatingly handsome 24-year-old poet she had just met was 'bad, mad and dangerous to know'. She paused, then slowly added, 'But that beautiful pale face is my fate ...'

The beautiful face belonged to George Gordon Noel, Lord Byron, and no one was more aware than he of the power it gave him over women. He worked on his good looks; he was said to wear curling papers to bed to keep his dark auburn locks in order, and he kept his splendid figure trim with exercises, hot baths and purgatives. He maintained his poetic pallor with a diet of mashed potatoes and vinegar. Despite a clubfoot, of which he was overwhelmingly sensitive, he had tremendous sexual magnetism: 'Ladies almost fainted at the sort of under look he used to give,' remarked one contemporary.

His talent was as remarkable as his appearance. In 1812 he took fashionable London by storm with poetry that was as sultry as his looks. He had just returned from two years' travel in the romantic Near East, with a handful of poems 'not worth troubling about' in his pocket. But within three weeks of publication these first cantos of *Childe Harold's Pilgrimage* had sold out seven editions. Now the dark, limping poet was lionised by every salon hostess and idolised by every artistic young lady in London. Byron was quick to respond to female advances, and his promiscuity was already a scandal in polite society.

In Lady Caroline Lamb he finally met a woman whose fiery, passionate nature more than equalled his own. A slight, tomboyish woman with a tousled crop of short curls, she loved to dress up as a man – when she wore clothes, that is. A perennial exhibitionist, she horrified guests at her wedding to William Lamb (later Lord Melbourne) by tearing off her gown after an argument with the officiating bishop. The imperturbable William put up with this, but even he was startled while giving a dinner party, when his wife had herself carried in on a silver serving plate – stark naked.

Her affair with Byron was conducted with the same blatancy. Two days after meeting at a ball, the pair were spending blissful hours together in her bedchamber, right under William's nose. The cuckolded husband tried to laugh off his chagrin. When Caroline mischievously asked him at the breakfast table, after a night spent in her lover's arms, 'William, what is the seventh commandment?' he lightly replied: 'My dear, thou shalt not bother.'

But Lady Caroline did bother – she poured all her energies into the pursuit of her poet. If he were invited somewhere that she wasn't, she would wait outside for him in her carriage, or else come in looking for him dressed as a page, pretending to have a message for him. They went through a mock marriage ceremony, writing their vows in a book and signing them 'Byron' and 'Caroline Byron'. They heaped one another with gifts, and were frequently to be seen sitting in her carriage, openly kissing and fondling one another.

Byron's love for his lady shines through in a letter he wrote to Caroline:

> *Then your heart, my poor Caro (what a little volcano!), that pours lava through your veins; and yet I cannot wish it a bit colder ... you know I have always thought you the cleverest, most agreeable, absurd, amiable, perplexing, dangerous, fascinating little being that lives now or ought to have lived 2000 years ago.*

But Byron was not as patient and understanding as William Lamb, and before long Caroline's increasingly erratic behaviour began to grate. Her jealous tantrums were making her the laughing stock of London. William's mother, Lady Melbourne, was quick to pour scorn upon her daughter-in-law. 'She is now only troublesome in private and a great bore in public,' she wrote to Lord Byron.

Lady Melbourne had an ulterior motive for running Caroline down, however; in common with half the society women of the day, she fancied Byron for herself. Despite the difference in their ages Lady Melbourne was an attractive woman, and she had little difficulty fascinating the susceptible young poet. He began seeing less of Caroline, and she realised she had a rival for his affections. Now her jealousy knew no bounds. She staged hysterical scenes. She wept. She screamed abuse at him. She was utterly

Lady Caroline Lamb became unhinged by her passion for Byron.

transformed from the blithe tomboy who had stolen his heart, and finally Byron had had as much as he could take.

'Correct your vanity which has become ridiculous,' he wrote to her coldly. 'Exert your caprices on others ... and leave me in peace!'

Peace was the last thing Caroline wanted, for herself or anyone else. She wept for a fortnight after receiving this unfriendly letter, and then she made an enormous bonfire on which she publicly burned his effigy, along with locks of his hair and other mementoes. She issued her servants with new livery, complete with buttons upon which were engraved the words: 'Do not believe Byron'.

When Byron did not react to this, Caroline resorted to even more direct action. She took to storming in on him at all hours of the day and night. 'You talk to me about keeping her out,' he wrote wearily to Lady Melbourne. 'It is impossible, she comes in at all times, at any time; the minute the door is opened, in she walks.'

Even closed doors couldn't stop Caroline. On one occasion she sneaked in, disguised in her favourite pageboy outfit, only to find Byron in the arms of another woman. She stormed out in tears, and Byron rammed home the message by sending her a cruel present –

a bracelet woven out of the golden hair of another of his lovers.

But passion had unhinged Caroline. She simply couldn't accept that Byron no longer loved her. She haunted his rooms like a plaintive ghost, leaving notes like: 'Remember me?' Byron retorted poetically, if ungraciously:

> *Remember thee! Aye, doubt it not*
> *Thy husband too shall think of thee*
> *By neither shalt thou be forgot*
> *Thou false to him, thou fiend to me!*

But still Caroline refused to believe that Byron had abandoned her – until, almost in self-defence, he took a wife, Annabella Milbanke. They separated after a thoroughly unhappy year together, and the ensuing scandal was blown up by Caroline's spiteful revelations that among Byron's legions of lovers was his half-sister, Augusta Leigh. The public outcry was such that Byron was forced to flee England in disgrace.

Then Caroline sat down and wrote *Glenarvon*, a fictionalised account of her fling with Byron. A rattling Gothic yarn full of murderers, maniacs and ghosts, it made her as much of a laughing stock as him, but it also made money – within weeks, three editions had sold out. Caroline

Lord Byron, 'bad, mad and dangerous to know.'

established a promising career as a popular novelist, but with every year her grasp on reality grew weaker. She still had a weakness for taking off her clothes; on at least one occasion her long-suffering husband had to retrieve her from the streets of Brussels, where she had been promenading half-naked. William tried to entertain her with frequent trips abroad, but finally even he reached the end of his tether. In 1825, after fifteen years of marriage, he separated from Caroline. She was overwhelmed by this final rejection. She became ill, and within three years was on the point of death from dropsy. Dutiful William came rushing to her bedside when he heard the news.

Just as she died Caroline whispered to her nurse: 'I wish I could have loved him more.' But of course she couldn't. All her passion was reserved for her errant poet.

Ever the romantic, Byron had something of a weakness for lost causes. He became obsessed with the struggle of the Greeks against their Turkish overlords, and when Greek liberals mounted an uprising, he placed his considerable fortune at the rebels' disposal. Then he himself joined in the fighting, at the head of his own privately equipped expedition. A gallant and decisive leader, he advanced as far as Missolonghi. There he succumbed to a chill and, worn out with war and privation, he died on 9 April 1824.

'Let my body not be hacked or sent to England,' he begged shortly before his death. But it was not to be. His friends quickly arranged for his body to be returned home for burial in the family vault, but first his heart was removed and given to the citizens of Missolonghi – that heart which Lady Caroline Lamb had once so confidently believed belonged to her.

PERCY BYSSHE SHELLEY
AND MARY GODWIN

'I was not yet in love and was in love with loving,' wrote Percy Bysshe Shelley as an Oxford undergraduate. 'I was looking for something to love, loving to love ...'

One of the greatest Romantic poets of the early nineteenth century, Percy Shelley was in love with love. All his short life he was obsessed with his ideal of the perfect woman, one 'who can feel poetry and understand philosophy'. He found her in Mary Godwin, daughter of the radical philosopher William Godwin and his wife, the feminist writer Mary Wollstonecraft. She was only a 16-year-old schoolgirl when they met, but she understood the restless poet, philosopher and social idealist in a way few others could in the stodgy, conservative England of the post-French Revolutionary era.

Even his friends called Percy 'Mad Shelley'. He was born into an eccentric family: his grandfather, Sir Bysshe Shelley, erected an £80,000 mansion only to dwell in a humble cottage in its grounds, squirrelling enormous sums of money into odd corners. Percy's father, Sir Timothy Shelley, reacted against his father's oddness by becoming a conservative bigot. Alarmed by young Percy's vivid imagination and incessant scribbling, he packed him off to school at Sion House where, according to one account, 'He seemed like a girl in boy's clothing, fighting with open hands and rolling on the floor when flogged, not from pain but from a sense of indignity.' No amount of flogging could stop him writing poetry, it seemed.

Shelley had a highly developed social conscience, and he was already aware of the injustices of life. Later, while attending Eton, he organised a revolt against fagging, the practice of having younger boys wait upon older students. He was still rebellious when he went up to Oxford, a tall, stooped young man with large blue eyes and a shock of russet curls. He published a pamphlet called *The Necessity of Atheism*, in which he attempted to disprove the existence of God on 'geometric grounds'. It had only been circulating for a couple of hours before he was sent packing by his outraged tutors, vainly protesting that he 'had never met with such unworthy treatment'. His father, horrified by Percy's expulsion from Oxford, kept him on a short rein, and he was reduced to borrowing pocket money from his young sisters.

During one such financial mission to his sister Elizabeth's select academy, he met her friend Harriet Westbrook. The romantic schoolgirl was soon under the young poet's spell. She wrote to him that she was being tormented at school, and he rushed chivalrously to the rescue, eloping with her to Gretna Green. She seems to have loved him, but he, ever the libertarian, was only concerned with saving her from apparent tyranny. He soon infected Harriet with his revolutionary fervour, and together the teenage newly-weds descended upon Dublin 'to emancipate Irish Catholics'. But the Dubliners simply laughed at the earnest young reformers.

They returned to England and set up house in Lynmouth, where a daughter was born to them in June 1813. They named her Ianthe, after a character in Percy's epic poem *Queen Mab*, which he had just completed and was to make him famous. Before long, Harriet found that the demands of motherhood left her little time to spend on Percy's dreams of a better world. Gradually they drifted apart, and Percy began to despair of his ideal of a perfect union.

Then came another schoolgirl on the scene to set him on fire again – with love, not chivalry, this time. Mary Godwin, the radical child of radical parents, had ideas just as advanced as Percy's, and her fair hair and intense hazel eyes were equally appealing to the passionate poet. They met when he called on her father to discuss philosophy, and each immediately recognised a kindred free spirit.

Despite his marriage – Harriet was in fact expecting their second child at any moment – Percy and Mary eloped, bolting to the Continent. As an afterthought, Mary's stepsister Jane Clairmont came along for the ride, which was the couple's first mistake. The second was the donkey that Percy pawned his watch to buy in Paris. Intending to walk from France to Switzerland, they wanted the donkey to carry their luggage, but it was so small that Percy ended up carrying it in his arms, leaving the two

Percy Bysshe Shelley, 'in love with loving.'

women to carry the bags. The journey across Europe was made more difficult by Jane falling for Percy and declaring her love every step of the way. Fortunately, her affections were soon deflected to the even more attractive romantic poet Lord Byron, but Mary was already beginning to see that her life with Percy would not be an easy one.

When they returned to England, they set up an unconventional household with the tiresome Jane, who had changed her name to Clare. Soon Mary discovered that she was going to have a baby. She was unperturbed by the prospect of bearing a child out of wedlock. After all, had not her famous mother Mary Wollstonecraft denounced marriage as slavery in her controversial book *A Vindication of the Rights of Women*? But she was extremely upset when the child died just three weeks after birth. Both she and Percy were devastated, but they were consoled by the birth of another child, William – 'little Willmouse' – in January 1816.

Percy, full of love for all humanity, asked his estranged wife Harriet to join their unconventional household, but she refused.

This didn't cramp their style, however; later that year they journeyed to Geneva, where Clare met up with Lord Byron again. She became pregnant and gave birth to his daughter, Allegra.

This overseas stint was a productive time for the Shelleys. Percy published a number of poems, including the autobiographical *Alastor*, while Mary, not yet 20, dashed off the classic horror story *Frankenstein*, an extraordinary tale of a monster

Mary Godwin, a free spirit after Shelley's own heart.

created by a scientist without a conscience. But tragedy struck again when they returned to England in the autumn of 1816. Harriet, jilted by a lover, drowned herself in the Serpentine River, and Percy was denied custody of his and Harriet's children, Ianthe and Charles, the child who was born after his elopement with Mary. No less a personage than the Lord Chancellor declared him morally unfit to be a father.

Percy's image was not much redeemed when he wed Mary a fortnight after Harriet's death. Despairing of social acceptance, he threw himself into his work, producing the epic poem *The Revolt of Islam*, an idealisation of platonic love and friendship, in 1817. Around the same time Mary gave birth to a daughter, Clara, and for a while the couple's happiness seemed complete.

Then Percy's old restlessness set in and the odd ménage – Percy, Mary, William, Clara, Clare and her daughter Allegra – took off for a long tour of Italy. Tragically, each of the children perished of various diseases during the trip. Percy found some outlet for his misery in his dramatic verse *Prometheus Unbound*, but Mary's despair seemed bottomless. She sank into a deep depression from which she was only roused by the birth of another child, little Percy Florence Shelley, named after his birthplace, Florence. The journey got underway again, now with the addition of Percy's friends Jane and Edward Williams, and finished up at the Casa Magni, a house on the waterfront of the Gulf of Spezia. There, Percy and Edward spent many happy hours sailing a small boat, the *Don Juan*, which they had had built in Genoa.

Then came the day when Percy decided to visit his old friend Byron, now living at Leghorn, a seven-hour sail around the coast. The visit was a success but a storm blew up when Percy and Edward were making the homeward trip. The boat vanished, never to be seen again, but some time later two bodies were washed up on the shore, half-eaten by fish. One was identified as Percy Bysshe Shelley only by his jacket, which held a copy of Keats' poems in one pocket and a volume of Sophocles in the other.

Percy's wanderings were finally at an end. He was only 32. His body was burned on a funeral pyre of pinewood, but after three hours the flames had still not consumed his heart. It was removed and later buried in the Protestant cemetery in Rome, under a headstone inscribed with Shelley's self-composed, remarkably prophetic epitaph. It read: 'Here lies one whose name was writ in water.'

After his death, a heart-broken Mary returned to England to devote herself to raising their one surviving child, little Percy Florence. She was only 25, and she spent the next 29 years of widowhood tending Percy's memory, editing his poems and publishing new editions of his works. She became a noted novelist, biographer and travel writer in her own right, although none of her later works had the sensational success of her earliest effort, *Frankenstein*, in whose monstrous protagonist later writers saw parallels with her husband.

Like Frankenstein's monster, Percy Shelley had been misunderstood and ostracised by a callous, uncaring society. Ultimately Percy could only find peace in flight from his homeland – and in the arms of his schoolgirl bride, Mary. And she could only find peace with him. Many men wished to marry the attractive authoress after Percy's death, but she always replied smilingly: 'I think Mary Shelley so pretty a name I wish to have it on my tombstone.'

Victor Hugo
and Juliette Drouet

As Victor Hugo lay dying, he whispered to his grandson Georges: 'Love ... Seek love ... Give pleasure and take it in loving as fully as you can!'

This was a maxim which Hugo himself had followed all his life. In the four months before his death at the age of 83, he proudly recorded no fewer than eight affairs in his diary. Today, Victor Hugo might well have been diagnosed as suffering from satyriasis, the male equivalent of nymphomania, but to the citizens of nineteenth-century France such compulsive sexuality was what they expected from their foremost poet, novelist and dramatist.

The son of one of Napoleon's generals, Victor established himself as leader of the Romantic movement with some 25 volumes of fiery, passionate verse. His reputation was reinforced by his great novels, including *Notre Dame de Paris*, *L'Homme Qui Rit* and *Les Misérables*. The latter was based on his own experiences as an impoverished student in Paris, the city he immortalised with his prose, calling it 'the birthplace of my soul'.

Though his philandering brought him nearly as much fame – or infamy – as his writing, Victor was a virgin the day he married Adèle Foucher in 1822. But he soon made up for lost time: according to his biographer André Maurois, 'he had knowledge of his wife nine separate times in the course of his wedding night'.

It was an eventful evening in more ways than one; Victor's brother Eugene, who had courted Adèle himself, went mad from jealousy and had to be clapped into a lunatic asylum. Exhausted by all the emotional tension, to say nothing of Victor's lovemaking, Adèle withdrew from her husband and embarked on an affair with his best friend, the author Sainte Beuve.

Although the Hugos' marriage continued in name until Adèle's death in 1869, Victor made no secret of the fact that he was seeking consolation elsewhere ... everywhere. He never seriously pretended fidelity to any woman, but the great love of his life was undoubtedly Juliette Drouet, a *demi-mondaine*, minor actress and great beauty. She was his emotional anchor for half a century, and inspired some of his greatest work.

The daughter of a humble Breton tailor, Juliette was orphaned at the age of two and grew up wild under the guardianship of a bachelor uncle, one Lieutenant Drouet. Expelled from convent school at sixteen, she ran away to Paris, where her voluptuous figure ensured her success as an artist's model. Before long Juliette had graduated to prostitution, and she became the mistress of a succession of wealthy and powerful men. Then she took to the stage, winning a role in Victor's play *Lucretia Borgia*.

Victor Hugo, a great writer and a great philanderer.

The young actress looked 'like a bird of flame' according to Victor, who was immediately captivated by Juliette's wonderful figure, lustrous black hair, beguiling smile – and by her expertise at lovemaking, which equalled his own.

'The ritual of love, like poetry, is an art, and in that art Juliette was deeply skilled,' wrote Maurois. Their love was first consummated, according to Victor's diary, on 16 February 1833, and from then on Juliette devoted her formidable skills exclusively to him. Every February for the following 50 years Victor marked this date with a passionate avowal of his feelings in Juliette's anniversary book.

Victor was hardly Juliette's first lover, but he was her last. She gave up everything for him, abandoning her acting career to be at his beck and call, becoming a voluntary prisoner of love. For the first thirteen years of their relationship, she refused to step outside the flat which Victor called 'the ante-chamber to paradise' in case he should need her. Juliette was Victor's secretary, his cook, his nurse and his muse, as well as his lover.

She had no regrets: 'My clumsy shoes, faded curtains, my cheap spoons and the absence of ornament and pleasure, apart from our love, testify at every hour and every minute that I love you with all my heart,' she declared in a letter dated 1840.

Whenever they were parted, Juliette entertained thoughts of suicide. 'After the two months of love which have just passed, I fear like death the life in

Juliette Drouet couldn't live with Victor Hugo and couldn't live without him.

Paris,' she wrote during a separation in 1840. Upset by Victor's numerous infidelities, she was roused to uncharacteristic fury when she found he was two-timing her with the writer Léonie Biard, wife of the court painter François Biard. Informed of the affair by Juliette, François organised a police raid on Victor and Léonie, catching them *in flagrante delicto*. Léonie was promptly imprisoned for adultery, but Victor claimed immunity on the grounds that he had just been made a peer for his service to literature.

To spite Juliette, Adèle Hugo paid 1000 francs to bail Léonie out of Sainte Lazare jail, while King Louis Philippe personally intervened to scotch the scandal, ordering François Biard to withdraw his complaint.

Juliette was more supportive when Victor's political fortunes declined. A member of the French Assembly, he was outspoken in his condemnation of Louis Napoleon's 1851 *coup d'état*, and the police put a price of 25,000 francs on his head. Terrified, Juliette organised a series of hideouts for her lover, then produced a forged passport to enable him to flee Paris in her carriage, disguised as a common labourer. He escaped to the Channel Islands where Juliette joined him – at a distance. Victor's estranged wife Adèle still shared his home, even in exile, and Juliette had to rent a neighbouring house for herself. After Adèle's death, Juliette was finally accepted by Victor's family, and she was now officially mistress of his home as well as his heart.

In 1870, with the collapse of the French Republic, the lovers returned in triumph to Paris to start a new life together. But Victor was still philandering, even competing for the favours of his own son's mistress. After an episode involving a 22-year-old copyist called Blanche, Juliette decided she had finally had enough and walked out. Heartbroken, Victor scoured the country for her, declaring, 'My life and soul are gone!' But not for long – after three days Juliette relented and returned to him. She found she couldn't live without him, so she simply accepted that Victor was faithful to her in spirit, if not in action. 'To make a speech is more exhausting for me than making love three times, even four times,' he confessed in his seventies.

'Let us commence our 50th year together with this divine saying: "I love you",' he wrote on the anniversary of their first meeting. But the love that had endured half a century had not much further to run. Juliette's health had been failing for some time, and she died in 1883, aged 77.

Victor never wrote another word. Scarcely two years later he followed her to the grave, buried, according to his wish, in a pauper's coffin. But while his coffin may have been plain, his funeral, attended by tens of thousands of Parisians chanting his verses, was not.

Street lamps were swathed in black crêpe along the route of the funeral procession, which was lined with a guard of honour of young French poets carrying shields inscribed with the titles of their hero's works.

GEORGE BERNARD SHAW
AND ELLEN TERRY

George Bernard Shaw was terrified of sex. He claimed to be unable to understand how any self-respecting man and woman could face one another in the morning after making love. So he was happy to conduct his long, passionate friendship with the actress Ellen Terry almost entirely by post. For George Bernard Shaw, a Nobel Prize winner and the most prolific playwright of all time, believed a perfect relationship existed only on paper.

'My correspondence with Ellen Terry was a wholly satisfactory love affair,' he said. 'I could have met her at any time but I did not wish to complicate such a delightful intercourse.'

Dame Ellen Terry was no slouch in the letter-writing department herself. The greatest Shakespearean actress of the nineteenth century, Ellen was strikingly lovely – 'A being of an exquisite and mobile beauty', according to a critic for *The Times*. Unlike Shaw, she did not disdain physical love – she had no fewer than five husbands – but there was a cerebral side to the sensual actress.

Their celebrated correspondence began when she approached him on behalf of a young musician when Shaw was working as a professional music critic. She immediately sensed a soulmate in the eccentric Irishman with the flaming red hair. The fact that they rarely met only strengthened the relationship.

'It must be borne in mind that long and intimate correspondence can only occur between people who never meet one another,' explained Shaw. 'Ellen and I lived within 20 minutes of each other's doorstep, yet lived in different worlds; she in a theatre that was a century behind the times, and I in a political society [the Fabian Society] a century ahead of them. We were both too busy to have any personal intercourse except with the people we were working with.'

Shaw may have been busy, but he still found time to churn out over a quarter of a million letters during his 94 years on earth, a great number of which were addressed to Ellen Terry. He poured out his heart and all his thoughts to her, including this amusing account of the loss of his virginity:

> *Up to the time I was 29, I was too shabby for any woman to tolerate me. I stalked around in a decaying green coat, cuffs trimmed with the scissors, terrible boots and so on. Then I got a job to do and bought a suit of clothes with the proceeds. A lady immediately invited me to tea, threw her arms round me and said she adored me. I permitted her to adore, being intensely curious on the subject … Since that*

> *time, whenever I have been left alone in a room with*
> *a female, she has invariably thrown her arms round*
> *me and declared she adored me. It is fate.*
>
> *Therefore beware. If you allow yourself to be left*
> *alone with me for a single moment, you will*
> *certainly throw your arms around me and declare*
> *that you adore me, and I am not prepared to*
> *guarantee that my usual melancholy forbearance*
> *will be available in your case.*

To which Ellen, who signed herself 'your lover', coquettishly replied:

> *Oh, mayn't I throw my arms round you when (!) we*
> *meet? Then I shan't play … I'll wait until you need*
> *me, and then I'll mother you. That's the only*
> *unselfish love. I've never been admired or loved*
> *(properly) but one-and-a-half times in my life, and*
> *I am perfectly sick of loving …*

'[Ellen] got tired of five husbands,' Shaw smugly told his biographer Hesketh Pearson, 'but she never got tired of me.' Nevertheless, he was jealous of her long theatrical partnership with the distinguished actor/producer Henry Irving, and he did his best to sabotage it. But he didn't allow his marriage, at the age of 42, to the Irish heiress Charlotte Payne-Townsend to interfere with his mailbag romance with Ellen. In fact, he asked Ellen's advice about it:

> *Shall I marry my Irish millionairess? She …*
> *believes in freedom, and not in marriage; but I think*

I could prevail on her and then I should have ever so many hundreds a month for nothing. Would you ever in your secret soul forgive me, even though I am really fond of her and she of me? No, you wouldn't.

Ellen must have forgiven Shaw, for when he took the plunge with Charlotte on 1 June 1898 she wrote wistfully: 'Oh, I see you two walking in the damp and lovely mist, a trail of light from your footsteps, and – I don't think it's envy, but I know my eyes are quite wet, and I long to be one of you, and I don't care which …'

Shaw even described his wedding day in a wittily self-deprecating letter to Ellen:

The registrar never imagined I could possibly be the bridegroom, taking me for the inevitable beggar who completes all wedding processions. Wallas [Shaw's witness], over six feet tall, was so obviously the hero of the occasion that the registrar was on the point of marrying him to my betrothed.

But Wally, thinking the formula rather too strong for a mere witness, hesitated at the last moment and left the prize to me.

Charlotte may have believed in freedom, but she was rather piqued by the correspondence flourishing between her new husband and the famous actress. 'She will be pretty curious about you,' Shaw told Ellen, 'not only on the usual grounds of your celebrity, but because she has discovered that "work" and "important business" on my part means writing long letters to you.'

Ellen Terry. Words sustained her relationship with Shaw – and destroyed it too.

Poor Charlotte may also have been 'curious' about the fact that George Bernard Shaw decreed that their marriage would not be consummated. He preferred platonic relationships – though he was fascinated by female beauty – and he liked women to keep their distance. This could have been the reason why his and Ellen's romance ultimately foundered when they finally spent a great deal of time together, rehearsing one of his plays.

In an 1899 letter to Shaw, Ellen lamented the fact that there were no decent roles for actresses of her age (she was then 52, and a grandmother). Shaw promptly wrote *Captain Brassbound's Conversion* for her, basing the character of Lady Cicely on her letters to him. 'In every other play I have ever written – even in *Candida* – I have prostituted the actress more or less by making the interest in her partly a sexual interest,' he told her. 'In Lady Cicely I have done without this, and gained a greater fascination by it.'

This was the greatest tribute Shaw could pay a woman and an

artist, and so his chagrin was great when she wrote to say that the play wouldn't make a penny, and that the part didn't suit her and would be better played by another actress. 'Of course you never *really* meant Lady Cicely for me,' she added waspishly, 'but to be published along with your other plays!'

'Oh you lie, Ellen, you lie,' Shaw wrote back angrily. 'Never was there a part so deeply written for a woman as this for you, you silly, self-unconscious,

George Bernard Shaw liked women, but preferably at a distance.

will o' the wisp beglamoured child actress as you still are … I honestly thought that Lady Cicely would fit you like a glove … And so farewell our project – all fancy, like most projects!'

And farewell Ellen. With the vanity of a great actress, she never forgave Shaw his portrait of her. 'She became a legend in her old age; but of that I have nothing to say, for we did not meet and, except for a few broken letters, did not write; and she was never old to me,' he commented sadly on her death at the age of 81 in 1928.

Characteristically, Shaw had the last word on their odd relationship, which could withstand time but not propinquity: 'Let those who may complain that it was all on paper remember that only on paper has humanity yet achieved glory, beauty, truth, knowledge, virtue and abiding love.'

REBECCA WEST
AND H.G. WELLS

H.G. Wells went into his study one day and found a young woman lying across the hearthrug. She was wearing a raincoat, which she flung open, revealing herself naked except for shoes and stockings. 'You must love me,' she said, 'or I will kill myself. I have poison. I have a razor.'

Wells stared down at the hysterical woman and swore softly to himself. Why did women find him so damned attractive? Why were they always making scenes? He didn't want this woman. He wanted his lover, Rebecca West.

Herbert George Wells was something of a literary prophet. He wrote about aerial warfare in 1902, when aeroplanes were still crazy, kite-like contraptions. He wrote fancifully of 'iron-clad road fighting vehicles' taking part in a war, anticipating the invention of the tank by more than a decade. And most spectacular of all, in his book *The World Set Free* he described the destruction of cities by atomic bombing. That was in 1914

– 31 years before the obliteration of Hiroshima by just that method.

Wells wrote his first book in 1895 and from then on he never stopped writing. His first success was *The Time Machine*, which tells of how a Victorian scientist builds a machine that, after some trial and error, transports him to the year 802701. That was the beginning of one of the most astonishing literary outpourings the world has known. He wrote an average of nearly one and a half books a year for 50 years, as well as thousands of articles, pamphlets, papers, lectures and radio talks.

It was little wonder that the beautiful young Rebecca West fell passionately in love with this literary lion. They met in 1913. He was 46. She was 20. She was a young newspaper reporter who had been sent to interview the great man. There was an immediate attraction between them, in spite of the considerable difference in age. Rebecca was romantic; she wanted adventure. She began to pursue H.G.

Rebecca was born Cicily Fairfield on Christmas Day 1892. She moved to London when she was eighteen to become an actress, but she quickly tired of playing to empty theatre houses and decided to abandon the theatrical life. She did, however, keep one thing – her new name. Rebecca West was the strong-willed heroine of Ibsen's play *Rosmersholm*. So overnight, Cicily Fairfield disappeared and Rebecca West took her place.

Rebecca began to write for a feminist newspaper, *The Freewoman*, and then moved to political writing for *The Clarion*, a socialist newspaper. Although only 20 years old, she was already becoming known for her intelligence and wit. It was no coincidence that she had chosen to identify herself with Ibsen's dazzling and rebellious heroine. It was as though she was willing her whole life to become a defiance of what men thought a woman ought to be. George Bernard Shaw commented: 'Rebecca can handle a pen as brilliantly as ever I could, and much more savagely.'

When she decided to embark on an affair with H.G. Wells Rebecca was a young, beautiful, liberated woman. She knew that he was married and had children but she didn't care. She wanted to have an adventure. She wanted to feel alive, outside the narrow conventions that society placed on its women. She wasn't asking for marriage. She was asking for love.

H.G. Wells was surprised when the young journalist made the first move. He writes:

> *I liked her and found her very interesting, but I was on my good behaviour and we kept the talk bookish and journalistic. Until … face to face with my bookshelves, in the midst of a conversation about style or some such topic, and apropos of nothing, we paused and suddenly kissed each other. Then Rebecca flamed up into open and declared passion. She demanded to be my lover and made an accusation of my kiss. It was a promise, she said. I, too, was by way of thinking that a kiss ought to be a promise. But it was a very unexpected kiss.*

And so began a ten-year affair that was passionate, fiery and brilliant. It was a meeting of minds and bodies. They called each

H.G.Wells, 'Jaguar' to Rebecca West's 'Panther'.

other by pet names – Rebecca was 'Panther' and Wells was 'Jaguar' – names that symbolised the animal side of their relationship. They delighted in the sheer physical well-being of being in love. Wells wrote to Rebecca that he wanted to be 'loving but obscene'. He eulogised her 'dear fur' and spoke of coming up to London for 'a snatch at your ears and a whisk of the tail'.

Very early in the affair Rebecca fell ill. Wells was at home with his wife but he reacted characteristically. He wrote: 'You must get well because sickness and illness take the Magic out of life. Sick Panthers become little Rebeccas and Jaguars become kind and attentive Fathers and there can be no more love making until the creature is bounding well again.'

Rebecca soon discovered that she was not in fact ill; she was pregnant. This was 1913. Nice young women did not get pregnant to married men. But Rebecca was pregnant and she decided with her usual determination to have the baby. She was a free spirit and quite capable of breaking the middle-class rules of her generation. Marriage was obviously out of the question, as H.G. Wells was already married. But, together, they proposed to lead a secret life. Wells would have two homes: one with his wife and one with Rebecca.

Rebecca West risked her reputation for Wells when she bore him a son.

'Rebecca had never wanted anything more than a richly imaginative and sensuous love affair with me,' writes Wells, 'and now we have to attempt all sorts of vaguely conceived emotional adjustments.'

Most of the adjustments were made by Rebecca. She moved from rented house to rented house. She had nothing but Wells – from time to time – and her writing. She had not planned to become pregnant. She saw herself primarily as a writer, and she never stopped experimenting with the written word. She wrote articles for various newspapers and began to tackle novels.

Anthony Panther West was born like some sort of after-thought to the grand affair on 4 August 1914, the date on which England declared war on Germany. Anthony was a miserable boy, who was shunted from continent to continent and home to home. Sometimes he was known as Rebecca West's son, sometimes her nephew, and sometimes a young friend. Life was hard for a young woman with an illegitimate son. Anthony had a strange, lonely childhood, the heritage of a lifestyle of two brilliant but selfish parents.

The affair continued, but as Rebecca flowered into her twenties and became more certain of herself and her writing, she became less dependent on Wells. She was sick of spending her youth virtually in hiding as Wells' mistress. She wanted to lead an exciting, open life in the centre of English literary society. She continued to love Wells, but now she began to go out to parties and literary functions.

Soon society came to accept the brilliant young woman on her terms. But Wells was furious at her new success. He sulked, refusing to see her for weeks on end. He fantasised that she was having an affair with an American writer, so he retaliated by embarking upon an affair with Frau Gatternig, the Austrian woman who was translating his work into German. That would bring Rebecca to her senses, he thought.

Jealous, tired, intent only on wounding his Panther, Wells had no idea of the devastating effect his enormous charm was having on the Austrian – until that fateful night when he entered his study to find Frau Gatternig naked on his hearthrug, holding a razor and demanding his love. Sick with longing for Rebecca, he curtly refused her.

And then it happened. The hysterical woman slashed at her own wrists and neck as the horrified Wells tried to wrestle the razor from her. Finally he called the police and Frau Gatternig was hustled away to hospital. The ensuing scandal threatened to engulf Wells' reputation. He begged Rebecca to help him face the music, and she agreed to stand by him, touched by his hideous predicament. For some time their affair continued almost as before. But the Gatternig business showed, more clearly than ever, that Rebecca's path did not lie with Wells. Remorseful, broken-hearted, Wells slowly realised that the affair that had consumed ten years of their lives was steadily drawing to a close. He knew he would always want his Panther, 'his lost love, the black hole in his heart', but he would never again have her as his own.

'We loved each other in bright flashes; we were mutually abusive; we were fundamentally incompatible,' he concluded sadly.

William Randolph Hearst
and Marion Davies

Filmgoers of the 1940s were intrigued by Orson Welles' masterpiece *Citizen Kane*, with its thinly disguised portrayal of media mogul William Randolph Hearst and his lover, Marion Davies. But no fictional representation, however dramatic, could live up to the extravagant reality of the consuming love of one of America's most powerful men for a one-time chorus girl – a love that lasted over thirty years.

Marion Davies' origins were modest. Born in Brooklyn in 1897, the fourth daughter of a police magistrate (though Hearst newspaper accounts later upped his rank to 'Supreme Court Judge'), young Marion Douras dreamed of becoming a schoolteacher. To make ends meet she worked as an artist's model, achieving notoriety as the subject of artist Howard Chandler Christy's nude study *Morning*. This painting created such a sensation that she was given a part in the chorus of the Broadway musical *Chu Chin Chow*. The fresh-faced, blonde teenager promptly adopted the stage name Marion Davies, and was next seen high-kicking in the chorus line of New York's famous Ziegfeld Follies.

But not for long. Night after night, a pale, hulking middle-aged man bought two tickets to the show – one for himself, the other for his hat. Marion didn't know it then, but her golden good looks and dancer's body had caught the eye of newspaper proprietor William Randolph Hearst, one of the most wealthy, loathed and lonely men in the land.

Then in his fifties, Hearst was king of his own empire of trashy tabloids and sensational scandal sheets. The son of US Senator George Hearst, young William Randolph did not excel at school, and was later expelled from Harvard University. He then decided to try his hand at journalism, and asked his father to make him a present of the San Francisco *Examiner*, a daily newspaper Hearst senior had been using as part of his political machine.

William shocked his father – and the city – by transforming the ailing *Examiner* into a sleazy paper obsessed with sex and crime, boosting its circulation to phenomenal levels. This was a formula he was to follow successfully as he bought up newspapers all over the country, turning himself into a political powerbroker and multi-millionaire along the way. But while his distinctive brand of gutter journalism made presidents tremble at the sound of his name, Hearst was an intensely shy and private man. He had something of a weakness for showgirls; he married the actress Millicent Wilson in 1903, and the union produced five sons. But that was before he visited the Ziegfeld Follies in 1917. That's when he became obsessed by the all-American loveliness

William Randolph Hearst lavished gifts on the young actress Marion Davies.

of Marion Davies. Before long, he had lured Marion from the chorus and made her his mistress – and a movie star for good measure.

For five years Marion and 'WR', as she called him, pretended that she was merely his 'actress protégée', and so he installed her as president and star of her own production company, Cosmopolitan Films, spending over $5 million to launch her career. For the premiere of her first film, *Cecilia of the Pink Roses*, WR had the theatre filled with flowers and rose-scented perfume pumped through the air-conditioning. The critics raved at her acting debut – but they were all critics employed on Hearst newspapers. Independent observers weren't so kind: Miss Davies couldn't act, they sniffed. But the Hearst publicity machine drowned them out as Cosmopolitan Studios cranked out film after mediocre film: *Runaway Romany*, *Beverley of Granstark*, *It's a Wise Child* and *Five and Ten*.

Marion gradually learned her craft acting opposite such up-and-coming leading men as Clark Gable, Gary Cooper and Bing Crosby, and finally developed into a gifted light comedienne. It was this that induced Metro-Goldwyn-Mayer to offer her a contract for a weekly salary of $10,000 – that, plus the little extra incentive of unlimited free advertising in Hearst publications.

WR's gifts to Marion were as lavish as his efforts to push her career. He gave her a collection of gems that made eyes pop even among his millionaire cronies – including an American flag entirely made up of choice rubies, sapphires and diamonds. But he maintained the fiction that he was merely her patron –

Marion Davies remained devoted to Hearst for over thirty years.

until the night in 1922 when their cover was blown by the publicity generated by a wild party thrown by Marion's sister Reine, which culminated in millionaire guest Oscar Hirsh being shot at by his estranged wife. Both Hearst and Marion had attended the party, and their relationship was put under the spotlight by non-Hearst newspapers covering the scandal.

Appalled by the lurid headlines, Hearst's wife Millicent walked out on him – though she refused to consider divorce – and Marion moved in. Now that the necessity for discretion was gone, WR's generosity towards Marion knew no bounds. He built a palace for her – Los Angeles' legendary San Simeon, a $30 million complex of Moorish buildings crammed with another

$40 million worth of European and Oriental furniture and works of art. Marion's rooms were decked out with solid gold fittings, and the 150,000-acre garden was filled with exotic livestock like zebras, giraffes, lions and tigers. As San Simeon's unofficial 'empress', Marion was expected to play hostess to an endless succession of notable guests. President Calvin Coolidge, George Bernard Shaw, Winston Churchill and the Duke of Kent were just some of the celebrities eager to sample Hearst's spectacular hospitality – but even they must have been awed by San Simeon's dining room, which was an entire Spanish church that had been dismantled and then reassembled stone by stone on American soil.

Whenever Marion presided over the lavishly laid dining table there was a footman standing to attention behind her chair, holding her make-up bag in readiness should she wish to touch up her powder and lipstick between courses. San Simeon boasted one hundred rooms, including 58 bedrooms and dozens of bathrooms, which doubled as bars. Because WR was teetotal, whenever Marion felt the need for a glass of champagne she had to retreat to the ladies' rooms, where she kept her own private stock.

In case Marion found the grandeur of San Simeon a trifle oppressive, WR built her a more modest hideaway in Beverly Hills – a 47-room retreat with a mere seventeen bathrooms. But even its main salons had been imported directly from European palaces that WR had gutted for her.

The price that WR demanded for lavishing this extraordinary lifestyle upon Marion was that she remain forever the golden ingénue, the 20-year-old chorus girl who first captured his heart in 1917. So she made her long yellow ringlets and unsophisticated manner her trademarks, although in reality she was no dumb blonde but a very astute businesswoman. She invested her film earnings in real estate, to such good effect that she was soon a millionairess in her own right. Occasionally, the King Copetua and the beggar maid roles were reversed. During the Depression even Hearst's huge holdings felt the pinch, and his empire was only saved by Marion coming to the rescue with a million-dollar cheque.

WR wasn't the only one to experience Marion's generosity. The public saw only the society hostess whose fountains ran with pink champagne and whose swimming pools were filled with rare orchids during her extravagant parties, but there was a softer side to Marion Davies. She secretly endowed two children's homes and donated hundreds of thousands of dollars to hospitals all over the country. And she truly loved WR. At first the cynics scoffed at their May and December union, but as decade followed decade, it became obvious that much more than mere money was keeping them together.

In 1947 Hearst suffered a massive heart attack, and he became a virtual recluse. Marion became his right hand, running his business affairs, conveying his decisions to his news editors, and frequently making decisions for him. The former chorus girl became one of the most powerful women on earth during Hearst's final years. She nursed him devotedly until the end, which came in August 1951, when he was 88.

The night before he died, worn out with worry, Marion was

persuaded by a sympathetic nurse to take a sedative to ensure sleep. When she awoke the next morning, it was to discover that WR had died during the night and his body had been removed by his sons, who strongly resented her influence over him. They had also ransacked his bedroom, leaving only a photograph of Marion on which she had scribbled some lines from *Romeo and Juliet*.

> *My bounty is as boundless as the sea, my love as deep;*
> *The more I give to thee, the more I have, for both are*
> *   infinite.*

Marion was almost as devastated by the cruel treatment she received from WR's sons as she was by his death. 'He belonged to me,' she told a friend bitterly. 'I loved him for 34 years and now he was gone. I couldn't even say goodbye.'

And she didn't say goodbye. When Hearst was buried a little later at the family vault in San Francisco, the love of his life was not among those present. 'I thought I might go to the church,' she said later, 'and then I decided to stay here. He knew how I felt about him and I know how he felt about me.'

The great and the powerful attended WR's funeral, but the blonde Ziegfeld Follies girl who had captured his heart over three decades before remained sitting in his darkened bedroom, holding his pet dachshund – all she had left to her of William Randolph Hearst.

SCOTT AND ZELDA FITZGERALD

Lieutenant Francis Scott Fitzgerald took a deep breath of the scented breeze that wafted across the flowerbeds, and strode up the stairs to the Montgomery Country Club. Soft music and the laughing voices of young people dancing on the verandah mingled with the humming chorus of insects in the sultry summer air. Standing with some of his superior officers, Scott looked around the gathering. His eyes lit on a blonde girl surrounded by admiring young men. Intrigued, he continued looking at her. She turned her head and Scott saw her face clearly for the first time. She had the face of 'a saint, a Viking Madonna'.

In that one moment, Scott Fitzgerald knew he had found the only woman in the world for him. Brushing aside the formalities, he crossed the room and introduced himself to her, finding out that her name was Zelda Sayre and that she came from Montgomery, Alabama. On that July evening in 1918 began, as Scott later described it, the 'romance of the century'. He was a struggling writer of 22, she was a southern belle scarcely 18 years of age. Together they became the couple who epitomised the era known as 'The Jazz Age'.

Scott Fitzgerald was born in St Paul, Minnesota, in 1896. He went to Princeton University but did not graduate. In 1917, like so many of his generation, he joined the army in the hope of fighting in Europe. However, his two years in uniform were spent on American soil. He started his first novel, *This Side of Paradise*, while he was still in the armed forces.

Zelda Sayre was the daughter of a judge and had grown up in the heartland of the old Confederate South. From childhood she had known a lifestyle of leisure and elegance. However, she was not a traditional southern woman. Her sparkling wit and vivid imagination marked her for different things.

Scott Fitzgerald, with his cleancut features and cornsilk-coloured hair, was an unusual and famous figure when he appeared in her life. Not unnaturally, she was attracted to him. But when he asked her to marry him she pointed out that the likelihood of his being able to support her with his writing was slim for, despite his fame as a short-story writer, he was not making much money. After being rejected, Scott left Alabama for New York in despair. But he soon resolved to win Zelda over, which meant succeeding financially. 'By heaven and Lorimer [the editor of the lucrative *Saturday Evening Post*],' he promised Zelda, 'I'll make you a fortune.'

After months of rejection slips and grinding poverty, Scott sold a revised version of *This Side of Paradise* to Scribner's Publishers in New York. Overnight he became a celebrity, and his future as a writer seemed assured. He married Zelda in April 1920.

Scott's first book, which he called 'a novel about flappers, written for philosophers', sold 40,000 copies in six months. Suddenly, the young Mr and Mrs Fitzgerald were rolling in money. That year, 1920, Scott made $18,000 from book royalties and short stories for magazines – an enormous amount for those times. Zelda and he lived a wild lifestyle on the money Scott made. They resided in expensive hotels and went to parties almost every night. Scott

Scott and Zelda Fitzgerald: 'the romance of the century'?

used to light his cigarettes with five dollar bills and Zelda would dance on restaurant tabletops. It was the age of jazz, flappers, flaming youth and bathtub gin, and Scott and Zelda Fitzgerald were its living symbols.

It seemed they could never be touched by misfortune in those days. Lillian Gish, a famous actress of the twenties, said on meeting the Fitzgeralds: 'They were both so beautiful, so blond, so clean and so clear – and drinking straight whisky out of tall tumblers.'

Together, their physical likeness made them look like twins. Their emotional dependence on each other mirrored this outward similarity. In 1921 Zelda became pregnant, and in October she bore Scott a baby daughter. He nervously paced the corridors outside the delivery room and said that if Zelda died he would kill himself. She didn't, and Scott celebrated the arrival of his daughter, Scottie, in uproarious fashion.

Despite the large sums of money Scott was earning, his drinking habits and Zelda's extravagant demands meant that he was constantly in debt. They moved into a mansion at Great Neck, Long Island, where Scott tried to work on his second novel, *The Beautiful and Damned*, between parties and drinking binges. The Fitzgeralds quickly developed a reputation for eccentricity among their respectable neighbours. Once, Scott drove his Rolls Royce into a local duck-pond because 'it seemed like fun'. Zelda capped this exploit by calling the fire brigade to their house late one night. When the firemen impatiently demanded the location of the blaze, Zelda theatrically struck her breast and cried: 'Here!'

When *The Beautiful and Damned* came out in March 1922 it was a great success. Unfortunately, Scott had to keep writing short stories for magazines to pay for his and Zelda's lifestyle. In one year alone they had spent $36,000. On the advice of a friend, author Ring Lardner, Scott decided to get away from 'the ash heaps and millionaires' on Long Island and write a novel about them. In 1924 he took his wife and daughter to Europe and worked on his third novel, *The Great Gatsby*.

Although he was now at the height of his career and lauded

by such notables as Gertrude Stein, T.S. Eliot and Ernest Hemingway, Scott was not a happy man. He became jealous of Zelda's effect on other men. When she became involved with the French flyer Edouard Jozan on the Riviera, Scott threatened to 'wring the aviator's neck'. Trying to solve their marital problems, the Fitzgeralds travelled constantly in search of diversion. Zelda used to say: 'I hate a room without an open suitcase in it – it seems so permanent.' But nothing could hide the cracks that were widening in their marriage. Scott drank more and more heavily and took out his frustrations on Zelda, who began to retreat into a world of fantasy.

In April 1925 *The Great Gatsby* was released to worldwide acclaim. Scott and Zelda should have been the happiest couple on earth, but something was wrong in 'Paradise'. Their 'romance of the century' was beginning to turn sour. Zelda and Scott often quarrelled bitterly – hurting each other as only two estranged soulmates can. 'It's no fun anymore,' Zelda complained. 'If we go out at night Scott gets pie-eyed; and if we stay at home we have a row.' Zelda realised that Scott and she were chasing a romantic dream that was growing fainter as they grew older. 'Scott and I had it all – youth, love, money – and look how we've ended up: sitting around cafés, drinking and talking and quarrelling with each other.'

Scott Fitzgerald was not to complete another novel for nine years after *Gatsby*. During those years, the disintegration of his life and marriage paralleled that of the Jazz Age. Periodically he worked in Hollywood to stay afloat, but the collapse of the Wall Street Stock Exchange in 1929 had signalled the end of his era as a successful writer. Zelda by now could no longer cope with the real world and spent most of her time in expensive sanatoriums. Although they were no longer living together, Zelda's love for Scott endured through the dark years of the Depression. After one of his visits she wrote to him:

> *Dearest and always Dearest Scott,*
>
> *… All I can say is that there was always that deeper current running through my heart; my life, you.*
>
> *… I love you anyway – even if there isn't any me or any life – I love you.*

Scott's fourth novel, *Tender is the Night*, was published in 1934, but his stories of the Jazz Age were no longer in vogue. Desperately disappointed, Fitzgerald lapsed deeper into alcoholism. Tragically, when he roused himself to write another book, *The Last Tycoon*, in 1940, it was too late.

He died of a heart attack in California, a continent away from his Zelda in Alabama. It was not until 1948, when Zelda died, that they would be together again. Their two graves were marked with one simple headstone:

> *Francis-Scott Key Fitzgerald*
> *and His Wife Zelda.*

AGATHA CHRISTIE
AND MAX MALLOWAN

'I'm not going to let you go, do you hear? You're my woman. If I let you go away, I may lose you. I'm never sure of you. You're coming with me now – tonight – and damn everybody!' exclaims the dark and handsome hero in Agatha Christie's *The Man in the Brown Suit*. Needless to say, the heroine melts in his arms.

Agatha Christie had written dozens of love scenes, but when it came to her own she found herself painfully shy. She stared across at the intense young man who had just asked her to marry him. Max Mallowan was her closest and dearest friend. He made her happy in a way she had never been happy before – but she had doubts. They were so different. She was a writer of detective stories and he was an archaeologist. She was a divorced woman with a small daughter to support and he was a carefree bachelor. Worst of all, she was 40 and he was thirteen years younger.

Suddenly, despite her reservations, Agatha felt that nothing in the world would be more delightful than to be married to Max. But she still held back. If only he had been older or she younger ...

If this had been a scene from one of Agatha's novels, it would have run very simply: Max would have grabbed her in his arms and kissed her passionately until she agreed to marry him. But Agatha was frightened. She didn't want to make another mistake. Her first marriage to Archibald Christie had left too many scars.

'It's a terrible risk,' she said.

'It's not a risk for me,' Max answered. 'You may think it's a risk for you but does it matter, taking risks? Does one get anywhere if one doesn't take risks?'

Agatha was still undecided. She asked Max for time to think. He reluctantly agreed, and left her to make up her mind. 'I think you will marry me, you know – when you have had plenty of time to think it over,' he said.

Why was she so scared of life? She hadn't always been so unsure of herself. Here she was, the acknowledged queen of detective fiction, and she was frightened to make a decision. She was frightened to say 'Yes' to the man she loved.

Agatha Mary Clarissa Miller was born in the English seaside town of Torquay in 1890. Her childhood was extremely happy. She loved her older brother and sister and adored her slightly eccentric parents. Her mother decided that Agatha would be educated at home, but since she also believed that no child ought to be allowed to read until he or she was eight years old (better for the eyes and also for the brain) it is doubtful whether Agatha would have learned very much at all if she hadn't taken matters into her own hands. She taught herself to read when she was four. Her father was so impressed with his small daughter that he taught her to write. And that was the beginning of her affair with the written word.

While she was an introverted child because of her sheltered upbringing, she was in no way a frightened person. Her fear of life and lack of self-confidence only began after her marriage in 1914 to a handsome army officer, Colonel Christie. At first she was happy. Christie was actively involved in the First World War and she was nursing and training as a pharmacist in the Red Cross hospital in Torquay. More as a hobby than anything else, she wrote her first detective novel, *The Mysterious Affair at Styles*. In this book she created her famous Belgian detective Hercule Poirot (much later in her life she was to look back on her creation and ask: 'Why, why did I ever invent this detestable, bombastic, tiresome little creature?')

Christie returned to England from the Front at the end of the war and he and Agatha set up house and began married life. They were both delighted when Agatha gave birth to their daughter, Rosalind, whom they affectionately nicknamed Teddy. For the next five years life went well for the Christie family. Agatha wrote book after book, Christie appeared content and Rosalind thrived. Then, suddenly and quite out of the blue, the marriage was over. Christie had fallen in love with another woman. He told Agatha that he wanted a divorce so that he could marry Nancy Neele. He began to openly court the young woman as Agatha watched in helpless silence. Something deep inside her snapped. She couldn't go on.

One night when Christie was visiting Nancy, Agatha got into her car and drove away from her house. The car was found abandoned the next morning. Agatha had disappeared. The police believed that she had committed suicide. Five hundred policemen and 15,000 volunteers combed the country to find her body. The mystery of the disappearing author became front page news. The entire nation waited breathlessly as the plot unfolded in true detective story style. There were rumours that her husband had murdered her, and even suggestions that it was a gigantic hoax to gain publicity to sell Agatha's latest book, *The Murder of Roger Ackroyd*.

The truth of the matter was in some ways more fantastic than the wild theories. Agatha had been living quietly in a holiday hotel in Harrogate in Yorkshire. She had registered as Mrs Teresa Neele of Cape Town and was reported as acting like an amnesiac. Grief at her husband's brutal rejection had caused her to lose her memory. She was obviously in the grip of some strong fantasy when she chose to call herself Neele – it was the surname of the woman whom Christie loved.

Despite the intense public interest in the case, Agatha maintained her silence at the time. She simply didn't know what had happened to her. But years later she told a reporter: 'When suffering becomes too great some people commit suicide. In my case loss of memory was the escape. When I was discovered at Harrogate I was still alive but my mind had cut twelve years out of my life.'

Agatha divorced Christie in 1928 and tried to reassemble the shattered ruins of her life. She had always been shy but now she lived in a strange twilight world of fear of rejection. She began to bury herself in her work, writing an average of two books a year. But work was not enough. She decided to try and forget the pain of her divorce and the wreck of her marriage by constant travelling.

She was invited to visit the Persian Gulf, where some archaeologist friends were excavating the ancient city of Ur. It was here that she first met Max

Agatha Christie. Her fear of love was overcome by the younger Max Mallowan.

Mallowan. They were attracted to each other immediately, but all too soon Agatha had to return home to her daughter Rosalind. Max followed her, determined to make her his wife.

Max was persistent. He argued that the difference in their ages and backgrounds was irrelevant. He said that the only problem to him was that Agatha would have to spend her future with a man whose job was to 'dig up the dead'. She replied, 'I adore corpses and stiffs.'

And so, in 1930, they were married. And, despite Agatha's initial reservations, the marriage proved to be a very happy one. During the summer Agatha would assist Max on archaeological digs in the Middle East, then in winter she would return home to England to write her books. So successful was the blend of detective-fiction writing and archaeology that Agatha used many of the archaeological sites as settings for her novels, such as *Death on the Nile* and *Murder in Mesopotamia*.

Agatha Christie wrote over seventy novels and became the biggest-selling author, apart from Shakespeare, of works written in the English language. She was made a Dame of the British Empire in 1971 for her literary efforts. But despite all the fame and the accolades Agatha remained a shy and humble person. She frequently wrote adventure stories that ended with the handsome hero swearing his undying love for the beautiful heroine, but in her own autobiography she chose to write far more truthfully and lovingly.

She wrote of Max: 'I am proud of him and happy for him. It seems a kind of miracle that both he and I should have succeeded in the work we wanted to do ... we complement each other.'

BARBARA CARTLAND
AND HUGH MCCORQUODALE

His voice was deep with desire. 'I want you Diana,' he said. Wildly Diana sought to escape. She glanced feverishly around the room, but she was imprisoned.

'I despise and detest you,' she said, slowly and feelingly. 'Does that attract you?'

'Immensely,' he answered, smiling. 'A complacent woman is often a bore ...'

His arms enclosed her, she fought against him wildly and there was the sound of rending.

This is an excerpt from Barbara Cartland's novel *Sweet Punishment*. The heroine, Lady Diana Stanlier, gets her comeuppance when she trifles with the affections of the handsome, silent hero, Ian Carstairs. He promptly kidnaps and ravishes her, thus ensuring her undying love. A strange courtship, one might think, but somehow it works. At the end of the novel the flighty Diana and the taciturn Ian are united blissfully in marriage.

Barbara Cartland wrote over four hundred romantic novels, and although the names and locations change, the endings remain the same. Assertive womanhood is tamed by its rightful master, the dominating male.

At the time of her death at the age of 98 in May 2000, Barbara had become a legend in her own lifetime. She enraged feminists all over the world with statements like: 'A career girl is a second-rate pseudo-man who looks her worst in trousers. All that a woman really wants is the protection of marriage.' But Barbara had always been an anomaly. She preached female subjugation and practised just the opposite as a self-made career woman in an era when it wasn't always fashionable – or even possible. As she put it:

> *The truth is that there are really two quite separate 'Me's'. One is the crusader, who is impatient, rather aggressive, sometimes over-powerful, with a tendency to bulldoze everything before her. But at the same time, I have always had this other image of myself as a sort of flower-like creature, very delicate and feminine and always looking to be protected by a superior man.*

Luckily for Barbara, she was able to reconcile these two 'Me's' due to the fact that she met 'a superior man' who was more than willing to protect the 'flower-like' side of her nature. Her second marriage to Hugh McCorquodale was a deeply romantic and happy one. It had so many of the ingredients of the classic 'happy ever after' story, with the beautiful heroine falling in love and marrying the strong silent man of her dreams, that it might very well have sprung from Barbara's fertile imagination. But all had not been happy in her love life up to that point.

By 1926 Barbara had given up all hope of finding true love. She was a successful young novelist, a dazzling socialite, and had received 48 marriage proposals. She lacked nothing except a handsome husband. In desperation, Barbara accepted her forty-ninth proposal. Alexander McCorquodale was a strong, silent Scot whom Barbara assumed was pulsating with dark, hidden passion. Unfortunately, no such passion lurked in Alexander's bosom. He was just strong and silent. The marriage ended in a messy divorce in 1932 with both Barbara and Alexander fighting for custody of their small daughter, Raine. Barbara won the custody battle and set up house as a single mother. For the next few years she threw herself into her career. She wrote her romantic fiction and lived her pragmatic life, until fate – in the person of her ex-husband's cousin – stepped in and rescued her.

Hugh could well have stepped straight from the pages of any one of a number of Barbara's novels. He even composed love letters in the style of a true Cartland hero. He wrote her a note that was to be opened on the morning of their wedding.

> *My Darling One,*
> *Very soon now you will be my own very darling wife ... Darling, a little secret. Ever since I met you, I have wanted to marry you and I have never even given a single thought to any other girl. I thought then that you were the loveliest person I had ever seen – now you are more lovely still ... The loveliest*

> *creature God ever made loves me … It's so wonderful*
> *I can't believe it's true. I fear it may be a dream and*
> *I shall wake up and find I was just dreaming of a*
> *wonderful fairyland that does not exist at all. God*
> *bless you my angel,*
> *Your adoring Hugh*

After a simple marriage ceremony the happy couple set off for a romantic honeymoon in Paris. Barbara described herself as being 'caught up in an ecstasy which was divinely inspired'. Their marriage was a happy one. Hugh need not have feared that he was going to wake up and find that the 'wonderful fairyland' had been an illusion. Barbara adored and needed him as much as he did her. Her daughter, Raine, loved her new stepfather. They were a happy family. There was only one thing that Barbara still wanted – a son. Her dreams came true when she gave birth to Ian in 1937.

'I always wanted a son more than anything else in the world,' Barbara said of this event. 'When Ian was born it was the most exciting moment in my entire life … He was so beautiful that I thought he was an angel and would soon die.'

Luckily, Ian was not an angel and survived, growing up to take on the role of Barbara's business manager. Two years after his birth, Barbara had another son whom she called Glen.

Hugh was heavily involved in the way the children grew up. He totally supported Barbara in everything she did, from her writing to her choice of childcare. A quiet man, Hugh was the calm centre of the McCorquodale/Cartland household. He was Barbara's inner strength, more than happy to indulge her every whim.

One whim, Barbara contended, miraculously prolonged his life. She placed Hugh on a health-giving diet largely made up of honey. Although Hugh had never been a physically robust man, his intake of honey did indeed seem to give him vigour. He and Barbara had been married nearly 27 years and they were still lovers. Barbara believed that honey was not only an unbeatable source of energy, it was also 'one of the most important factors in keeping people sexually competent'.

Barbara Cartland found love with her first husband's cousin.

Honey may have helped their romantic life but it could not prolong Hugh's life indefinitely. Just before Christmas 1963 he caught bronchitis. His constitution was not able to weather the disease, and on 29 December he collapsed and died, bringing to an end a romance to eclipse any that Barbara could have written. She was desolate. Although she had the children, she felt alone without her beloved Hugh. She wrote a poem to express her sense of loss, simply entitled *To Hugh*.

I love the silver of the mist at dawn,
I love the shadows underneath the trees.
I love the softness of the velvet lawn,
The fragrance of syringa on the breeze.

I am so lonely without you here,
You who loved everything the garden grew.
The birds, the flowers are very dear,
But it's an empty beauty without you.

HERMAN TARNOWER
AND JEAN HARRIS

Jean Harris felt for the pistol in her handbag as she drove up the driveway of her lover's luxury New York home. She was relieved and surprised to find that the gun was still there. But how could it not be there? Hadn't she carefully loaded it and put it in her bag before she started the long five-hour drive? Of course she had. She was just confused, that's all.

She'd been confused since she'd run out of her daily amphetamine dose of Desoxyn five days earlier. Why hadn't Hi sent her the precious drugs he knew she depended on so much? Was her lover punishing her, or had he simply forgotten to prescribe her usual dosage?

'What if Hi says something to spoil my resolve to die?' she thought as she got out of her car. 'I won't let him know what I'm going to do, I won't stay too long, and I won't spoil my resolve.'

As she made her way through Hi Tarnower's garage and quietly let herself into the house Jean was wondering about the gun. Was

Dr Herman Tarnower, murdered for love.

she going to commit suicide in front of the man whom she'd loved for fourteen years? Was she going to kill him and then herself? Or was she going to stage a dramatic scene that would end with Hi taking her in his arms and telling her that he loved her?

All she knew was that she was hurting inside and that she had to see Hi. She wanted to tell him her problems. After all, he was a doctor and doctors made things better, didn't they? She climbed up the steps to his bedroom and called to him softly, 'Hi, Hi, Hi …' Herman Tarnower woke and stared sleepily at the fragile blonde who was standing over his bed. 'Jesus,' he snapped, 'it's the middle of the night and you wake me up.'

'I only want to talk,' pleaded Jean, 'and anyway I won't be long.'

Tarnower sighed heavily and rolled over on his side. Jean began nervously pacing around the room. There were things that she had to talk about. Hi couldn't just ignore her. She flicked on the lights and saw an unfamiliar greenish-blue negligée hanging on the bathroom door. Her eyes filled with tears. Did Hi have to flaunt his affair with Lynne Tryforos so obviously? In the past he had at least got his housekeeper to tidy away the evidence that he shared his bed with another woman. Jean walked into the bathroom and saw Lynne Tryforos's plastic box of electric hair curlers. Angrily she picked up the box and threw it out into the bedroom. She was sick and tired of being humiliated.

Jean Harris: 'I never meant to cause him any ill.'

She was sick and tired of being 57 years old and watching her long-time lover take up with a woman 30 years younger than she was. She must make Hi understand how he was hurting her. She took a deep breath and walked back into the bedroom.

An hour later Hi Tarnower lay dying, trying but unable to speak, his right lung filling with blood from a tiny but deadly hole made by a .32 calibre bullet. A year later Jean had been arrested, indicted, tried for murder, found guilty and sentenced to fifteen years' imprisonment. It was a tragic end to a passionate and bizarre love affair. In the words of Jean's defence attorney, Joel Aurnou, 'This is a story of love … love gone wrong … love from a woman who had more to give than one man could handle. She loved a man incapable of accepting the greatest gift a woman can give.'

To discover how that love went wrong it is necessary to find out what sort of people Jean Harris and Dr Herman Tarnower were before her overpowering love destroyed them both.

Jean was a divorced woman with two sons to support when she first met Hi. She was an elegant, almost excessively genteel person who wore her hair pulled back in an Alice band, neat strands of pearls, cashmere sweaters and expensive tweed skirts. When she shot and killed Tarnower in 1980 she was the headmistress of Madeira, one of the most prestigious girls' schools in the country. She was known as a firm disciplinarian, causing her pupils to nickname her 'Integrity Jean'. She wasn't looking for a man when she met Hi at a dinner party in 1967, but once she'd found him she was determined never to let him go.

Tarnower was a rich and famous cardiologist who was also single. He was not a handsome man, but he had an urbanity and acid wit that made him deeply attractive to women. Jean was no exception. She fell for him hook, line and sinker. She admired the fact that he was a self-made man who had become rich as the founder of the Scarsdale Medical Group, and when he later allowed her to help write his book, *The Complete Scarsdale Medical Diet*, she was enormously flattered. The fact that the book, with its simple message for losing up to 20 pounds of excess weight in two weeks, made millions of dollars was of no concern to Jean. What really pleased her was that Hi had allowed her to help him.

The courtship began in 1967. Jean described her first date with Hi: 'He left like he always did – like Cinderella – when his man [chauffeur] came at 11 ... He wrote ... sent lots of roses ... he began to call every night at 6.30 and he sent roses.'

Hi wrote:

> *Darling, I love you very, very much. You know it!!*
> *There are so many times when I am tempted to call*
> *just to hear your voice, but that could easily be*
> *annoying or embarrassing. As it is, the boys [Jean's*
> *sons] probably think we are 'wacky' ... You have on*
> *occasion criticised my cryptic style. As I re-read this*
> *letter, the frankness of it all scares the hell out of me.*
> *Since you like to live dangerously, I hope it suits you*
> *just fine ... See you soon, my darling. I love you.*

And then came Jean's happiest moment. 'He asked me to marry him,' she said from the witness box as she stood trial for Herman Tarnower's murder in 1981. It was her best moment in court. The jury sympathised with her, as did the press. Reporters called her 'Miss Prettyface' and wrote of her 'pale shred of beauty wrapped about her like a shawl'. Jean's happiness was not to last. Tarnower took back his marriage proposal: 'Jean, I just can't go through with it,' he said.

If this rejection hurt Jean, she didn't show it. At the trial she said that she had told Tarnower 'it was too bad he thought marriage was the last requirement of middle-class respectability

… by that time I was very much in love with him.' Tarnower rewarded Jean's restraint by taking her on a luxury holiday to Jamaica. The pattern of their relationship was set. Jean was free to adore Hi provided she didn't make a nuisance of herself. He took her to Kenya, Khartoum, Ceylon, Bahrain and Vietnam in 1971. Even though Hi had rejected her as a marriage partner, Jean believed that he loved her and that they were true soulmates. She was convinced that Hi was her man. It didn't matter that he wouldn't marry her, so long as they had an ongoing relationship. He was there to help her when she had problems at school, he was there to advise her on how to bring up her sons, and he was there to love her. And then Hi started a serious affair with his office assistant, Lynne Tryforos.

As time went on, Jean spent more time waiting than she did anything else. For at least three years Lynne and Jean shared the doctor, but it was the younger woman who was getting the lion's share of his attention. And then, in March 1980, things came to a head. Jean had serious problems at Madeira that forced her to expel a group of students. Hi was refusing to answer her phone calls. She was running out of Desoxyn. Suicidal and strung out as a result of the withdrawal of her medication, Jean made a will and wrote Hi a letter. This letter has become known as the Scarsdale letter, and it was to become important evidence during Jean's trial. The letter, written in red ink, was a ten-page plea for attention. It was often abusive and often disjointed, but its message was clear: 'Please love me.'

As soon as she had sent the letter Jean was shocked that she had revealed her feelings so openly. She must get the letter back before Hi had a chance to read it. She would drive to his place, remove the missive, have a last chat with her lover and then drive to some quiet park and commit suicide.

It didn't quite work out that way. She never got the letter back. Hi was angry with her and there was no quiet chat. Instead, there was a violent struggle that resulted in four bullets being pumped into Herman Tarnower's body. Jean maintained that it was an accident. Hi had fought to remove the gun as she tried to turn it on herself – the bullets she was hoping would end her own life tragically misfired and killed her lover.

The jury did not believe her. Whatever the truth of the matter is, there is no doubt that Jean Harris deeply and passionately loved Herman Tarnower. As her defence lawyer said, her story is one of love going wrong. Hopelessly and fatally wrong.

Jean's last words in court indicate her feelings for the man she killed: 'I did not hurt Dr Tarnower. I loved him very much. I never meant to cause him any ill.'

POLITICAL
UNIONS

CHARLES STEWART PARNELL AND KITTY O'SHEA

Kitty O'Shea was determined that Charles Stewart Parnell would become her lover from the moment they first met. Unwittingly, she was to plunge the two of them into one of the most sensational scandals of the nineteenth century. Their affair was to become the subject of vulgar gossip in the British House of Commons, drastically change the course of Anglo-Irish history, and ultimately destroy Parnell's political career. And all this because a pretty woman chose to fall in love with a handsome young man.

Kitty wrote of their first meeting:

> *A rose I was wearing in my bodice fell out on to my skirt. He picked it up and, touching it lightly to his lips, placed it in his buttonhole ... This rose I found long years afterwards done up in an envelope, with my name and the date, among his private papers, and when he died I laid it upon his heart.*

Charles Parnell: 'I will give my life to Ireland but to you I give my love.'

Kitty was the English wife of Captain William Henry O'Shea, and Parnell was the leader of the Irish Parliamentary Party in the House of Commons. He was the 'Uncrowned King of Ireland' and she was a married lady. A union between two such people would prove a perfect recipe for disaster.

Parnell was born at Avondale, County Wicklow, on 27 June 1846. His parents were landed gentry who believed that all good Irish boys should receive an English education. In 1869 he returned from Cambridge to find his native land in dire straits. The Irish people were starving and rebellious. They wanted two things – repeal of the 1801 Act of Union with Great Britain, and reform of the Land System.

Since the Potato Famine in the 1840s the Irish agriculture system had been bankrupt. Most of the Irish were on the land as tenants of English landlords who held their title deeds under confiscations by Queen Elizabeth I, King James I and Oliver Cromwell. The poor tenants were forced to pay exorbitant rents or face eviction that meant starvation and almost certain death. Not surprisingly, the Irish wanted their land back. In 1858 the

Fenian movement was created, a secret society that espoused armed revolution against the British. Members had to take an oath of allegiance to the Irish Republic. The movement later became known as the Irish Republican Brotherhood, which gave birth to the Irish Republican Army, the IRA.

The execution of three Fenians, the 'Manchester martyrs', in 1867 changed Parnell from a country squire into a political agitator. He decided to enter politics as a Home Ruler. He was going to fight to free Ireland. He was 31 years old when he was elected president of the Home Rule Confederation of Great Britain.

It was at this time that he met Kitty O'Shea. Her husband was just beginning to dabble in Irish politics. O'Shea was something of a dilettante who had so far failed to establish himself in any reasonable or lucrative career. His wife was lonely and bored. She turned to Parnell for warmth and affection, and revelled in his passion and dedication. He was so different from her weak, philandering husband.

In 1880, shortly after they first met, Parnell was writing to Kitty: 'My dear Mrs O'Shea. I cannot keep myself away from you any longer. My own love, you cannot imagine how much you have occupied my thoughts all day and how greatly the prospect of seeing you again very soon comforts me.'

In the autumn, Parnell went to stay with the O'Sheas. According to Kitty, he was ailing and William O'Shea had invited him to stay so that he could be nursed back to good health. Kitty and Parnell began to sleep together. Kitty wrote later:

I had fought against our love, but Parnell would not

fight and I was alone. I had urged my children and his work, but he answered me — 'For good or ill I am your husband, your lover, your children, your all. And I will give my life to Ireland but to you I give my love, whether it be your heaven or your hell. It is destiny.'

Kitty claimed that O'Shea knew about her affair with Parnell from the outset, writing:

He actually encouraged me at times. I remember especially one particular occasion very early in the affair when he wanted to get Parnell's assent to something or other he said — 'Take him back with you to Eltham and make him happy and comfortable for the night and just get him to agree.' And I knew what he wanted.

While he adored Kitty, Parnell still burned for Ireland. He continued to fight against landlordism, and in a public speech to his countrymen he created an historic new weapon of protest — the boycott:

When a man takes a farm from which another has been evicted, you must shun him on the roadside when you meet him, you must shun him in the streets of the town, in the fair and in the market place, even in the house of worship, by leaving him severely alone, by putting him into a moral Coventry, by isolating him from his kind as if he were a leper of old.

> *You must show him your detestation of the crime he has committed.*

Captain Charles Boycott was the first landlord to be ostracised in this manner. The British Government was not happy about Parnell's interference, but Parnell didn't care. He continued to campaign for Home Rule. He gained the firm support of the clergy, most of Ireland and a great number of the moderate English voters.

In 1881 Gladstone created the Land Bill, which granted the tenants their three major demands: fair rents, free sale and a fixity of tenure. But Parnell wanted more. He didn't just want reforms, he wanted the British landlords out of Ireland altogether. He continued to agitate, and in 1881 was jailed because he 'made speeches couched in violent language'. His internment only served to make him more popular. He was hailed as Ireland's saviour and conquering hero.

His love for Kitty O'Shea had deepened with time. He was besotted with her. Kitty was now expecting Parnell's child, and that was the only thing that concerned him as he languished in prison. He knew that he would only be there for a short while but he worried about Kitty and his unborn baby. He wrote to her on the day of his arrest: 'My own Queenie. I have just been arrested by two fine-looking detectives, and write these words to wifie to tell her that she must be a brave little woman and not fret about her husband. I worry that this may hurt you and our child.'

The baby was born in February 1882, but lived only a couple of weeks. Kitty wrote:

> *Mr O'Shea was very good; I told him my baby was*

> *dying and I must be left alone. He had no suspicion of the truth and only stipulated that the child should be baptised at once … I had no objection to this. Parnell and I had long before agreed that it would be safer to have the child christened as a Catholic.*

It didn't take Parnell long to arrange his release from prison. He rushed to Kitty's side to comfort her over the loss of their child. By now Kitty was totally alienated from her husband. Although she had pretended that the dead child was his, she now rescinded the story and admitted that the baby had been Parnell's. From then on Parnell and Kitty lived as man and wife, and they openly declared their two subsequent children as their own.

In 1885 Parnell had his biggest political victory. He and his 39 Irish Nationalist MPs brought down Gladstone's Liberal government. Parnell had failed to get a satisfactory Home Rule statement from the Liberals so he turned his allegiance to the Tories to force Gladstone's hand. The Tories were no more satisfactory than the Liberals, however, so in 1886 Parnell sided with Gladstone once more. This time he held the balance of power. Gladstone knew he needed Irish support if he was going to stay in office.

Kitty thought it was time to get a divorce from William O'Shea and to marry Parnell and settle down. She approached O'Shea who promptly filed for divorce, naming Parnell as co-respondent. In court, Parnell was described by the judge as 'a man who takes advantage of the hospitality offered him by the husband to debauch the wife'. The judge granted the decree nisi and awarded O'Shea custody of all the children under sixteen – including Parnell's two daughters.

Overnight, Parnell became a public villain. People had been gossiping about his affair with Kitty O'Shea for years, but after the messy divorce they came right out into the open. The priests openly campaigned against him, and his colleague Michael Davitt called for his retirement 'to deliver Ireland from the deadliest peril by which it has yet been assailed'. Gladstone also put pressure on Parnell to resign, threatening that if he didn't, Ireland could forget about Home Rule.

Obscene jokes and filthy rhymes about Kitty O'Shea were the order of the day. 'Will the petticoat of Kitty O'Shea be the flag of Ireland?' sneered Parnell's erstwhile supporters. Parnell refused to resign. He defiantly went ahead and married Kitty before a registrar in Sussex on 24 June 1891. Kitty wrote of her wedding day:

> As a rule Parnell never noticed what I wore but that morning he said, 'Queenie, you look lovely in that lace stuff and the beautiful hat with roses. I am so proud of you.' And I was proud of my King, of my wonderful lover, as we drove through that glorious June morning.

And that was the last happy moment that Parnell had. He returned to Ireland where he was constantly and publicly vilified. On 6 October he became critically ill. He said to Kitty: 'Kiss me, sweet wifie, and I will try to sleep a little.' He closed his eyes and lapsed into unconsciousness. He died that night. The cause of death was heart failure.

Parnell was given a public funeral in Dublin. Thirty thousand people filed past his coffin before the funeral procession began, and a crowd of 100,000 people watched the procession. It was all over for a man whose only faults were that he had loved his country and his woman too well.

JOSEPH LYONS
AND ENID BURNELL

When Joe Lyons first met Enid Burnell he scarcely noticed her. He was a 28-year-old schoolteacher and she was a precocious 11-year-old much given to reciting poetry and stories to assembled groups of her elders. Joe yawned as he listened politely to the pretty child emoting about the evils of alcohol. Her story about some monster who had ruined his home and murdered his own children under the influence of the demon drink was becoming tedious. He wondered when he could leave.

Enid, on the other hand, was considerably interested in Joe. She was piqued that he seemed indifferent to her harrowing tale. She was used to applause. Years later she confessed: 'When little Blossom was slaughtered and I could see the tears of the audience, I had my first heady draught of power.'

It was a different story the next time they met. This time it was Joe who was interested in Enid and she who didn't seem to notice him. Enid was sixteen, and was finishing her training at

Hobart Teachers' College. Joe had left teaching and had embarked on a political life. He was now Treasurer and Minister for Education for the Tasmanian Labor Party.

On the day Enid and her sister visited Parliament House with their mother, Enid knew she was looking her best:

> *Sixteen is the age of vanity. I had a dark grey velvet frock, trimmed with silver-grey braid and further enhanced by tiny touches of blue. With it I wore a large grey hat, lined beneath the brim with a blue almost matching my eyes. This costume suited my fair complexion and blonde hair extremely well.*

She wasn't as impressed by Joe's looks:

> *I re-met the ex-schoolteacher for whom I had recited some years earlier. I decided that he was not very handsome. He was above medium height but inclined to be overweight. He had a mess of black curly hair touched lightly with grey and beautiful, vividly blue eyes, but – and this was an awful thought – he had a Roman nose, slightly out of line!*

The minister began to pursue the trainee teacher. He visited her and her family, and wrote weekly letters to the girl he called his 'pretty, blue-eyed, cheeky kid'. Enid grew fond of Joe but because of the difference in their ages she found it impossible to call him by his Christian name. Joe and her family found it amusing that she called her admirer Mr Lyons or Minister. Finally she was persuaded to address him by his first name. Blushing and embarrassed, she managed to stutter out the word 'Joseph …*ine*'. Joe smiled and her family hooted with laughter. Gradually it became easier, and by the time Joe finally asked her to marry him she was easily able to call him 'my Joe'.

Enid had been won over by Joe's persistence and charm. She was convinced that he loved her, and that conviction helped her to love him. He awoke an unexpected passion in her. The public, however, were not in favour of the engagement. Because Joe was a senior member of the government, people assumed he was older than he was. Neighbours knew that Enid was only seventeen and they were shocked. Among members of Tasmania's extremely conservative society Joe was criticised as a cradle-snatcher, while Enid's mother was accused of surrendering her child to the arms of an ageing roué. Another problem for the lovers was that he was a Roman Catholic and she was a Protestant. Neither of their respective families wanted a mixed marriage, so Enid solved that problem by converting to Catholicism.

In response Joe wrote:

> *The tears are in my eyes as I write, blinding my vision. Your reference to the ceremony you have been through … the kindness of Father O'Donnell to my little queen, and your anticipation of the happy ceremony to come, all wrung from me the tears I have tried to keep back … Oh, Enid, was any man ever blessed as I am without deserving it or was any man happier than I am today?*

They were finally married in 1915. The happiest day of Enid's life was followed by a honeymoon at a premiers' conference. 'Scarcely the kind of honeymoon to be recommended for general adoption,' Enid remarked dryly. 'That is not to say I was miserable: indeed, I was absurdly happy.'

The honeymoon was an indication of things to come. Both Enid and Joe were destined, together and separately, to live their lives in the public arena. A man cannot become Prime Minister of Australia, as Joe did in 1931, and a woman cannot become the first woman member of the House of Representatives, as Enid did in 1943, and later the first female member of the Federal Cabinet, if they are not prepared to sacrifice their privacy.

Political life was not the only thing that kept Enid busy. In between running her own official affairs, helping Joe with his, and writing books and articles, she also managed to give birth to twelve children. One of the saddest events that can happen in a parent's life is the death of a child. The Lyons lost one of their children when he was just ten months old. Enid wrote despairingly:

> After the baby's death, when the first storms of my grief had passed, I lived for some days in an unreal world ... Even the sunshine had a quality of unreality, like artificial lighting. How could everything go on as usual in the face of tragedy as I knew it now? And then I received an anonymous letter. It accused me of killing my baby with neglect, and it almost broke me.

Luckily it did not. Enid never got over the death of the child, but

Enid Burnell stands in front of her husband's portrait. She outlived him by 43 years.

her own strength and Joe's love pulled her through the tragedy. They set about trying to have another baby straight away. Enid often joked about her fecundity: 'When we were first married, I asked a good friend to pray we would be blessed with a family. Four years later and four children later I chased all over the countryside looking for him to ask him to stop praying.' Jokes aside, Enid's love of children was phenomenal.

Just as life began to stabilise, Joe was involved in a car accident that hospitalised him for nine weeks and left him permanently lame. During this time Enid gave birth to their eighth child. It was a moment of jubilation mixed with extreme fatigue and worry. She was only 30 years old.

There were moments of great heartbreak in their life together, but these were balanced by moments of great joy and love. Enid remembered the family arrival in Canberra when Joe first became Prime Minister as one of their most colourful moments:

I arrived at the Lodge wearing only a petticoat under my coat. We came by train from Melbourne ... After 7am breakfast at the railway station we headed for Canberra and the four young children were violently sick. I vacated the car, rolled my dress into a ball and tossed it into the boot.

She was beside Joe all the way. She was there when he attended the coronation of King George VI in London. She was there when he discussed the Second World War with President Roosevelt. And she was there when he resigned from the Labor Party and formed a new party, the Australian Party (UAP), which became the principal opposition party.

She was also there to provide a little light relief. 'When I met Pope Pius XI – a singularly humorless man – I disgraced myself yet again,' she wrote. 'I overbalanced during my curtsey. Not many people have been hauled to their feet by a Pope, but I was.'

And she was there when Joe died on 7 April 1939, after a massive heart attack. Just before he finally stopped breathing he held out his hand to Enid and, in her own words: 'Across the gateway of eternity, for a long moment, our eyes met and held.'

In 1980 Enid became a Dame of the Order of Australia. She died in 1982, but her love for Joe lives on in her writing. In the introduction to her book *So We Take Comfort* she remarked: 'This is not a biography. It is the story of a marriage; of two people who loved each other and set out on the great adventure ... They met with giants, slew dragons and took part in great events.'

And so they did.

WINSTON AND
CLEMENTINE CHURCHILL

Clementine Hozier stared across the room at Winston Churchill and wondered whether he remembered her. They had met once before but Clementine doubted that the charming man with the fiery red hair and blazing blue eyes would recall the meeting. After all, he was one of the most eligible bachelors in Britain. And who was she? An impoverished aristocrat who was reduced to giving French lessons to supplement her annual dress allowance.

Clementine wished she hadn't come to Lady St Helier's dinner party. She felt very young and very ill at ease. Why should the Tory rebel who had crossed the floor of the House of Commons in 1904 to join the Liberals be remotely interested in an inexperienced and shy suffragette? However, Winston knew exactly who Clementine was. He had only recently read in the society magazine *The Bystander* a reference to Clementine having 'lovely brown hair and the most delicate aquiline features, fine grey eyes and a delightful poise of the head'. For once the popular

Winston Churchill and Clementine Hozier in 1908, a week before their marriage.

press had not lied. Clementine was one of the most beautiful women Winston had ever seen. He determined then and there to make her his wife.

They were married a few months later – the ceremony was the gala event of 1908. Sixteen hundred guests turned up for the wedding at St Margaret's Church, Westminster. Even the suffragettes who had fought and pelted Winston with rotten fruit were there, cheering his choice of a bride. Winston's romance with Clementine had created a truce between the militant feminists and the Liberal politician.

Since Winston was not a believer in women's rights, the truce was to be a temporary one. In 1910, Sylvia Pankhurst announced that 'in Winston Churchill the Liberal Government will receive the weight of the women's opposition'. Before her marriage, Clementine admitted to friends: 'Being married to him couldn't be easy.' It certainly couldn't be, and it wasn't. Winston's radical politics made him one of the most hated men in the country.

The couple were also poor. Winston had to work hard as a journalist and author to support his family. So what made the marriage work? What made Clementine stand by her husband's side while he was hissed and booed by hostile crowds?

The answer was that Winston and Clementine were passionately devoted to each other. Their married life can be summed up by the final seven words of Winston's autobiography, *My Early Life*: 'I married and lived happily ever afterwards.'

Clementine was the power behind the throne. She helped Winston with his speeches, bolstered up his confidence in himself and calmed him when he was gripped by his 'black dog' – the chronic depression he suffered from in times of stress.

Winston's political life was a series of magnificent victories and crushing defeats. In 1910 he was made Home Secretary, but although he showed a keen interest in social reform he proved politically accident-prone. His actions in calling the military to aid the police during the Welsh miners' strike in Tonypandy lost him much of his radical following. In 1911 he was transferred to the Admiralty, where for a while things went well. But disaster struck when he was forced to resign as First Lord of the

Admiralty because of the failure of the Dardanelles expedition in 1915. Winston was distraught.

'I think it must have been, above all, the belief of his wife in him that was his rock during that terrible time, because I cannot imagine what other comfort he could have had,' commented Lord Ismay.

Aware that her husband needed something to take his mind off his crushing defeat, Clementine suggested that Winston take up painting. The suggestion proved therapeutic. From then on, Winston was never without his paintbox and easel. They accompanied him everywhere – even on his wartime missions around the world.

If Winston's political profile was erratic, his domestic side was not. 'It would not be possible for any public man to get through what I have gone through without the devoted assistance of what we call one's "better half",' Winston said proudly. In their letters, they addressed one another as Pig and Cat. Clementine was always the Cat or Kat, and her missives were invariably adorned with drawings of cats in various moods and poses. Initially, Winston was the Pug, then the Amber Pug, and finally the Pig. When Clementine was expecting her first child the couple referred to the unborn baby as Puppy Kitten. Each one of their five children was given a similar pet name.

Clementine was not without flaws. While she was pregnant with her daughter, Diana, Winston was frequently away from home. Clementine was lonely and jealous. She became convinced that Winston was having an affair. She refused to talk to her husband, forcing him to write to her from his office – even though his office was just two miles from their home. The letter still exists. He wrote:

> *Dearest, it worries me very much that you should seem to nurse such very wild suspicions which are so dishonouring to all the love and loyalty I bear you and will, please God, bear you while I breathe. I could not conceive myself forming any other attachment than that to which I have fastened the happiness of my life. You ought to trust me for I do not love and never will love any woman in the world but you. Your sweetness and beauty have cast a glory upon my life.*

The Churchills had their own set of rules for a happy marriage. This did not mean that they shared the same tastes. Clementine preferred to breakfast alone, while Winston liked company at the first meal of the day. Winston once said rather ruefully: 'My wife and I have tried two or three times in the past years to have breakfast together but we had to stop, otherwise our marriage would have been wrecked.' They also had their arguments. Winston wrote about a family budgeting session:

> *Once a year Clemmie and I go over the accounts. I see an item – 200 guineas for Diana's dresses. 'This is ruinous,' I cry.*
>
> *'You can't speak like that,' retorts Clemmie. 'The girl is coming out and she is entitled to be dressed properly.'*
>
> *We proceed. Then my wife sees an item – £300*

*for whisky. 'This is outrageous,' she says. 'What?' I cry.
'That's the breadwinner's staff. You can't touch the
breadwinner's staff.' We scowl.*

Then came World War II. After years of mixed political
success, Winston was back in the main arena. In 1940 he became
head of the Government. On 13 May he faced the House of
Commons for the first time as Prime Minister. He warned
members, 'I have nothing to offer but blood, toil, tears and
sweat.' He announced his policy: '... to wage war by sea, land and
air, with all our might and with all the strength that God can give
us.' He proclaimed one aim: 'Victory – victory at all costs,
victory in spite of all terror: victory, however long and hard the
road may be.'

Winston proved to be just the right sort of leader for war-
torn Britain. He inspired people with courage and
determination. Whether he was visiting victims of the Blitz,
smoking his cigar, or giving his famous V-for-victory sign, he was
the epitome of hope for the British. No longer were people
bombarding him with bricks and rotten eggs – they were hailing
him as their saviour.

While Churchill proved a highly successful war leader, he
failed as a party leader. Once the war was over he was no longer
needed. Britain elected a Labour government and Winston was
out in the cold once more. He continued to serve as Leader of
the Opposition for the next six years. More and more, however,
he turned to his wife, his writing and his painting. He had had his
moment of glory as wartime leader and now it was time to rest.

In 1951 he was elected Prime Minister for a second time, but by now he was an old man and ill health forced him to resign in 1955. He died in 1965. The world mourned him as a great and often misunderstood man. Clementine mourned him simply as a great man. He had been her life and now he was gone. She knew that for all his achievements, there had only been one that Winston had openly boasted about.

'My most brilliant achievement,' he had frequently remarked, 'was my ability to persuade my wife to marry me.'

ANGELA DAVIS
AND GEORGE JACKSON

'I think about you all of the time. This is one slave that knows how to love. It comes natural and runs deep. Accepting it will never hurt you. Free, open, honest love, that's me ... You've got it all, African woman.' – Letter from George Jackson to Angela Davis, 1970.

At 26, Angela Davis did seem to have it all: she was a beautiful, talented young teacher with a brilliant academic career unfolding before her. But there were four counts against Angela in the troubled, racially divided America of the sixties and seventies. She was black. She was female. She was a communist. And she loved prison activist George Jackson, a man who, like Angela, threatened the complacent white system too much to be allowed to walk free.

The road to revolution began for Angela in the ghettos of Birmingham, Alabama, where she was brought up never to look a white in the eye: 'One was taught to look at the ground when a white person passed.' She was radicalised by the 1968 bombing of a Birmingham church by a racist mob in which four of her friends were killed. Angela escaped from Birmingham the only way she knew – using her brilliant brain. By her mid-twenties she was Assistant Professor of Philosophy at the University of Los Angeles. But the more Angela studied, the more she realised how harshly the American system discriminated against blacks.

George Jackson was an underprivileged, highly intelligent young black who was imprisoned for life at 19 for stealing $70. Each year he applied for parole, each year it was denied, for George, as far as the authorities at California's Soledad prison were concerned, was a troublemaker.

The countdown to ultimate tragedy began in January 1970, when a white guard fired wantonly into a group of convicts, killing three blacks. Prison inmates were enraged when this unprovoked act was dismissed as 'justifiable homicide'. A few days later, another white guard was found killed. Three black prisoners – George Jackson, Fleeta Drumgo, 24, and John Clutchette, 27 – were charged with his murder. Suspicion flared that the three had been framed because of their outspokenness against prison conditions.

The cause of the Soledad brothers, as the three became known, was an emotional one for American blacks. Angela was caught up in the fight to get them a fair trial, touring California to raise money for their legal defence. She visited George in prison, and fell in love with the 'beautiful black warrior' at first sight.

'I came to know George through his letters,' she said. 'The

Angela Davis under arrest. She risked her career and her freedom for love.

closer I felt to George, the more I found myself revealing a side of me I usually kept hidden except from the most intimate of friends.'

'Should we make a lover's vow? It's silly, with all my tomorrows accounted for, but you can humor me,' wrote George. 'I love you, African woman. If you really need me, I'll rush to your side – right now, through steel, concrete, all that sort of stuff.'

But it wasn't Angela who went to war, it was George's brooding, introspective 17-year-old brother Jonathan. A baby at the time of George's arrest, he grew up idolising the brother he rarely saw. He attached himself to Angela like a shadow during her campaign for George's release. On 7 August 1970, Jonathan single-handedly invaded a San Rafael courthouse with a satchel full of handguns, a rifle and a sawn-off shotgun under his raincoat. 'All right, gentlemen, I'm taking over now,' he told the court as he handed guns to the prisoners being tried. Then, shouting, 'Free the Soledad brothers by 12.30!' Jonathan fled with the prisoners and five hostages, including 65-year-old Judge Harold Haley.

They didn't get far; Jonathan, the judge and two others were killed in a gun battle with police in the courthouse carpark. Angela wasn't at the courthouse, but the guns were registered in her name – which under California law made her as guilty as Jonathan of murder and kidnapping.

A massive national police hunt followed. Angela was a fugitive for eight weeks, her face plastered on posters in every police station in America, the only woman on the FBI's 'Ten Most Wanted' list. On 13 October 1970, she was arrested at gunpoint at a New York hotel, and charged with murder, conspiracy and kidnapping. She was held on one of the highest bonds in American history – $250,000 – and kept in solitary detention for six months. If found guilty, Angela faced the electric chair, but she approached her trial with gallant defiance: 'If I have to give my life to the struggle, then that's the way it has to be!'

In prison, still awaiting trial for the warden's murder, George was fiercely proud of his baby brother. 'Man-child, black man-child with submachine in hand, he was free for a while. I guess that's more than most of us can expect,' he wrote. 'I want people to wonder at what forces created him: terrible, vindictive, cold, calm man-child, courageous, scourge of the unrighteous ...'

Those forces were the same ones that killed George himself, a year to the day after Jonathan's death. Shortly before he was to come to trial, George Jackson was shot dead while allegedly trying to escape from the maximum-security wing of San Quentin Prison.

Angela's trial for murder, conspiracy and kidnapping commenced on 28 February 1972. An unprecedented international campaign was waged for her release: there were 54 'Free Angela' committees around the world, and 100,000 letters of support flooded in from East Germany alone. Prominent black Americans such as Coretta King, Ralph Abernathy and Aretha Franklin voiced their fears that Angela wouldn't receive a fair trial, due to her race, politics and sex.

After a trial lasting seven weeks, Angela was acquitted, due in part to the efforts of her supporters. She went back to her academic life, and continues to spread her political messages through her books. She lectures all over the United States as well as Europe, Africa and the Caribbean. Building on the momentum of the 'Free Angela Davis Campaign', she co-founded the National Alliance Against Racism and Political Repression, which continues its work today.

The pity of it is that for all her achievements, she was still powerless to save her imprisoned love, George Jackson, from a cruel death.

ANATOLY AND
AVITAL SHCHARANSKY

This is a love story with an almost biblical ring to it. A man is released from prison at the eleventh hour to wed the woman he loves, but they spend only a single day together before she sets out for the Promised Land, expecting him to follow her. But he is unjustly detained, and she travels the world seeking his release. Like Jacob waiting for Rachel, he will wait many years to see her again.

But all this happened in the present day, not in Old Testament times. The man is Anatoly Shcharansky, after Andrei Sakharov the Soviet dissident best known to the West. The woman is his devoted wife Avital, who fought tirelessly for twelve years for his release from the Russian Gulag. Condemned as a traitor to the Soviet way of life, Anatoly's sentence was the longest imposed on any Russian Jew since Stalin's death, but both he and Avital knew that his only crime was his passionate espousal of the right to emigrate to Israel.

Anatoly Shcharansky didn't look the part of a hero or a

martyr. Very short – just over five feet tall – and balding, he was nevertheless intensely charismatic, enormously optimistic, highly intelligent and incapable of being discouraged. It was these qualities that raised him to the forefront of the dissident cause – and which won the heart of Avital.

A mathematician, computer programmer and chess champion, Anatoly's interest in Zionism was stirred by the Yom Kippur War of 1973. Jewish sympathies everywhere were inflamed by Israel's near defeat. Even the traditionally anti-Semitic Russian authorities softened to the extent of issuing 45,000 exit visas that year to Russians emigrating to Israel. But for every Jew granted permission to leave, others were denied. These 'refuseniks' often found themselves harassed and bullied, removed from their jobs and even arrested on trumped-up charges. Anatoly Shcharansky was one of them. His quirky sense of humour and willingness to talk to Western reporters made him a natural target for the KGB.

By the time he met Avital in 1973, Anatoly was an old hand at dealing with the police. She approached him for help when her brother Michael Stiglits was arrested for taking part in a demonstration, and she was immediately struck by his warmth and ready wit.

'He could see I was afraid,' she recalled later, 'and he tried to comfort me. He asked me all about myself, my work, my plans to go to Israel ...'

Anatoly soon managed to secure Michael's release. He was deeply attracted to Avital, in whom he sensed a kindred spirit despite their very different personalities. Avital was a shy art student, whose revulsion against the Soviet system dated back to her childhood, when she stumbled upon a political prison camp deep in the forests of Siberia. Her dissatisfaction crystallised when she read Boris Pasternak's forbidden novel, *Doctor Zhivago*, at the age of seventeen. Around the same time she discovered her Jewish background, which her parents had concealed from her. She felt that she would only find the freedom she craved in Israel, and she decided to emigrate. But, like Anatoly, she was refused permission to leave Russia.

Mesmerised by her icon-like beauty – all dark, brooding eyes and luminous, Slavic cheekbones – Anatoly asked Avital to marry him. They moved into an apartment together, planning their wedding, teaching themselves Hebrew and dreaming of escape to Israel. Again and again they applied for exit visas, but were always refused. Anatoly had been too vocal for his own good, had talked to too many foreign correspondents about the state of human rights in Russia. He was denounced as a traitor by his colleagues and thrown out of his mathematician's job at the Moscow Research Institute. He and Avital were followed everywhere by KGB 'tails' who were so determined not to lose sight of their quarries that one even jumped into a taxi Anatoly had hailed and rode with him to his destination, splitting the bill with him. 'To talk freely we used to walk around Moscow for hours together,' said Avital.

Their wedding preparations weren't getting any further than their emigration plans. Their marriage application at the neighbourhood administrative office was simply ignored. 'They never said no,' said Avital. 'They said we must wait.' Finally, despairing of a civil ceremony, they opted for a Jewish wedding, but most Moscow rabbis were too frightened to marry refuseniks. Finally Avital managed to track down one brave enough to perform the ceremony, and the date was set for 4 July 1974. But then disaster struck – Anatoly simply disappeared.

On 19 June, on the eve of US President Nixon's visit to Moscow, Anatoly and seventeen other prominent dissidents were arrested to get them out of sight of the American correspondents who were accompanying Nixon. Avital was frantic. But then came a new twist to her agony – she was told that her exit visa had finally been granted, but only on condition that she leave the Soviet Union within ten days; otherwise it would be revoked forever. Desperately trusting in providence, Avital went ahead with the wedding preparations, and miraculously, Anatoly was released at 10am on the appointed day. They were married at 4pm that afternoon.

'It was such a happy wedding,' recalled Avital, even though Anatoly was unshaven and grubby from prison. 'After the ceremony we all started to sing Hebrew songs … We felt like big winners – so excited.'

Avital told Anatoly that her exit visa was to expire within 24 hours, and added that she had been told that if she went quietly, 'without fuss', Anatoly would be allowed to follow 'within a few months'. Overjoyed at this news, he insisted that she should go, and so the next day, after a honeymoon lasting a single night, Avital flew to Israel. Ominously, she mislaid her wedding ring, then discovered that the wedding photos hadn't come out. These could have been signals that worse was to come, for the authorities had tricked the Shcharankys; for month after month they refused Anatoly's emigration application, giving no reasons.

Two weary years crawled past, and Avital attempted to re-enter Russia to rejoin her husband – only to be turned back. By now Anatoly had incurred further official wrath by joining the Helsinki Accord Watchdog Group, set up to monitor Moscow's human rights record and report to the West. He was harassed by the KGB and finally arrested in 1977, snatched in front of two American reporters. A year later he stood trial on the capital charge of treason and spreading anti-Soviet propaganda. Holding a photograph of his wife in his hand, Anatoly conducted his own spirited defence at the nightmare trial, concluding by addressing his absent Avital with the words: 'Next year in Jerusalem!'

But he would not see her next year, nor for many years to come. He languished in a series of grim prisons, ranging from the remand cells of Lesurtovo, the high security fortress of Vladimir, the isolation of Christopol in faraway Tartary, and a remote prison farm in Term. He endured hundreds of days of solitary confinement, in temperatures as cold as 50° centigrade below freezing. He kept sane by singing Hebrew songs, studying a smuggled copy of the Psalms, and writing countless letters to Avital. Very few of them reached her, and even fewer of hers reached him. 'Avital wrote to me twice a week, but I received two letters a year – and that was a good year,' he later commented ruefully.

Finally he went on a hunger strike to protest against being forbidden to write to his wife, or even to mention her name in correspondence. He was beaten and force-fed, but finally some of his letters were allowed to trickle through.

> *When I see his letters they make me really excited.*
> *They make me see how the spirit of a human being*

> *can win over everything. He pays for these letters*
> *with his body and the authorities know that our*
> *relationship gives him strength; they will do*
> *anything to undermine it … Anatoly is physically*
> *weak, but spiritually he's strong. I know we can both*
> *go on as long as we have to.*

But sometimes Avital had her doubts. As year followed year
apart, she began to wonder if her husband would even recognise
her any more. Anatoly reassured her:

> *Mama sent me your picture with friends in Jerusalem*
> *in the summer of 1978 … You have lost a lot of*
> *weight; you are visibly tired.*
>
> *Naturally something has changed, but that*
> *something is the wisdom which was given to us by*
> *these bitter years of our life and which added to your*
> *youth and beauty, my beloved wife … Even your*
> *silence helps, simply because you exist and you are*
> *waiting.*

Avital had every right to look tired. For while Anatoly had
been languishing in solitary confinement or in labour camps, she
had been endlessly agitating for his release. She doorstopped US
Presidents Carter and Reagan, France's President Mitterrand and
'three or four Italian heads of state', as she put it. She flew to
Washington to join in an all-night vigil with US Congressmen.
She haunted the world's newspaper offices.

Her unceasing efforts ensured that her husband was never

Avital Shcharansky holds a prisoner of conscience breakfast near the United Nations. On the left are two posters of her husband.

forgotten, and slowly a groundswell of international opinion put pressure on the Soviets to release Anatoly. While Avital became a symbol of stoic resistance in the battle against political repression, her efforts took their toll. At one point she commented glumly:

> *I don't live like a woman. I live like a soldier, all the time fighting for my husband ... I get my strength from Anatoly. I never feel separated from him – somehow we're always together. The worst thing is that we don't have any children, and I wanted many ...*

She sought consolation in religion, keeping a strict kosher kitchen and covering her head in the pious Jewish manner so that her hair, her crowning glory, would be seen only by her husband. If he ever saw her again … Despite her brave front, over the years Avital often came close to despair. But her incessant campaigning and demonstrations were ultimately more effective than she realised, and by 1985 rumours were circulating that Anatoly would soon be released by the Soviets as a concession to international pressure. Avital redoubled her efforts, even approaching Raisa Gorbachev on her husband's behalf.

Anatoly realised his release must be imminent when his captors started feeding him up: 'Within a few weeks I gained 10 kg,' he said. But weakened by hunger strikes and more than a decade of ill treatment, he still scarcely weighed more than a child. His hair had almost completely fallen out and he had developed heart problems. But his spirit was unconquerable. When, on 11 February 1986, he was finally released in a preposterous 'spy swap' with the West – the Soviets insisted on maintaining the fiction that Anatoly was a secret agent for the CIA – he was flown to Berlin and told to walk in a straight line across the Glienicke Bridge to freedom. Characteristically, he insisted on zigzagging.

Waiting for him on the other side was the wife he hadn't seen in twelve years. Together they flew on to Israel's Ben Gurion Airport, where a gala state reception and an international press conference awaited them. Ebullient as ever, Anatoly rose to the occasion, flashing a broad grin and chatting to reporters. But Avital's emotions almost overcame her on this happiest day of her life. She blushed when Israeli Prime Minister Shimon Peres described her as a 'lioness'. She blushed even more when Anatoly attempted to embrace her at the conference, then wiped away tears as he told reporters how on their wedding night he had promised he would see her soon in Jerusalem. 'But the way to Jerusalem has been very hard,' he added.

Finally Avital broke down and wept when President Reagan rang to congratulate her. It was all too much. She whispered to Anatoly and they left the press conference together. She took him to the fabled Western Wall, all that remains of King Solomon's temple, built three millennia ago. There Avital had often scribbled prayers for her husband's release and slipped them into crevices in the ancient stones. As Anatoly prayed in front of the Wall, she slipped away to the private area set aside for women and offered up her own heartfelt gratitude for her husband's return to her. Now, after a night together and a dozen years apart, their marriage could finally begin.

In May 1986 Avital and Anatoly were awarded gold medals by the American Congress as its highest expression of national appreciation for distinguished achievements. This honour put them in exalted company: other non-Americans to receive gold medals have been Mother Teresa, Nelson Mandela and Winston Churchill.

Since his release Anatoly has worked tirelessly for Israel, founding a party to help Russian immigrants. He was appointed to the Cabinet as Minister of Industry and Trade in 1996, and served in both Ehud Barak's and Ariel Sharon's governments. And by his side, supporting him in all his achievements, has been his beloved Avital.

AFFAIRS
OF THE
ARTS

FRÉDÉRIC CHOPIN
AND GEORGE SAND

Frédéric Chopin had heard a lot about George Sand, and he knew that he didn't like the sound of this woman who masqueraded under a man's name. She, on the other hand, had never heard of the young Polish composer.

It was Paris, 1836, and George Sand, the romantic novelist, was the toast of the town. Everyone was talking about the woman who was born Amandine Aurore Lucile Dupin in 1804, who had married Casimir Dudevant in 1822 and left him in 1831 to 'find herself'.

When she found herself, she changed her name to George Sand. It was a man's world, she thought, and the only way to get by was to assume a male persona – hence the name George. She had borrowed the surname, Sand, from one of her young lovers – Jules Sandeau.

The first time Frédéric Chopin saw George Sand, she was surrounded by a coterie of literary admirers at a social function.

The elegant young Pole stared disdainfully across the room at the flamboyant author. She was dressed in a startling Turkish costume with wide purple pantaloons and had covered her black hair with a vivid red scarf. To top it all off, she was chain-smoking cigars. Chopin turned away, almost fearfully. But throughout the evening he found himself craning to catch a glimpse of the eccentric George Sand. Later he took his friend Ferdinand Hiller aside and commented, 'What an unsympathetic woman. Is she really a woman? Almost, almost, I doubt it.'

Hardly an auspicious beginning for one of the most curious love affairs of the nineteenth century, but it was a beginning. Two years later, Chopin and George Sand were involved in a torrid relationship that would last seven years. In one way, the affair was based on the attraction of opposites – Chopin was frail and shy, whereas Sand was liberated and extroverted. She was also six years older than the talented composer. But in another way the affair flourished on the grounds of their mutual idealism. Chopin was a romantic who was trying to compose the perfect piece of music, while Sand was also looking for perfection, albeit of a different sort. She wrote:

> *I have always believed above all else in fidelity. I have preached it, I have practised it, I have demanded it. Others have failed to live up to it and I too. And yet I have never felt remorse, because in my infidelities I have suffered a sort of fatality, an instinctive idealism which impelled me to abandon the imperfect for what seemed to be closer to perfection.*

Paris marvelled when Chopin and Sand became lovers. They all but laughed at the union between the fastidious composer and the bizarre novelist. Many sniggered at the thought of the elegant Chopin finding solace in the arms of a woman who dressed like a man and swore like a trooper.

George Sand was not a beautiful woman, she was short and stocky, but she did have one saving grace. She had the most lustrously beautiful eyes, which she used to her advantage at every opportunity. She also had charisma and the ability to stand up and fight for the things she believed in. She believed in Chopin and she fought for him.

Neither Sand nor Chopin had had a hard beginning. They had both come from families that were a strange mixture of royalty and peasantry. Chopin had been a child prodigy and his parents had happily fostered his talent on the piano. He made his debut in Vienna in 1829 but soon after moved to the centre of European culture – Paris.

Sand had had a carefree childhood and had married Casimir Dudevant when she was just eighteen. At first she had been happy. She gave birth to a son, Maurice, in 1823 and then in 1828 her daughter, Solange, was born. It is debatable whether Solange was also Dudevant's daughter, however. By this time the marriage was well and truly over and George had become famous for her scandalous love affairs.

In 1831 she decided to leave her husband and her rural home in Nohant and move to Paris to take part in the Romantic movement. In 1832 Sand found herself an immediate success with her first novel *Indiana*, which was a passionate protest

George Sand. 'Is she really a woman?'
Chopin commented on first seeing her.

against the social conventions that bind a wife to a husband against her will. She quickly followed up with *Valentine* and *Leila*, which entrenched her firmly on the side of militant feminism. Sand asked pertinent questions: 'Women differ from men but ought this difference, so essential to the harmony of life, constitute a moral inferiority? ... And does it necessarily follow that the souls and minds of women are inferior to those of men, whose vanity permits them to tolerate no other natural order?'

Sand didn't choose to dress as a man to shock society. She was trying to open doors that were conventionally closed to women. The simple act of eating in a restaurant was impossible for a woman on her own, hence her decision to wear male attire. She didn't know it, but she was blazing a trail for the women of today who choose to wear slacks and go to the theatre or restaurants unescorted. She also helped to liberate women from their traditionally passive position in a male society.

It was she who pursued Chopin with love letters and offers to help him with his musical career. She adored the beautiful young man and was openly worried about his constant coughing, which later proved to be a sign of tuberculosis. 'The poor angel needs me,' she wrote. 'Life in Paris is bad for his health. He must have country air and exercise. Above all, he must have affection.' She whisked Chopin off on a restorative holiday to Majorca, but unfortunately she picked the wrong place. The couple were subjected to disaster after disaster. It rained the entire time, there was a plague of fleas, they were evicted from their rented

Frédéric Chopin. His surprising affair with the flamboyant George Sand lasted seven years.

digs and Chopin came down with bronchitis. Despite all this, however, the lovers decided they would live together and they returned to Paris.

They never quite set up house together. In Paris they lived in adjacent apartments and in their summer vacations they went back to Sand's country property at Nohant. Chopin got on very well with Sand's children, and although he preferred city life he found that country air agreed with him. It was at Nohant that he conceived his *Fantaisie in F Minor*, widely regarded as his masterpiece. Although he longed for the excitement of Paris, most of his music was actually written at Nohant.

Sand and Chopin made an odd couple, she with her cigars and men's clothing and he in his satins and lace. But they were in love. She would leave notes for him among the sheet music on the piano: 'You are adored! Aurore.' He replied: 'Now I know what your eyes have said – those eyes so dark and so strange. You love me. Aurore, lovely name!' George Sand might have been known to her public by her masculine pen name, but to Chopin she was always the lovely Aurore.

Unhappily, it is only in fiction that odd couples find themselves living happily ever after. The differences between Chopin and Sand began to wear away at their relationship. By 1845 a visitor remarked of their life: 'Love is no longer here but tenderness and devotion, mixed with sadness, regrets and ennui.'

The problem for the couple was that they had been born in the wrong time. Chopin couldn't stand being the weaker of the two, and Sand found herself despising rather than loving her younger partner. Society had clear-cut roles for the sexes, and Sand and Chopin had reversed those roles for too long. They had one last, bitter fight and parted forever.

When Chopin died of tuberculosis in 1849, Sand refused to attend his funeral. The lovers had seen each other too clearly and knew each other's weaknesses too well to be able to forgive each other.

ARISTOTLE ONASSIS
AND MARIA CALLAS

Before she met Aristotle Onassis, Maria Callas had only ever wanted one thing – to be the first lady of opera. After meeting the Greek shipping tycoon, she had room for only one obsession – she wanted to be Ari's *prima donna*.

Maria had always been an obsessive person. She was born in New York in 1923, to parents who had moved to America from Greece to find fame and fortune. They found neither. Maria grew up with a passion to escape. She wanted to leave her quarrelling parents, her shabby home and the constant feeling that she was second best.

'I was the ugly duckling of the family,' she said, 'fat and clumsy and unpopular. It is a cruel thing to make a child feel ugly and unwanted.'

Luckily for Maria, she had an avenue of escape – her voice. She could sing like an angel. The miserable young girl perfected her talent to the point where she could leave home. She moved to Italy and began to establish herself as a potentially great soprano. Her first leading role came in 1942, when she sang *Tosca*. She was a resounding success, and from then on nothing could hold her back. By 1957 opera critics were raving about the girl with the 'miraculous throat', whose voice was described as 'phosphorescent beauty'. Maria had arrived. She was one of the most celebrated sopranos in the world.

And then she was introduced to Ari.

Onassis was fascinated by Maria's talent. He openly showed his appreciation by following her all over the world. He flew to London to see her as Medea, buying 30 tickets which he distributed among his friends. Nobody had any doubt that the wealthy Greek was pursuing the fiery opera singer. Least of all Maria's businessman husband, Giovanni Battista Meneghini.

Giovanni had married Maria when she first arrived in Italy. She had been fat, unattractive and gawky, but Giovanni had fallen in love with her. He was more than twice her age but they seemed happy. Giovanni abandoned his own career and spent all his time and money on his wife. He became her manager and agent, and set about making her a star. He succeeded admirably. During their time together Maria even managed to lose the excess weight that had plagued her all her life. By the time she met Ari she was a svelte, attractive woman.

Ari invited Maria and Giovanni for a holiday cruise on board his luxury yacht, the *Christina*. He tempted them with the fact that Winston Churchill would be one of their travelling companions, and he also said that his wife, Tina Onassis, would be delighted if they accepted. Since it was public knowledge that

Onassis was hell-bent on having an affair with Maria, it seemed doubtful whether Tina's invitation was totally sincere. Nevertheless, Maria and Giovanni accepted.

While he was on board the yacht Giovanni kept a diary, and his private thoughts indicate that he was ill at ease and unhappy:

> *Many of the couples split up and found other partners. The women and also the men often sunbathed completely nude and fooled around in broad daylight, in front of everyone.*
>
> *I had the impression of finding myself in the middle of a pigpen. One of the things that made the strongest impression on me was to see Onassis naked. He didn't seem to be a man, but a gorilla. He was very hairy. Maria looked at him and laughed.*

Sadly for Giovanni, Maria didn't laugh for very long. She fell passionately in love with Ari. She forgot her kindly husband's early help in establishing her as one of the world's most famous opera singers. She forgot that he had loved her at a time when she had been fat and unknown. And she forgot that Ari was already married.

She turned on Giovanni: 'You act like my jailer,' she said. 'You never leave me alone. You control me in everything. You're like some hateful guardian, and you've kept me hemmed in all these years. I'm suffocating!'

The cruise ended with Maria determined to leave her husband. As far as she was concerned, the marriage was over. She told Giovanni that she was going to move in with Ari. Giovanni tried to reason with her but she was adamant. She wanted out of the relationship. Less than a month later, they had their final confrontation. Maria asked Giovanni to join Ari and herself, to discuss the future. According to Giovanni, the meeting was disastrous:

> *I really lost my patience, I insulted him [Ari] and called him the epithets he deserved. Maria began to tremble and to sob convulsively. Then Onassis began to cry, saying: 'Yes, I'm a disgrace, I'm a murderer, I'm a thief, I'm no good, I'm the most revolting person on earth. But I'm a millionaire and powerful. I will never give up Maria, and I will take her away from whomever it's necessary, using whatever means, sending people, things, contracts, and conventions to hell … How many million do you want for Maria? Five, ten?'*

Giovanni bowed out of Maria's life and she officially became the mistress of Aristotle Onassis. The next nine years were a combination of idyll and nightmare. Ari showered Maria with love and affection but he refused to allow her to have the baby she so ardently desired. When she became pregnant at the age of 43, he insisted that she have an abortion. If she refused, he said, he would leave her. Maria agreed. The idea of losing Ari was impossible.

In the time they were together, Ari gave Maria millions of dollars of jewellery, clothing and real estate. He also gave her a lot of misery. He referred to her as 'nothing but a nightclub singer' – this when she was truly losing her voice. Maria's

Maria Callas's passionate affair with Aristotle Onassis was both idyll and nightmare.

great gift was gradually petering out. At concerts she was booed and hissed off the stage. But it was worthwhile as long as Ari loved her. She didn't mind the fights and the insults if they were alleviated by passionate reconciliations.

Which they were, until Ari met the glamerous Jacqueline Kennedy. Then Onassis began to pursue the beautiful young widow with a vengeance. He publicly humiliated Maria. He refused to have her on board the *Christina* when Jackie was there. He jeered at her lost voice. 'What are you? Nothing. You just have a whistle in your throat that no longer works.'

A heart-broken Maria tried to pick up the threads of her career. She arranged a series of grand concert tours. Anything to get away from the man who was making her life a misery. So while Ari cruised the world with Jackie, Maria was singing her heart out before audiences who often proved extremely unsympathetic. 'Get fat again, Maria. Get fat!' Those who had loved her singing when she was obese now blamed her lack of success on her new, slim figure. 'Like a monochrome reproduction of an oil painting,' was one critic's verdict on her comeback. Maria felt totally rejected. It seemed that the world shared Aristotle's opinion of her fading voice.

Ari and Jackie were quietly married in 1968 in a tiny chapel on the island of Skorpios. 'First I lose my weight, then I lose my voice, and now I've lost Onassis,' Maria lamented.

Even though Ari had rejected her, she still loved the Greek millionaire. In 1969 she told reporters: 'He was my love and at the same time, my best friend. Things have not changed just because we are separated. I am happy if he is happy – even with another woman.'

Within a couple of days of his marriage to Jackie, Ari realised that he had been wrong in repudiating Maria. He might have fallen in love with Kennedy's widow, who made him feel young again, but when all was said and done, he was distinctly middle-aged. Callas might have had her day, she had all but lost her voice and she wasn't as glamorous as Jackie, but the fact remained that Onassis wanted her back in his life. She was part of him. He openly began to court Maria. After all, they had both seen the hard side of life and they were beginning to mellow with age. Ari found he had trouble keeping up with his new young wife, and he turned to Maria more and more.

Then came the catastrophe that finally ended their happiness – Onassis died in 1975. 'All of a sudden I am a widow,' said a distraught Maria. Life without Ari was pointless, and she didn't bother to try to find a new meaning.

Maria died after suffering a heart attack in 1977. As her friends commented: 'After Ari's death she was never the same again. Her zest for life had disappeared. Maria just pined away.'

ELVIS AND PRISCILLA PRESLEY

The three bodyguards looked up. They could hear their master's voice, imperiously summoning them. And although it was the small hours of the morning, the well-drilled men tumbled obediently into the nearby master bedroom. There, squatting yoga-style on the opulent bed, was a dark-haired, bloated man, drenched with sweat, plainly in the grip of a manic rage.

'The man has to die,' he said, slurring his words badly. 'There is too much pain in me and he did it! Mike Stone has to die. You will do it for me. Kill the sonovabitch!'

The three men – Sonny West, Red West and Lamar Fike – looked at their boss in horror. For a long time now his behaviour had been increasingly erratic. And now that the only woman he had ever loved had left him for a man named Mike Stone, Elvis Presley seemed to have gone over the edge into murderous insanity.

Elvis Aaron Presley was born on 8 January 1935, the firstborn of identical twin boys. The second boy, Jesse, was stillborn. From the moment of his birth the bond between Elvis and his mother Gladys Presley was extraordinarily strong. Throughout his life Elvis wanted love – uncritical, unstinting love, like that which Gladys had lavished on him. As the world's hottest musical property, millions of adoring women would have given him anything he asked for. Girls blatantly offered themselves to him in their letters. Others threatened suicide if he didn't make love to them. He frequently obliged, but there was only one woman who left her mark on him – Priscilla Anne Beaulieu.

Outwardly the strutting, smouldering bad boy of rock and roll, Elvis's dramatic success as a teen idol had left him secretly bewildered and confused. Emotionally immature himself, he had a liking for very young, virginal women – but even those who knew him well were startled when, while serving in Germany, he fell under the spell of a radiantly pretty 14-year-old girl.

Priscilla Beaulieu was an army brat, the daughter of a US Air Force captain stationed in Germany. Poised and well-developed, she looked older than her years. Elvis was attracted by her good looks, and engineered a meeting. At first Priscilla couldn't believe she was being asked to date the US Army's most glamorous draftee. 'Someone asked me if I wanted to meet Elvis Presley and I said "Fine", thinking it was all a joke,' Priscilla recalled later. 'The next thing I knew I was on my way to Elvis's house ... He got up and shook my hand and the reality hit me.'

And the reality was that Elvis's charm was irresistible. He set out to woo the adolescent girl, arranging further dates, showering her with flowers and gifts. When his stint in the army was over, air force police would not allow him to kiss Priscilla

Pricilla and Elvis Presley on their wedding day

goodbye at the airport where he awaited a US-bound plane. Upset, he muttered angrily, 'They won't let me see her ... They won't allow me to see her.'

Back home in the States, he decided that he *would* see Priscilla – exactly when and where he wished. He wanted her by his side, with no more midnight curfews set by Captain Beaulieu, waiting up for his little girl to return from her dates with the king of rock and roll. Elvis called Priscilla's parents in Germany and talked them into allowing her to spend the Christmas holidays with his family in Memphis. They agreed to a short visit, but somehow Elvis neglected to send her home after the holidays. 'I ended up staying and going to school there at the Immaculate Conception High School,' recalled Priscilla.

At this time she had no idea there was anything strange about her situation. 'I wasn't worried,' she said later, 'because Elvis had assured my parents that no harm would come to me.' And Elvis made sure that his teen dream led a fairytale existence. He bought her a Corvair, and then a lavender Chevrolet sports car to drive to school. He had her flown to his side whenever he was away on location making a film or completing a concert tour. When they went to the movies, he would hire the entire cinema so that they could make as much noise as they liked together.

The grooming period came to an end on 1 May 1967. Priscilla was now 21, fit queen for the king, and they exchanged wedding vows at the Las Vegas Hotel in a hasty, impromptu ceremony. Exactly nine months later the couple's only child was born, Lisa Marie Presley. Now Elvis had two little girls to look after – except that one of them was growing up fast. Like the beautiful princess in a fairy story, Priscilla was beginning to wake up to her extraordinary lifestyle.

She became aware that Elvis was changing – for the worse. The hectic pace of his career had made him dependent on amphetamines to keep him going, and medication to help him sleep after giving a show. Elvis despised heroin and marijuana as symbols of weakness; he didn't seem to realise that he had become addicted to legal drugs, 'uppers' and 'downers' prescribed for him by unscrupulous doctors. His personality altered and he became paranoid. He was convinced that his legions of devoted fans were plotting to kill him, and he always carried a gun, on stage and off. Both he and the retinue of bodyguards who surrounded him day and night took karate lessons in case an attacker caught them unarmed. He went on eating binges and his weight soared, leaving him puffy, bleary and out of condition.

Ironically, it was his obsession with security that led to Elvis's undoing. He decided that Priscilla should also learn to defend herself, and he engaged a handsome young karate instructor called Mike Stone to give her some lessons. Before long the lessons got out of hand, and Priscilla found herself in love for the second time in her life. She was determined to be upfront about it. She told Elvis she was leaving him for another man and a simpler lifestyle, and moved out of Gracelands, Elvis's fabulous antebellum mansion in Memphis. 'I want to grow. I want to do things,' she told him.

Elvis became a virtual recluse at Gracelands, plotting revenge against Mike Stone, the man who had stolen his Priscilla. His aides learned to vet his television viewing, for they knew from experience that if he saw the popular series *The Streets of San Francisco*, in which actor Karl Malden portrayed a character called Mike Stone, Elvis was likely to shoot out the television screen with one of his arsenal of guns.

Then came the terrible night when, stupefied with drugs, he ordered his guards to kill Mike Stone. He seemed bent on self-destruction. He rarely got out of bed when he wasn't performing; he was regressing to the safe, warm world of childhood, back to when he was secure in his mother's love. He had to shut out the real world, and the twilight of drug-taking softened his pain.

He was regularly taking doses that would kill people not habituated to drugs, and finally he lost out on the odds. On 15 August 1977, five years after Priscilla had left him, he downed a bizarre cocktail of fourteen different drugs, including Quaaludes, Seconal, Demerol and Valium. The following day he was found dead of a heart attack in his bathroom. The King's reign was over. He was only 42.

Priscilla's relationship with Mike Stone did not stand the test of time. She had other relationships before falling in love with Marco Garibaldi, with whom she had her second child, a son she named Navarone, in 1987. She embarked on a successful acting career, appearing in several television series and the *Naked Gun* film trilogy. She has also proved to be an astute businesswoman, creating her own line of International fragrances. As executor of the Elvis Presley Estate and president of Elvis Presley Enterprises between 1979 and 1998, she took an estate worth $3 million and built it into a business valued in excess of $250 million.

She can never forget her extraordinary life as the only woman Elvis Presley loved enough to marry. 'It was a very strange relationship,' she has observed. 'It went beyond a normal life. It went beyond a normal relationship – it was much deeper … There's not a day goes by that we [she and Lisa Marie] don't think of him.'

JOHN LENNON AND YOKO ONO

She never smiles. She was taught by her aristocratic mother that only shopkeepers need to ingratiate themselves by smiling. She's small and shy, fragile and birdlike. She often wears sunglasses that cover half her face. She always wears dark clothes, as if she wants to be invisible. It's difficult to see how such an inconspicuous figure could have become one of the most reviled women of the twentieth century.

She is Yoko Ono, the woman the world blamed for breaking up the Beatles, for transforming John Lennon, the Cynical One of the Fab Four, into a bearded recluse who squandered his talents on half-baked schemes for world peace.

For a long time she was seen merely as John's Oriental temptress, but Yoko Ono was well established as an avant-garde artist long before they met. She was famous for making films like the notorious *Number Four* – two hours of close-up of hundreds of human backsides. She staged concerts at which the audience was invited to listen to electric clocks through stethoscopes. She held 'happenings' at which the participants cut the clothes from her body with scissors. The critics sometimes publicly wondered whether Yoko's artistic efforts weren't some enormous inscrutable joke, but John Lennon always took her seriously.

They met in 1966, at the opening of an exhibition of her sculpture, and were instantly drawn to each other. They had so much in common; John, the untamed intellectual of rock, like Yoko often felt misunderstood as an artist. They had both had desperately lonely childhoods – with one important difference. While John was a working class lad from Liverpool, Yoko was a Japanese version of the poor little rich girl. Descended from billionaire banker Zenjiro Yasuda, Yoko was brought up in a mansion with about thirty servants.

'We were so wealthy that I could never play in the street,' she once confessed. 'If I wanted friends I would send a servant to bring a child from a nearby cottage. I was always giving them toys, but they didn't smile, and I yearned for friendship ...'

She got more than friendship from John Lennon, who recognised a soulmate in the enigmatic artist. 'When I met Yoko, we were two poets in velvet coats, almost literally,' he recalled. 'We were full of positive ideas for the world ...'

But the world didn't always see it that way. The other Beatles were particularly disturbed by the extent of Yoko's influence over John. He and Paul McCartney, together the creative heart of the group, became increasingly at odds with each other. All the Beatles were feeling the strain of being the most successful pop act ever, and Yoko's constant presence at recording sessions only added to the tension. Some of John's frustrations were revealed in 'The Ballad of John and Yoko':

Christ, you know it ain't easy
You know how hard it can be
The way things are going
They're going to crucify me!

The Beatles split up, amid considerable bitterness, in 1970, and Yoko was singled out for the lion's share of the blame. Musically, John was in limbo. His first two solo albums had aroused a storm of controversy. *Unfinished Music No 2: Life With the Lions* and *Wedding Album*, on which he collaborated with Yoko, confused and alienated the legions of Beatles fans. It wasn't until later that the critics caught up with their musical innovations.

But that didn't bother John. Blissfully happy in his love for Yoko, he wasn't too concerned about reaction to his music; he was more interested in pushing the cause of world peace. When he and Yoko held a press conference on the subject, they famously appeared in bed. They seemed determined to shock people into changing their attitudes, appearing in the nude on one of their album covers. Almost everything they did made newspaper headlines, and just as it had in his Beatle days, the incessant publicity was beginning to take its toll on John. While he and Yoko had one of the most public love affairs of all time, John secretly could not bear to share her with anyone.

A desperately insecure man, like many geniuses, he was, in the words of his own song, 'just a jealous guy'. He resented anything that took Yoko away from him for even a minute. 'He didn't even like me knowing the Japanese language because that was a part of me that didn't belong to him,' she said later. 'After

John Lennon and Yoko Ono. They were soulmates, but their partnership bewildered the world.

a while, I couldn't even read any papers and magazines in Japanese …'

The strain became too much for the couple, and they split up for eighteen months in the mid-seventies. These were months of drunkenness and despair for John, months in which he learned that he needed Yoko even more than he needed music. They decided to give their love a second chance, and sort out their priorities. Domestic bliss now came first, and John happily retired from the music scene to look after their new son, Sean, while Yoko busied herself sorting out his tangled financial affairs.

'We were both self-destructive,' he said of their period apart. 'We came out of that by the gift of having the baby ... I don't think I would have been able to withdraw from the whole music business if it hadn't been for Sean.'

For five years he was a househusband, but finally his musical genius had to have its outlet. His love for Yoko and Sean blossomed into an outpouring of lyrical creation. He saw Yoko and himself as reincarnations of the legendary lovers Elizabeth Barrett and Robert Browning. Yoko was similarly inspired, and together they produced the album *Double Fantasy*, the first of a projected series of records they called 'heart plays', in which they laid bare their love for each other. But shortly after the album's release in 1980 John Lennon was dead, struck down by the bullet of a crazed assassin, Mark Chapman, who slaughtered him in front of Yoko's horrified eyes.

The world mourned the passing of a legend, but Yoko Ono's sorrow knew no bounds. She keeps John's ashes in a ceramic pot, and her walls are lined with his pictures and albums. She has built her own monuments to John. Some are inspirational, like her Strawberry Fields garden project dedicated to his memory in New York's Central Park. Some are bleak and bitter, like her controversial album *Season of Glass*, whose cover features a close-up of John's famous spectacles, bloodstained from the bullet that killed him. The lyrics of one of the album's songs, 'I Don't Know Why', end in a torrent of abuse aimed at John's assassin. It is clear that Yoko Ono is unlikely ever to forgive Mark Chapman.

Yoko has also continued her work as an avant-garde artist. During her 2003 *Cut Peace* performance in Paris, she invited an audience of two hundred people to each take a turn snipping at her clothes with scissors in the name of world peace, and to send a scrap of the fabric 'to the one you love'. It was fitting that John and Yoko's son Sean was the first to cut a scrap from her dress.

It is clear that neither he nor Yoko Ono will ever forget John Lennon, the man with whom she made such wonderful love and marvellous music for fourteen turbulent years.

KURT COBAIN
AND COURTNEY LOVE

Courtney Love's voice was jagged and out of control. Tears poured from her eyes as she read aloud the suicide note left by her husband Kurt Cobain, who had days earlier blown his brains out with a shotgun. It was his memorial service.

Kurt was just 27 and had everything to live for. As lead singer of the legendary group Nirvana he had the whole world eating out of his hand. He was adored by Courtney and their daughter Frances Bean. But somehow, it wasn't enough. Courtney's voice shook as she read her husband's note:

> I haven't felt the excitement of listening to music along with really writing something for years now. I feel guilty beyond words about these things. The fact is I can't fool you. It simply isn't fair to you or to me. The worst crime I could think of would be to put people off by faking it, by pretending I am having 100 percent fun. Sometimes I feel as if I should have

a punch-in time clock before I walk on stage. I still can't get out the guilt, the frustration, the empathy I have for everybody. There's good in all of us and I simply love people too much. So much that it makes me feel too ... sad, a little sensitive, unappreciative ... So remember: It's better to burn out than fade away.

Choking with emotion, Courtney ground out the words, 'God, you asshole!' She would never forgive Kurt for abandoning her.

They had so much in common, they were so much alike: both heroin addicts, both victims of abusive childhoods, both rock stars with a passion for music. Twin souls, and now he was gone. She didn't know how to go on. It was like a line in one of her own songs from the album *Live Through This*, released the day after Kurt's memorial service: 'If you live through this with me I swear that I will die for you.' But she couldn't die for him. She had to go on for the sake of their child, betrayed by his suicide.

Kurt Donald Cobain was born on 20 February 1967, in Washington State. His father Don, 21 when Kurt was born, worked as a mechanic, and his mother Wendy, just 19, was a high school beauty queen. They were young to have a child; too young for their marriage to survive.

'I can't put into words the joy and life that Kurt brought into our family,' remembered his aunt, Wendy's sister Mari. 'He was this little human being who was so bubbly. He had charisma even as a baby. He was funny and he was bright.'

He was also extremely sensitive to the increasing strain

between his parents. In February 1976, just a week after Kurt's ninth birthday, Wendy told Don she wanted a divorce. 'He thought it was his fault, and he shouldered much of the blame,' observed Mari. 'It was traumatic for Kurt, as he saw everything he trusted in – his security, family and his own maintenance – unravel in front of his eyes.'

Rather than outwardly express his anguish, Kurt turned inward. That June, he wrote on his bedroom wall: 'I hate Mom, I hate Dad. Dad hates Mom, Mom hates Dad. It simply makes you want to be so sad.'

Although Wendy had won custody, Kurt moved in with his father and visited his mother on weekends. By the time he was eleven, the family conflicts had begun to affect Kurt's behaviour. He talked back to adults, refused to do chores and, despite his small size, began to bully other children. Finally his father took him to counselling.

Holidays were always a problem, with Kurt shuffled between households at Thanksgiving and Christmas. He felt pure anger towards his mother's new boyfriend. One night the boyfriend broke Wendy's arm, causing her to be hospitalised. Kurt witnessed the incident. When Wendy refused to press charges, Kurt pitied his mother and hated her for having to pity her. His parents had been his gods when he was younger; now they were false gods, fallen idols not to be trusted.

Courtney had also grown disillusioned with her parents at a young age. She was born Michelle Courtney Love Harrison in San Francisco in 1965. Her mother was a hippie heiress named Linda Carroll and her father Hank Harrison, a publisher, an

*Courtney Love and Kurt Cobain with
their daughter, Frances Bean*

'abject sociopathic failure' of a man who hung out with the rock group Grateful Dead. He denied rumours that he gave Courtney drugs as a two-year-old, saying they were vitamin pills.

As she grew up, Courtney was expelled from a series of schools before getting caught shoplifting and being sent to a reformatory. At sixteen she left home, living on an $800-a-month endowment from her maternal grandmother while working as a stripper and singing in bands up and down the US West Coast. In 1989 she formed her band Hole.

It was Hole and Nirvana that brought Courtney and Kurt together; she went to see his band while recording companies were courting hers. This is how rock journalist Everett True describes their first meeting:

> *I can picture her now, walking across the empty dance floor to meet me: loud, bedraggled, all smudged make-up and tights full of holes, the neon light shining through her dirty yellow-blonde hair.*

> *I thought she looked like a drunken man's Madonna. She introduced herself, and within minutes she'd mentioned half-a-dozen famous people she claimed to be intimately acquainted with. She bought me a whiskey, and demanded that I buy her some back. Later, Nirvana showed up. They were in town recording sessions for what would later become* Nevermind, *the album that defined an era. Kurt could see that Courtney and I were engaged in some major misconduct. He naturally made his way across the room and started rolling round the floor with us. And that was it. Kurt met Courtney.*

It was pretty much love at first sight, as Kurt revealed in an interview soon after this encounter.

> *My attitude has changed drastically, and I can't believe how much happier I am and how even less career-oriented I am. At times, I even forget I'm in a band, I'm so blinded by love. I know that sounds embarrassing, but it's true. I could give up the band right now. It doesn't matter … I'm just so overwhelmed by the fact that I'm in love on this scale.*

It wasn't long before Courtney fell pregnant. They both wanted a baby, perhaps to right the wrongs of their own sad childhoods, or perhaps to have something to love in a world that so often seemed loveless. But they were both addicted to heroin. Courtney immediately went cold turkey to give the baby a chance.

In 1992 they married on Waikiki Beach at sunset. The romantic occasion quickly turned sour. Chain-smoking to combat her craving for heroin, Courtney wore a silk dress that had belonged to the tragic Hollywood actress Frances Farmer, who had been institutionalised and lobotomised against her will. Kurt showed less self-restraint. 'I wasn't very high. I just did a little teeny bit so I didn't get sick,' he said.

Their daughter, Frances Bean, was born later that year. They adored her, but it was too late for Kurt who fell into a deep depression that only ended when he committed suicide in April 1994.

Courtney went into a decline, abusing drugs once more and refusing to be parted from Kurt's ashes. But she had a drive to survive that Kurt did not. She began to pull herself out of her sorrow and look to the future. She moved to Los Angeles to get Frances Bean away from the Nirvana fans who kept a vigil outside the Seattle house where their idol had died. She went into rehab and dried out yet again. This time, she emerged a far more stable person than she had been while married to Kurt. She even made a pilgrimage to the Namgyal Buddhist monastery in Ithaca to finally lay his ashes to rest.

She continued to write and perform her own songs, and won critical acclaim as an actress, in 1997 winning an Oscar nomination for her role in the movie *The People vs Larry Flynt*. Courtney Love has proven to be an achiever as well as a survivor, one more than worthy of her talented, tortured husband, Kurt Cobain.

David Beckham
and Victoria Adams

She was an ugly duckling who grew up to become a pop princess. He was a working class kid who won worldwide fame for his wizardry with a soccer ball, who became her Prince Charming. They are David Beckham and his bride, former Spice Girl Victoria Adams – better known to their legions of fans as Posh and Becks.

They have been dubbed Britain's new royal couple, and certainly they perform the traditional regal role of leading by example; their wholesome images and love of family life would have done Posh's namesake, Queen Victoria, proud. For celebrities exposed to every possible temptation, they are remarkably straight. 'I'm what a lot of people would say is boring, old-fashioned and square,' Victoria confesses. 'I'm a very moral person and I don't like all that funny business that goes on. You know, people having sex and that.'

As David's old schoolmaster John Bullock once said, 'If you

put a football and a girl in front of David, he'd always pick up the ball first.' But that was before he met Victoria. It was love at first sight. David was smitten the moment he spotted Posh on a Spice Girls video. 'That's the girl for me,' he told his best friend, Manchester United team-mate Gary Neville. He asked her out when they finally met, at a charity soccer match. 'Good game, huh?' she'd said, but it was no game for Beckham. Nor for Victoria. 'I knew he was right for me,' she recalls. 'What I liked about him particularly is he's very family-orientated.'

They were soon dating (although, the perfect gentleman, he didn't kiss her until their fourth date). They went around together in disguise to avoid attention, but the media soon got wind of the romance. It went into a feeding frenzy after the pair announced their engagement in 1998, with David giving Victoria an $80,000 solitaire diamond ring (she gave him a gold band encrusted with 30 diamonds).

Their wedding was celebrated at Dublin's fifteenth-century Luttrelstown Castle in 1999, with an orchestra playing Spice Girls hits. Victoria was 25, David 24. Victoria released a hundred white doves into the air as a symbol of her love for David, who was supported by his old mate Gary Neville as best man. Among the three hundred guests were Elton John and the couple's tiny son Brooklyn, then just four months old.

The British glossy *OK* paid a record £1 million to cover their nuptials. And the media interest has only intensified since. Barely a week goes by without one or both of them featuring on magazine covers or television shows. As London's *Daily Mirror* editor Piers Morgan has said: 'If there was any doubt what to put on the front page, we'd put a royal on it. It used to be Diana; now we put on Posh.'

'I think we are seen as accessible,' David says in an attempt to explain their appeal. 'We are very much in love and we're not controversial. I think we're good role models.'

Victoria, meanwhile, is happy to send herself up, and has even satirised the Beckhams' pseudo-royal status by creating a mock website of their palatial country mansion, complete with shots of family thrones and monogrammed toilets. Despite her protests that 'My tongue is firmly wedged in my cheek,' such is the Beckhams' appeal that the site scored ten million hits in four days.

As fairytale romances go, theirs has been a Cinderella story in reverse, with Victoria a middle-class girl from Hertfordshire and David a poor boy from East London. The daughter of an affluent businessman, Victoria was driven to school in her father's Rolls, but, self-conscious about an acne problem (cruel schoolmates called her 'sticky Vicky'), she was a lonely teenager. 'I've always been insecure about how I look,' she has said.

Her self-consciousness didn't prevent her attending drama school – 'You don't have to come from an underprivileged background to be driven,' she points out – nor later auditioning to join the Spice Girls, who became the most successful female pop group of the 1990s with their infectiously catchy tunes and their mantra of 'girl power'.

Nicknamed 'Posh' for her dark, fine-boned beauty and aloof air, Victoria may have been the quietest of the Spices – 'Her voice can carry a tune, just not very far,' sniffed one critic – but her

Victoria and David Beckham, Britain's new royal couple. 'We're good role models.'

business savvy has made her the most successful of the girls. She vetted the group's contracts to win the best deal for herself and the other girls, and as Ginger Spice (Gerri Halliwell) has commented: 'She could keep our feet on the ground when our ambitions outstripped our abilities.'

Since the group split up in 1998, Posh has gone from strength to strength in her solo career. A millionaire many times over, she no longer needs to work, she admits, and her singing is a labour of love – none more so than with 'IOU' and 'Unconditional

Love', the tracks she wrote for David on her self-titled debut album, *Victoria Beckham*.

'Nobody is remotely attractive compared to David ... I idolise him,' she confesses. 'I want to wake up with him every morning and go to bed with him every night.'

What's the appeal? 'He makes me laugh a lot. He loves me for me, rather than me dressed up with make-up,' Victoria says. Like Victoria, David is 'confident in his work, but he's not confident about his looks,' she adds. 'I just look at him and I think, "You're perfect. What are you on about?"'

Like many modern couples, their lives are a complex juggling act of family duties and professional commitments. Victoria tries to tailor her singing career to David's football schedule; when this is impossible and they must spend time apart, the pair call each other dozens of times a day. She has bought him a Ferrari so he can speed to her side when their schedules permit.

Though still young, both have published autobiographies; his is entitled *My World*, hers is *Learning to Fly*, which triggered a bidding war between the glossies and scored a seven-figure amount. And there's even a book – *Talking* – devoted to the couple's pronouncements on various issues.

But their lives haven't always been blessed. They have weathered kidnap threats, and rumours that Victoria has anorexia. Their lowest point came in 1998, when a referee sent David off during a World Cup game against Argentina, a disgrace that prompted fans to burn his effigy (and a Nottingham vicar to put a poster on his church door proclaiming 'God forgives even David Beckham'). Devastated, David flew straight to Los Angeles to seek consolation from Victoria, then touring with the Spice Girls. She had her own problems – Gerry Halliwell had just quit the group and it was beginning to fracture.

But Beckham free-kicked his way back to favour. He redeemed himself by leading England to some creditable victories at the 2002 World Cup. Now the former Manchester United No 7 has joined the Spanish club Real Madrid, and all eyes will be on him and his new team during the 2006 World Cup. The hit comedy film *Bend It Like Beckham* celebrated his uncanny ability to land a ball where he wants it.

In recent years, David's appeal has transcended his sporting achievements. He earns millions in celebrity endorsements, but he is equally ready to lend his voice to good causes, speaking out against hooliganism and racism in sport. Secure in his masculinity, he's been credited with giving birth to the 'Metrosexual' – the straight man willing to explore his feminine side, equally at home on the sporting field and wearing a sarong or polishing his nails. His ever-changing coiffeurs – from cornrows to Alice bands within a week – are almost as legendary as his free kicks. 'I've got a bigger wardrobe than Victoria,' he boasts, and he makes no secret of his liking for raiding her lingerie drawer. Now, as happily married couples are said to do, they even look like each other, sporting matching watches, leathers and hairstyles.

David sports a tattoo of Victoria's name translated into Hindi, and he loves to cook for her. 'He's very good at Sunday dinner, vegetables and chicken and all that,' she says. 'And he knows I just snack all day so he makes me a packed lunch.'

For all their success, the Beckhams' feet remain firmly on the ground. Their idea of a nice night in is to 'get the food we really like and some Asti Spumante or Tesco Bucks Fizz', as Victoria says. 'Then we cuddle up and watch *Friends*.' They're ordinary people leading extraordinary lives, and it's their very ordinariness that makes them so special. In 2002, their happiness was crowned with the birth of another son, Romeo.

As Victoria has vowed, 'I'm with the man I know I'm going to grow old and wrinkly with.'

HOLLYWOOD LIVES

CHARLIE CHAPLIN
AND OONA O'NEILL

'Either I'm going to be a star or I'm going to marry one,' 17-year-old Oona O'Neill pronounced after she had been in Hollywood all of a week. Exactly one year later, she was married to the greatest cinema star of them all – Charlie Chaplin, comic genius, mime artist and founding father of the silver screen. It didn't matter to her that at 54 he was three times her age, nor that he was in the middle of fighting a sordid paternity suit, nor that he already had three failed marriages behind him, as well as a legion of broken hearts. He was the only man in the world for her.

The fact that her adored father, noted playwright Eugene O'Neill, disowned her for her liaison with a man older than himself didn't stop her. 'I will never love any other man,' she told her mother, New York socialite Agnes Boulton. And she never did. The unlikely May-and-December union confounded the cynics by lasting well over thirty years. After several false starts, the moody middle-aged comedian had finally found the woman of his dreams.

Perhaps it wasn't as unlikely as it appeared at first. On the surface, the darkly beautiful Oona seemed the antithesis of the erratic, impatient Chaplin, who had struggled out of a London slum to make millions with his touching, humorous portrayal of the downtrodden little tramp. Oona, shy, sensitive and cultured, appeared happiest when fading into the background. Unlike Charlie – and most unusually in an aspiring actress – she had a relatively undeveloped ego. Their marriage seemed a union of opposites.

Both had had more than their fair share of family tragedy, however. Drink, drugs and suicide had dogged the talented O'Neill family for three generations. Oona's grandmother, Ella O'Neill, was a hopeless drug addict. Her uncle James was an alcoholic. Her father, Nobel and Pulitzer Prize winner Eugene O'Neill, was also a compulsive drinker who tried to exorcise the family demons by writing them up in plays like *Long Day's Journey Into Night*. Oona's brother, Eugene junior, a brilliant classical scholar, killed himself by opening his veins while taking a hot bath. Shane, another brother, also attempted suicide, and was committed to various narcotics institutions for heroin addiction.

Only Oona was able to escape the curse dogging the 'doomed O'Neills', as they were called. Her dark Irish good looks led to her being nominated 'Number One Glamour Girl of 1942'. She was not only startlingly beautiful, with shoulder-length raven hair, a dazzling smile and a model's figure, she had poise well beyond her seventeen years. It wasn't long before she was being squired around fashionable nightspots like New York's Stork Club by beaux such as boy genius Orson Welles. It was Orson who introduced Oona to Charlie, then going through one of the lowest points of his life.

Although she didn't know it then, Charlie had a penchant for very young women. His first wife, Mildred Harris, was only sixteen when they wed. So was Lita Grey, his second wife; in fact, it was whispered that he had only married Lita to beat a morals charge for seducing an underage girl. His third wife, screen siren Paulette Goddard, was a little older, but their marriage also ended in divorce. And now Joan Barry, another pretty young actress, was claiming that Charlie was the father of her unborn child. Despite blood tests proving that this couldn't be the case, the cinema-going public, scandalised by Charlie's much-publicised libido, swallowed her story. It seemed that only teenaged Oona O'Neill believed in him now. And she demonstrated her faith in him by marrying him on 16 June 1943.

'It was at my insistence – I love him,' she declared. 'We had made all our plans before that suit was filed. He wanted to wait, for my sake, until he had established his innocence, but I said I wanted to be by his side.'

It was just as well she didn't wait, for the jury held that he was indeed the father of Joan Barry's child, for whom he was ordered to pay $75 a week maintenance for 21 years. It was a blatant injustice, as the blood test results were publicly known. Disgusted, Charlie and Oona turned their backs on America and headed for Europe. Oona wasn't just quitting her homeland, but rejecting stardom at the same time. Within weeks of arriving in

Charlie and Oona Chaplin: She stood by her man in the face of public outrage.

Hollywood she had taken it by storm, with a natural ability that promised to flourish into a great acting talent. But she never set foot in a studio, never appeared before a camera. Instead, she became Mrs Charlie Chaplin, feeling this was a role offering her infinitely more satisfaction than mere stardom.

Oona saw in Charlie what other women could not, the hurt child behind the clown's mask. Charlie had been born in Kennington, London, in 1889, to an alcoholic father and a mentally unstable mother, both small-time vaudevillians. His father died when he was three and his mother Hannah, unable to cope, was committed to hospital after a nervous breakdown. Abandoned, Charlie and his brother Syd slept in parks, foraged in rubbish bins for scraps and were finally bundled into a workhouse orphanage. Charlie retreated into his own fantasy world of pantomime and comic creation. He learned to laugh so he would not cry, and by the time he was in his teens London was laughing with him. His talents at dancing, singing and mimicry landed him a succession of engagements in English theatres, and his reputation started to build.

By his early twenties he was in Hollywood, on the first rungs of a dazzling career writing, directing and starring in his own films. By 1916 he was earning the then fabulous sum of $670,000 a year, and enjoying a lavish lifestyle to match. But his early experiences had left their scars, which could be seen in the character that became his trademark – the little man, the underdog whose modest gallantry in the face of inhuman odds was a feature of films like *Mabel's Strange Predicament*, *The Pilgrim*, *A Dog's Life*, *Shoulder Arms*, *The Gold Rush*, *The Circus*, *City Lights*, *Modern Times* and *The Great Dictator*. 'The little chap I want to show,' he said, 'wears the air of romantic hunger. He is for ever seeking romance, but his feet won't let him.'

He was referring to his creation's comical pigeon-toed walk, caused by a combination of baggy trousers and oversize shoes, but he might just as well have been describing his own hang-ups. He yearned for love and the security of a stable family life, but his early traumas meant he didn't dare admit it, even to himself. In real life he played the libertine, but his true feelings towards women, a shy reverence and tender devotion, shone through in his films. Above all, they showed in his masterpiece, *Limelight*, in which he played a broken-down clown bringing life and hope to a little dancer who wanted to die.

Although short and chunky, the young Chaplin was extremely

attractive, and his reputation as a love-'em-and-leave-'em Lothario didn't deter a bevy of film beauties like May Collins, Claire Windsor, Lila Lee, Pola Negri and Peggy Joyce from falling for him. He was still charming even when his hair had turned silver, but it was his vulnerability that won Oona's heart.

And he was feeling very vulnerable indeed in the aftermath of the paternity suit. Joan Barry's lawyer's insults still rang in his ears; he had described Charlie as a 'lecherous swine', a 'runt of a Svengali', a 'cheap Cockney cad', and a 'master mechanic in the art of seduction'. Charlie knew what store Hollywood placed upon public probity. He had seen what had happened to fellow star Fatty Arbuckle, broken on the wheels of a sex scandal and reduced to directing B-grade movies under an assumed name. He didn't want that for himself and Oona. Their private wedding had already caused a sensation, and newshounds followed them everywhere. He decided to make his home abroad, and he and Oona settled in Switzerland.

Before too long it was clear that their self-imposed exile had an official imprimatur – US immigration authorities made it plain that the Chaplins were not particularly welcome to return to Hollywood. Charlie's radical politics, even more than his morals, had offended an America even then slipping into McCarthyist conservatism. But this didn't really bother the Chaplins, who were busy fashioning a lifetime of bliss together. Despite the fact that they had separate bedrooms – Charlie liked to pace around at night, thinking up ideas for movies – they produced child after child: Geraldine, Michael, Josephine, Victoria, Eugene, Jane, Annette and Christopher, each as striking looking as their mother.

'We live for [the children] but we try not to spoil them,' said Oona, although she admitted it was difficult at times. Charlie was still receiving around $11 million a year in royalties on his old movies alone, and there was a staff of 22 to keep their luxurious villa at Corsier-sur-Vevey, near Geneva, in order. Oona herself worked hard to ensure that mundane matters did not encroach on Charlie's creativity. She made sure he ate well and rested regularly, and took care of all the household accounts – for Charlie, like royalty, never carried money. 'I talk over everything with her, business and otherwise. We have no secrets,' he said.

Charlie died on Christmas Day 1977, and was quietly buried in a heavy oak coffin in the village burial plot. A devastated Oona, now 51, made daily visits to his grave. Then came an additional heavy blow. Three months after the burial Charlie's body was stolen from its simple grave, and a large ransom demanded. Oona courageously refused to succumb to this vile demand, and her husband's remains were found some eight weeks later, buried in a field not 20 kilometres from their original resting place.

They were lovingly reinterred – this time, in a concrete-lined grave.

BOGART AND BACALL

It was four o'clock in the morning when the Bacalls' phone started to ring. Betty picked it up. Humphrey Bogart was on the line and he was just a little under the influence. 'I'm walking back to town. Come and get me – I'll be on Highway 101.'

Betty, soon to be known to millions as Lauren 'Baby' Bacall, started to get ready for the drive. Her distraught mother, woken by the untimely phone call, tried to dissuade her 19-year-old daughter from running off in the middle of the night to meet Bogart. 'You can't jump every time he calls!'

Outside it was pouring with rain, but Betty didn't even notice. Getting into her car, she switched on the ignition and roared off into the California night. For what seemed an eternity she searched the lonely highway. Then, just as the rain eased off and the sun was coming up over the horizon, she saw Bogey. He was walking along the side of the road. His suit was crumpled and he looked unshaven. In his lapel was a huge sunflower.

Betty screeched to a halt. She jumped out of the car and ran over to Bogey. For just a moment they stood and looked at each other, then they fell into each other's arms.

Theirs was a story more romantic, more exciting than any of the blockbuster films they starred in together. The year was 1943. They had met on the set of famous director Howard Hawks' movie *To Have and Have Not*. This classic adaptation of Ernest Hemingway's great novel was to be the vehicle for one of America's hottest movie properties – Humphrey Bogart. With his brooding eyes and rough-hewn features, Bogey was an enigmatic screen idol. A loner. The epitome of rugged individualism.

He had been married three times, and the eleven weeks of filming *To Have and Have Not* saw the death throes of his last marriage to stormy actress Mayo Mehot. Theirs had been a violent and destructive relationship, and Bogart often turned to the bottle for solace.

At the age of 44 this cinematic legend, who had established his reputation playing ruthless gangsters, seemed an unlikely match for an ingénue like Betty Bacall. In fact, upon being introduced to her by Hawks, Bogey expressed doubts. 'I looked at her and wondered whether or not she could act,' he said later.

He was the complete professional, a veteran of 20 years of stage and screen. She was a model only recently turned actress. Tall and slender, she had a type of sultry elegance that belied her youthful inexperience. She was nervous at the prospect of working alongside a veteran of over fifty films, but Bogart was to reveal the human side of his paradoxically tough exterior. Bumping into Betty before filming commenced, he was pleasant and encouraging.

'Saw your test. I think we'll have fun working together, kid.'

She thought he seemed friendly – not at all arrogant or aloof. At first it looked as if that was all there was to it. Then came the filming of the scene that became famous for establishing the legendary Bogart and Bacall chemistry. It was Betty's first scene in the movie, where her character, Slim, asks Bogey's character, Steve, whether he has any matches. He throws her a box and she catches it nonchalantly, murmuring, 'Thanks.' Underneath the laconic dialogue ran a strong undercurrent of sexual innuendo.

Betty was so jittery about doing the scene that she repeatedly fumbled the catch. In the end, it was only because of Bogart's calming, supportive manner that she was able to complete the scene. Gratefully, Betty thanked him and he laughed away his contribution as being the least he could have done. A real friendship was formed between the two of them that day. They seemed to have so much in common, despite the gap in their ages. Bogart had little time for 'femmes' – as he called the excessively feminine type of actress he usually worked with. But Bacall was different. As he said, 'The reason I liked Betty was that she didn't remind me of a woman.'

Bogey was not the type of man who flirted with starlets. He was no Errol Flynn. But someone as innocent and unaffected as young Betty Bacall appealed to his bluntly honest nature. Hollywood, for all its glamour and mystique, was just a place to work for Humphrey Bogart. As an actor first and foremost, he had little time for stars who believed the hype they read about themselves in the gossip columns. Betty was like a breath of fresh air for Bogey.

In Betty's eyes, Bogart was everything a man should be ... strong, but caring and considerate. Together they were always

Humphrey Bogart and Lauren Bacall: 'I think we'll have fun working together, kid.'

laughing and making jokes on the set. Their relationship clicked into place like two pieces of the same puzzle. The more they saw of each other, the fonder they became. In a letter to her mother Betty wrote, 'Bogey has been a dream man. We have the most wonderful time together. I'm insane about him. We kid around – he's always gagging [joking with] me – trying to make me break up, and is very, very fond of me.'

It had to happen. One evening, after they had been filming together for three weeks, Bogey came into Betty's dressing room to say goodnight. Betty was sitting in front of the mirror, combing her hair. Bogey stood behind her, telling a joke and looking at her laughing reflection in the mirror. Suddenly, she stopped laughing and saw his eyes in the mirror. There was a smile of such tenderness on his face that she quickly turned around to him. Betty's green eyes softened. Bogart gently placed his hand under her chin and raised her mouth to his.

On-screen their developing passion for each other became more evident each day of filming. Director Howard Hawks took advantage of this and shot the movie in chronological order so that Bogart and Bacall's burgeoning love affair paralleled that of their screen characters, Steve and Slim. However, Bogart had a problem. He was still married. Admittedly, his wife was mentally unstable and a violent alcoholic. But Bogey believed in the institution of marriage and he thought he should give Mayo, his wife, a chance to change. But she didn't. More and more he needed the relief of Betty's soothing, affectionate company. Hedda Hopper, the notorious Hollywood gossip columnist, warned Bacall that Bogart's wife 'may drop a lamp on your head one day'.

The situation was tearing Bogey in two. He wrote to Betty: 'It's tragic that everything couldn't be all clean and just right for us instead of the way it is ... I love you so much ...'

After eleven weeks, *To Have and Have Not* was completed. Bogart made his farewells to the cast and crew and walked with Betty out to his car. She smiled and waved as he drove away, but inside she was desperately unhappy. When would she see him again?

Then came the phone call that brought them together. On the deserted coastal highway, Bogey told Betty he couldn't live without her any more. At last they were truly alone with each other. They clung together as the sun rose over the Pacific Ocean.

Their marriage was one of the happiest in Hollywood. The cynics said it would never last, but it did. The only thing that could tear Bogey from his 'Baby's' side was death itself. Sadly, in 1957, cancer did just that. Betty went on through life knowing that in her heart no one could ever take the place of Bogey.

SPENCER TRACY
AND KATHERINE HEPBURN

When Katherine Hepburn and Spencer Tracy first met in 1942, on the set of the film *Woman of the Year*, she coolly looked him over. A tall woman who loved to increase her height with upswept hairstyles and specially made high heels, she towered over the chunky male star.

'You're rather short, aren't you?' she said condescendingly, smiling her sweetest, haughtiest smile. Tracy glared at her. Hollywood's hottest male property at that time, he wasn't used to that type of remark from his leading ladies.

'Don't worry, honey,' interjected the film's producer, Joe Mankiewicz. 'He'll soon cut you down to size.'

And he did. Throughout their long professional association, which included nine smash-hit films, Tracy's name always preceded Hepburn's on the billing. When asked by writer/director Garson Kanin whether gallantry didn't decree that the order be reversed, Tracy simply said, 'This is a movie, chowderhead, not a lifeboat!'

That was Spencer Tracy all over: plain talking, rugged and tough – and that was how his public loved him. Strangely enough, that was how the cool, aristocratic, beautiful Kate Hepburn loved him too. The sparks frequently flew between them after that disastrous first meeting, for they both had fiery tempers, but somehow their clashes ignited a dynamic chemistry between them, both on and off the screen. Together they made film after successful film – *Keeper of the Flame*, *Adam's Rib*, *Pat and Mike*, *State of the Union*, *Desk Set*, *Without Love* – but never could two actors have been less alike.

She was dazzling, original, eccentric – she wore men's clothes and personified women's independence long before it became fashionable. She was the well-educated daughter of a New England doctor; he came from a poor Irish family, and went to work for the first time at the age of eight. She was a thoroughbred who was prepared to discuss the finer points of the theatre for hours on end; he was a down-to-earth battler who, when asked his secrets at the height of his film fame, growled: 'Learning the blasted lines!'

On the screen, Tracy and Hepburn made movie magic, but off the set their intense relationship was one of Tinseltown's best-kept secrets, which only really came to light after his death in 1967. He was married but living apart from his wife, Louise, when he met Kate. An ardent Catholic, his respect for his church and the sacrament of marriage prevented him from publicly declaring his love for her. Their lives together were destined to be played out among the shadows.

Hepburn won acclaim for her roles portraying headstrong,

Spencer Tracy and Katherine Hepburn: an intense relationship, played out among the shadows.

independent women in films like *Christopher Strong* and *Bringing Up Baby*, but more than one friend noted that she rarely played a happily married woman – except when acting opposite Spencer Tracy.

Spence's own career had taken a long time to get going. When he first screen-tested for Fox, studio executives were unimpressed by his burly frame and open, Irish face. 'That guy has as much sex appeal as a watermelon,' one of them commented.

He certainly didn't see himself as a sex symbol, despite his hordes of devoted women fans. 'I was always the good-natured goof,' he recalled of his early screen roles. 'I did all the brave bits and Clark Gable got the girls.' Except that Clark never 'got' Hepburn – all her passion was reserved for 'goofy' Spencer Tracy.

She could have had her pick of men – millionaire Howard Hughes was just one of her legions of suitors – but she was overwhelmed by Spence's simplicity and integrity. 'Spence is the only pure person I ever met in my life,' she told a friend. 'No affectations, not a single selfish bone in his body.'

He had never had an acting lesson in his life, but he instinctively knew how to move audiences. He acted in over two hundred stage plays before he hit the big screen, driven not so much by the desire for fame as the need for money to get the best possible medical treatment for his son John, born totally deaf, with little prospect of ever learning to speak. The tragedy took its toll of Spence's wife, Louise, as she desperately tried to give little John a normal childhood, and their marriage disintegrated under the strain. Heartbroken, Spence moved into a modest cottage on director George Cukor's estate, and began drinking heavily. His personal life was in ruins, but his film stocks continued to soar.

Only Kate could bring him out of the deep depressions brought on by his drinking bouts. He had many pet names for her: Kathy, Kath, Flora Finch, Olive Oyl, Laura LaPlane, Madame Curie, Carrie Nation, Molly Malone and Coo the bird girl. Her love for him went beyond nicknames. 'He is like an old oak tree,' she once said of him, 'or the summer, or the wind. He has enormous integrity. He belongs to an era when men were men.'

Kate respected Spence's strict views on divorce, but she didn't share them. She had already been divorced from Ogden Ludlow Smith when she met Tracy – simply because she couldn't bear the thought of being plain Mrs Smith, according to unkind Hollywood gossips. But she went along with Spence's determination to spare Louise any pain and humiliation, and meekly slipped into the background over the 26 years spanned by their love affair.

More than once the truth about their relationship threatened to surface. On 31 July 1963 Spence collapsed from respiratory congestion while picnicking with Kate at Malibu. She kept her head and saved his life by rushing him to a hospital, then she called his family to take over and discreetly faded from the scene before the tabloids could exploit the situation.

While Kate managed to wean him off the booze, he was continually dogged by bad health. His unruly thatch of red hair turned pure white and his craggy face became ever more deeply etched with wrinkles deep enough, according to one of his contemporaries, 'to hold two days' rain'. He gave up working, becoming increasingly moody and reclusive. Then in 1967 he came out of retirement to make a final film with Kate – *Guess Who's Coming to Dinner*, a taut comedy/drama about racial prejudice. He knew it was his swan song and his life ended just a few days after filming was completed. He died, as he had lived, alone. But soon, as word got out, those who loved him gathered at his small house on George Cukor's property to pay their last respects by his deathbed. There stood Louise and Kate, side by side, the wife and the lover. Tragedy had brought them together for the first time – and the last.

The final chapter of Kate and Spence's secret relationship was played out on the day of his funeral. Six hundred mourners attended the ceremony, but Katherine Hepburn was not among them. She knew that pride of place belonged to Louise Tracy in this hour of grief, so she stayed away, working through her sorrow alone. Her only consolation was to tell herself that, somehow, Spence still lived through his work on film.

When she received the news that she had won the second of her three Oscars for her moving performance in *Guess Who's Coming to Dinner*, she immediately asked if Spencer Tracy had also won one. When told that he had not, she was silent for a moment. Then she said quietly, 'Well, that's okay, I'm sure mine is for the two of us.'

She continued to achieve success after success, winning a third Oscar for her role in *The Lion in Winter*, and critical acclaim for her parts in *Love Among the Ruins*, starring Laurence Olivier, and *Rooster Cogburn*, starring John Wayne. But she never forgot the days when her leading man was Spencer Tracy. 'I'll miss him every day as long as I live,' she once said. And she did. Her love for Spence continued to colour her life right up to her own death, at age 96, in June 2003.

BARBARA HUTTON
AND CARY GRANT

In the 1930s, the life and loves of Woolworth heiress Barbara Hutton, America's 'million dollar baby', exercised the same fascination over the public mind as Princess Diana did during the 1990s.

She was not only one of the wealthiest women in the world, thanks to her $50 million inheritance from her grandfather, chainstore founder Frank Winfield Woolworth, but she was hauntingly beautiful, being blessed with huge violet eyes, black velvet brows to contrast with natural blonde curls, a porcelain complexion and a wistful, heart-breaking smile. Yet even with all this going for her, she was so desperately insecure that she was convinced she had to pay people to love her.

'When you inherit as much money as I did, it destroys whatever incentive or goal you might want,' she would say sadly. 'I inherited everything but love. I've always been searching for it because I don't know what it is.'

She certainly received little enough of it from her own tormented family. Her mother, Edna Woolworth, committed suicide when she was five, and Barbara's discovery of her mother's body traumatised her for life. Grandfather Woolworth died a couple of years later, and Barbara's grandmother had a complete mental breakdown. Her father, New York stockbroker Franklyn Hutton, resented the fact that Barbara inherited the Woolworth millions, and continually told her that only fortune hunters would ever be interested in marrying her. This not only destroyed her self-confidence, it became a self-fulfilling prophecy. She was to marry seven times, and six of her husbands were to demand extortionate amounts to marry her, and even more to leave her.

The exception was her third husband, Hollywood heart-throb Cary Grant, the one man who was even more famous than she was, whose movie earnings were so fabulous that he could more than afford to pay his own way. He was also the one man in Babs' life who truly loved her and came close to rescuing her from her pathological insecurity.

The erosion of Barbara's self-esteem was well advanced by the time she met the Tinseltown charmer. The tabloids' relentless chronicling of her fantastic lifestyle made her a hated woman during the drab days of the Depression. When she was still under age, she set up her own New York apartment at the cost of nearly half a million dollars, a fabulous sum in those austere times. Her glittering debut party at New York's Ritz-Carlton hotel cost $60,000, and her splurges on clothes, travel, ornaments and artwork made almost daily headlines. People flocked to see her pass, but they also reviled her for her conspicuous consumption. She once said that she expected to be spat at in the streets, and she was a favourite butt of Woolworth's shop assistants, who loved to compare her unearned inheritance with their meagre salaries. Her astonishing generosity, which would end by almost paupering her, went unnoticed, even though she gave huge sums to causes dear to her heart, including a staggering $1 million donation to the Free French movement during the Second World War.

Rejected by her family and the public, Barbara poured out her loneliness in her poems. She yearned for love from a man – any man. She was barely 20 when she married white Russian aristocrat Prince Alexis Mdivani, a polo-loving playboy who made something of a habit of wedding wealthy girls. 'It's going to be fun being a princess,' she gleefully told reporters on their wedding day in 1933. But the union turned out to be more fun – and more profitable – for the impecunious prince. There was the million-dollar wedding settlement she made on him for starters, and the two million dollar pay-off when the marriage foundered a couple of years later. But what cost Barbara most dearly were his casual, cruel words on their wedding night. 'Barbara,' he said as she stood before him clad in silken lingerie, 'you're too fat.'

Barbara was indeed rather plump at this time – she weighed 10 stone 10 lb – and this remark almost destroyed her. She went on a crash diet, losing over three stone, then found she couldn't stop. She had developed the slimmer's disease, anorexia nervosa, and it completely ruined her health. For the rest of her life one of the world's richest women subsisted on little more than black coffee, cigarettes and cocktails.

Her next, equally disastrous marriage was to Danish nobleman Count Reventlow. The father of her only child, Lance, Reventlow talked her into becoming a Danish citizen for tax reasons, leading to further disapproving headlines in her homeland. Unlike Mdivani, who simply neglected her, Reventlow tried to dominate Babs, who was only half his age. Eventually she rebelled, and after a child custody wrangle that dragged on for three years, she divorced him in 1941 – at the cost of a $1.5 million settlement.

Poorer and wiser, Barbara vowed never to marry again. But still she dreamed of a knight in shining armour who would release her from the hell of self-loathing. She began to spend all her time in movie houses, for in the anonymous darkness she could forget who she was and lose herself in romantic fantasies. Then she saw *Philadelphia Story*, in which a suavely handsome Cary Grant paid court to a wilful heiress – an heiress whom she instantly identified with herself.

'He was a dream at that point,' she later told a friend, but the dream became a reality when they met at a party and the dashing British star found the haunted heiress just as appealing as she found him. To the star-struck Barbara, it came as a revelation to find a man who could pay his own bills, who lavished gifts on her – but didn't send them COD like her two husbands. For Cary, Barbara's warmth, sweetness and touching self-deprecation were balm to the wounds left by the break-up of his first marriage to actress Virginia Cherrill.

Cary and Barbara married in Beverly Hills on 8 July 1942. It was 'a marriage made in a bank', according to gossip columnist Louella Parsons. The wits dubbed the happy couple 'Cash and Cary', but this was unfair, for alone among her husbands, Cary insisted on signing a pre-wedding agreement relinquishing any claim on Barbara's money.

They set up house in Douglas Fairbanks Junior's old Hollywood mansion, and for a time things went blissfully. 'They were like two puppies together,' noted one observer. But even then Barbara feared the worst, that her new husband would leave her as everyone else seemed to. She clung to him, almost smothering him with her affection. 'I loved Cary the best; he was so sweet, so gentle,' she later told a friend. 'It didn't work out, but I loved him … For a time it gave me infinite solace and strength to belong to Cary, and I prayed that my feelings for him would endure forever.'

Barbara's feelings did endure, but the reason the marriage ended, just as she feared it would, was because she had no real understanding of the very different world from which Cary had come. Fans saw him as the personification of the gallant British gentleman, but he had been born plain Archie Leach, an impoverished Cockney, in Bristol in 1904. His father was an alcoholic and his mother was institutionalised in a mental home when he was just a child. For a while he worked as an acrobat, then broke into acting, crossing the Atlantic to Hollywood to find stardom as the leading man for screen goddesses like Mae West, Carole Lombard, Rosalind Russell and Marlene Dietrich.

He was as charming and sexy as his image, but he found it hard to come to terms with the high-flying café society friends with whom Barbara insisted on filling their home. A hard-working actor with a reputation to maintain, his idea of a night's entertainment was learning his lines for the next day's filming, then going to bed early. He simply couldn't afford to party all night with Barbara's hangers-on, a motley collection of dubious international aristocracy and Yankee *nouveaux riches*.

'If one more phoney earl had entered the house, I'd have suffocated,' he explained later. Ever the entertainer, he was determined to prick the stuffy guests' pretensions, coming to Barbara's parties dressed in pyjamas, or on stilts. At one particularly posh supper, where the multi-national guests were served carefully prepared meals from their native countries, he humiliated his wife by yelling in pure Cockney: 'Now h'I comes from Lime'ouse, and h'I's just a bloody Cockney. Where's me fish and chips?'

But some aspects of their marriage were beyond a joke. Both Cary and Barbara ardently desired children, but Barbara had become infertile through years of dieting. Unable to sleep, she would gulp down pills and booze, then spend the day in bed, incapable of movement. Then there were the uppers and downers, the painkillers and tranquillisers she swallowed to get her through the day. It became clear to Cary that, despite his best efforts, the marriage was disintegrating.

He threw himself into his work, making film after film: *Mr Lucky*, *Destination Tokyo*, *Once Upon a Time*, *None But the Lonely Heart* and *Arsenic and Old Lace* in 1943 alone. With Cary at work all day, Barbara increasingly turned to alcohol to fill her lonely hours. But still she cared for him. 'I'm afraid that my terrible

Barbara Hutton and Cary Grant. He was the only one of her seven husbands who was not a fortune hunter.

unpopularity might spread to Cary – wouldn't that be awful?' she sadly told a friend.

Cary's popularity remained intact, despite her fears, but their marriage was on the rocks. He moved in and out of their home dozens of times, playing revolving mansions in his attempts to revive the romance, but by July 1945 he finally called it quits, and they were divorced. The only explanation Barbara would give was, 'He did not like my friends,' but the truth was that all the charm and good looks in Hollywood couldn't halt the course of Barbara's self-destructiveness. Her inner scars simply went too deep.

Now that her worst fears were realised, Barbara sought consolation in the only way she knew – buying men. In rapid succession she wed a series of aristocratic spongers: Lithuanian Prince Igor Troubetskoy; international playboy Porfirio Rubirosa; tennis star Baron Gottfried von Cramm, and finally Laotian painter Prince Doan – each of whom was reputed to have received a farewell gift of a million dollars from her.

Cary sadly watched her matrimonial merry-go-round from a distance. They remained close until the end. 'I still have a great feeling for Barbara,' he said. 'We are great and good friends. I wish her well. I wish she could be supremely happy. I shall be so pleased when I see her happy and smiling with someone – or even smiling without anyone.'

But this generous wish remained ungranted. As Barbara spiralled into lonely, sickly old age, she was reduced to sending her servants out to scour the streets for teenagers to talk to her – for a fee of $1000 a time. Still she refused to eat, dwindling in her final years to a mere 60 lb. Worn out by years of self-imposed privation, her heart finally failed on 11 May 1979 – the centenary of the opening of the first Woolworth store – but it had been broken for a long, long time.

If only the blighted 'dollar princess' had managed to hold on to Cary Grant, the only man who loved her for herself and not her millions, she may well not have ended up lonely and alone, literally starving for affection.

CLARK GABLE
AND CAROLE LOMBARD

Clark Gable looked at the balloons and streamers festooning the dining room of his Californian home and smiled. 'Ma' would get such a thrill when she walked through the front door. Huge bunches of red roses filled every corner of the ranch house with their sweet perfume. He had set dozens of candles so that when his wife, Carole Lombard – 'Ma', as he lovingly called her – arrived, the house would be filled with a twinkling, welcoming glow.

Impatiently, Gable glanced at his watch. It was nearly eight and he wondered why he hadn't had a message from the airport yet. Surely Carole's plane should have arrived by now.

That was when the phone rang. A close friend, Eddie Mannix, was on the line.

'Can I call you back?' said Gable, looking at his watch again. 'I'm expecting word on Ma's arrival any minute.'

There was a short, painful silence on the other end of the line.

Clark Gable and Carole Lombard. He was the only man who could control her fiery temperament.

Then Mannix spoke. 'King, that's why I'm calling. Larry Barbier just phoned from the airport. Carole's plane went down a few minutes after it left Las Vegas.'

Gable's face went white as the dreadful message continued. His 'Ma' in a plane crash? Somewhere, high on a lonely snow-covered mountain in the Nevada Desert, his wife Carole

Lombard lay in the twisted, burning wreckage of an aeroplane.

The love affair between Clark Gable – the 'King of Hollywood' – and his glamorous consort Carole Lombard was the stuff of which legends are made. Theirs was an era in which movies provided a glittering fantasyland where ordinary people could escape for a short while from the harsh realities of the Depression and its aftermath. Actors and actresses became a kind of nobility, chosen by the public to live in the limelight until their popularity at the box-office waned. Their lifestyles were often even more splendidly extravagant than the roles they played on-screen.

At a time when movie stars seemed larger than life, none were to capture the public's imagination more than Clark Gable and Carole Lombard. By the time he met Carole in 1936, Gable had become the most popular actor in the movies, earning more money than any other actor in the country. He was the Great American Dream Man of the Depression era. His virile manner and rugged good looks, combined with that wicked Gable smile, had made him the sort of screen idol not seen since Valentino's death in the twenties. Women dreamed about him and men dreamed of being like him. Still married to his second wife, Ria Langham, when he first met Lombard, Clark Gable seemed to be a man that no woman could tame.

Carole Lombard, originally Jane Alice Peters, was 27 when she fell in love with Gable. The beautiful zany blonde was one of Paramount Studios' hottest properties, rivalled only by such stars as Mae West, Marlene Dietrich and Claudette Colbert. In 1932 Lombard had played opposite Gable in a movie called *No Man of Her Own*, but at that time it had been a case of mutual dislike.

Clark found the beautiful blonde too boisterous and profane for his taste; Lombard thought the tall, swarthy Gable was a stuffed shirt. At the completion of the film she presented him with a large smoked ham with his photograph on it.

Then, on a Saturday night, 25 January 1936, the pair were to meet again at a formal ball in Beverly Hills. Gable was looking his dashing best in white tie and tails as he entered the party with some show-business friends. Lombard, who was helping stage the ball, came across the room to greet them. In a white silk dress that clung to her body like a second skin, Carole looked fantastic. Gable gazed at her admiringly as she said hello. He smiled and winked at her. She winked back, and her blue eyes looked at him tantalisingly. Later, Gable asked Lombard to dance and as they moved on to the dance floor he grinned shyly and said, 'I go for you, Ma.' 'Ma' was one of the nicknames he had given her during the filming of *No Man of Her Own*. Lombard looked up at him and said, 'I go for you too, Pa.'

As they danced together the closeness of their bodies and Lombard's intoxicating loveliness made Gable desire her more than any woman he'd ever known. He invited her for a spin in his new sports car and she, wanting a breath of fresh air, agreed. They drove to the Beverly Wiltshire Hotel where Gable lived and he asked Lombard if she would like to come up to his place for a nightcap. An ironic smile played on Lombard's lips. 'You're pretty sure of yourself, aren't you? Who do you think you are, Clark Gable?' she laughed, utterly deflating the big man's ego. The evening that had begun so well ended with the two quarrelling.

The next morning, however, Lombard sent Gable two white doves as a peace offering. There was no denying the attraction between them. Though still married to Ria Langham, Gable wanted to see more of Lombard. Carole could not help herself any more than the rest of American womanhood. She started to fall in love with Clark Gable. When Valentine's Day came around she sent him a beaten-up old Model T Ford painted white with red hearts all over it. Gable was completely captivated by Lombard's delightfully unpredictable personality. Before long, the two were madly in love.

The publicity their affair generated was enormous. The heads at Gable's studio, MGM, feared a scandal that would harm the 'King's' reputation and tried to put the reins on the relationship. They couldn't. Nothing could. Gable began divorce proceedings against his wife but they were to prove too slow. Defying moral censure, he decided to live with Lombard, herself a divorcée. Finally, in 1939, Gable's divorce came through. Instead of a grand show-business wedding, he eloped with Lombard to a remote town in Arizona. The happy couple sent a telegram to MGM and Paramount Studios that simply said, 'Married this afternoon. Carole and Clark.'

Their marriage was to prove a tempestuous one. Gable, unable to resist the advances of beautiful starlets, was not always faithful to Carole. But she always forgave him, even after their most bitter quarrels. As long as 'Pa' still loved her, she could overlook his infidelities. And he was the only man big enough to keep her fiery temperament under control.

Once, when Lombard, upset at delays in the renovation of

their new home, abused a workman, Gable took her into the next room and shook her hard. 'Listen, baby,' he said sternly. 'If there's any cursing to be done, I'm man enough to do it myself.' Lombard was rigid with fury. Then suddenly she burst into tears and sobbed, 'I've waited a long time for somebody to do that. Oh, Pa, I'm glad I love you. I'm so glad I married you.'

The Gables were the uncrowned royal couple of Hollywood. In 1935 Clark had won an Oscar for *It Happened One Night*, and his appearances in such movies as *San Francisco*, *Mutiny on the Bounty* and *Saratoga* established him as a huge box office drawcard. Then came his famous role as Rhett Butler in *Gone With the Wind*, one of the most profitable movies of all time. That made him more than just famous; it made him a living legend.

It seemed that Gable and Lombard had everything: money, fame, and their love for each other. But the shadow of the Second World War fell across their lives in 1941 with the destruction of Pearl Harbor. Lombard was intensely patriotic and threw herself into helping sell War Bonds. At the same time she urged Gable to join the army in a real capacity, not just accept a phoney Hollywood commission, as many other actors had done.

Sadly, in January 1942 just before Carole was setting off on a bond tour, the couple quarrelled and Gable did not see her off at the airport. He was never to see her again. Carole Lombard was killed in a plane crash that was so violent no recognisable trace of her could be found, except a pair of diamond and ruby earrings Gable had given her. Gable had them mounted in a tiny gold box that he wore around his neck from that day on.

He never really recovered from Carole's death. Tired with life, he joined the American Air Force and flew bombing missions over Europe as a gunner and a cameraman. When he returned at the end of 1943 as a war hero he was welcomed back to MGM studios with open arms. But something was missing from his life. He tried to find it in the company of women who were always strangely similar to the late Carole Lombard: blonde hair, blue eyes. He remarried. It didn't work. He simply couldn't forget Carole.

When Clark Gable died in 1960 shortly after starring in *The Misfits* with Marilyn Monroe, his fifth wife, Kay Williams, had him buried next to Carole Lombard's monument in the Forest Lawn Cemetery in Los Angeles. She wasn't jealous. For like everyone else, Kay knew that Lombard had been Gable's one true love.

LAURENCE OLIVIER
AND VIVIEN LEIGH

From the first moment Vivien Leigh set eyes on Laurence Olivier she knew she had to have him. She was in the audience, watching him play the part of the dashing Tony Cavendish in *Theatre Royal*. It was 1934, and young Larry Olivier was the crown prince of the London stage.

With his dynamic approach to theatre and his classic good looks, he was a natural actor. On stage he projected such energy, such sexual magnetism, that every woman in the audience instinctively responded to him. Vivien Leigh was swept along as helplessly as the rest. Never mind that she was married to kindly, stodgy barrister Leigh Holman, or that Larry was married to pretty actress Jill Esmond. Or that Larry himself had no idea yet that Vivien even existed.

At this time, she was a respected actress in her own right. While her greatest professional success was still to come, her beauty was already legendary. With her huge slanted green eyes, heart-shaped face and bewitching smile, she captured the heart of every man she met. She was accustomed to being admired, pursued. She had never gone after a man. Not until she saw Laurence Olivier.

She managed to arrange a meeting, and the famous actor was plainly smitten by the enchanting young ingénue. Before long they were playing opposite each other as the young lovers Michael Ingolby and Cynthia in the award-winning film *Fire Over England*. The love they acted out by day became real by night. By the time they went to Denmark to star in Tyrone Guthrie's controversial production of *Hamlet*, staged at Elsinore, the sparks that flew between them had built to an unquenchable flame. There was no way out but marriage.

There was no real problem asking the understanding Leigh Holman to divorce Vivien: he knew they were not suited, so he gracefully relinquished her and managed to remain her friend for life. But Jill Esmond had sacrificed her career for Larry's and had only lately given birth to his son, Tarquin. She was not going to go quietly. When the lovers returned to England, Jill visited Vivien to beg her to give up Larry. Such was Vivien's enormous charm that nobody – not even Olivier's scorned wife – could deny her anything she wanted. When Jill arrived, Vivien took her affectionately by the arm and ordered her maid to bring champagne. Jill found she simply could not bring herself to reproach Vivien and she quickly left, her mission unaccomplished.

She soon realised the inescapable truth: Vivien and Larry's love for each other was of such intensity that it could not be denied. They could not keep their eyes – or their hands – off each other, in public or in private. They devoured each other.

Then Larry was summoned to Hollywood to star in Sam Goldwyn's film *Wuthering Heights* and Vivien followed him, determined to play Cathy to his Heathcliff. She lost that role to Merle Oberon, but was soon consoled when she landed the plum role of Scarlett O'Hara in *Gone With the Wind*, David Selznick's blockbusting film of Margaret Mitchell's classic Southern novel. She won an Oscar for her work in the film, which made her an international screen star. Now all the world was at her feet – and so was Larry.

They married at Santa Barbara, California, in August 1940. They had chosen a private ceremony, shunning publicity, but the news electrified a war-torn world, hungry for romance. They were the theatre's golden couple. Their obvious delight in each other's company, both on stage and off, was infectious and the public adored them.

It all seemed too good to be true – and it was. Vivien was a fascinating, beautiful woman, but she was also a highly complex one. Her sweetness and charm made her a well-liked actress in a notoriously bitchy profession, but beneath her careful facade raged a turmoil of emotion. Her love for Larry was just one aspect of the passion that was to destroy her life. All who saw her as Blanche Dubois in Tennessee Williams' harrowing masterpiece *A Streetcar Named Desire* marvelled at her compelling impersonation of a woman spiralling into insanity. They thought it was just acting; they could not know it was for real.

For some time Vivien's health had been breaking down and then, to her horror, the doctors diagnosed tuberculosis. What they didn't tell her – then – was that her symptoms were exacerbated by incipient manic-depression and schizophrenia. Vivien Leigh was going mad.

She became increasingly erratic, alternating fits of deep depression with terrifying hysterical outbursts during which she would blindly attack those she loved best – in particular Larry. There were often happy, loving months between attacks, and she was invariably charmingly contrite afterwards. But the strain her illness placed upon her marriage was enormous. She was capable of almost anything when in the grip of an attack – tearing her clothes off in public, screaming obscenities, sleeping with strangers, assaulting her husband. She broke down completely in Ceylon, where she was filming *Elephant Walk* with Australian actor Peter Finch. She couldn't go on with the role, which was taken over by a young Elizabeth Taylor.

Now began a round of gruesome medical treatments. She was packed in ice to allay her symptoms. She was given electric shock treatment. She was force-fed raw eggs to build up her strength. She became a little better, then a little worse, over and over again. Her health fluctuated, but in two things she remained steadfast: her acting work was always faultless and her deep love for Larry remained unchanged. But her illness made terrible demands upon them both, and finally the strain was too much for him. He had been transformed from ardent lover to nursemaid, and he began to look elsewhere for consolation. He found it in the attractive young actress Joan Plowright, who played opposite him in John Osborne's play *The Entertainer*.

Soon Vivien was horrified to see that the sparks that had flared between herself and her husband on stage were now flying

Vivien Leigh and Laurence Olivier. The intensity of their love delighted the world during the war-torn 1940s.

between Larry and Joan. She of all people could recognise sexual chemistry at work. She feared that they would soon become lovers – and they did. History was repeating itself. Larry asked Vivien for a divorce, begging her to release him from a marriage that had become a nightmare to him.

Their glittering relationship, which had spanned a quarter of a century, was legally ended in a London court on 3 December 1960. Vivien wept as she was granted a *decree nisi* on the grounds of Larry's adultery with Joan. After the hearing, she left the court in a silver Rolls-Royce with a number plate that bore mute testimony to the love that had just been officially extinguished: VLO [Vivien and Laurence Olivier] 123.

Her long-time friend, actor Jack Merrivale, had lunch with her that day and reporters eagerly asked if Vivien and he might now wed. Nonplussed, he replied: 'I cannot say.'

Of course he could not say. For while he became Vivien's constant companion during the few years remaining to her, they both knew that there had only been one true love for her and he could not be replaced by any other man.

Her divorce from Olivier broke her heart. She was found dead in her London flat on 7 July 1967. Although the official cause of death was tuberculosis, her friends knew she had been exhausted by the demands of her own restless nature, cruelly torn by her passionate love for Laurence Olivier.

Ingrid Bergman
and Roberto Rossellini

Senator Edwin C. Johnson of Colorado rose to his feet and addressed the assembled Congress of the United States of America. A powerful influence for immorality, he thundered in righteous tones, was threatening the moral fibre of their great nation. His face red with emotion, the Senator demanded that for the protection of the American public a special bill be introduced by Congress – to ban movie star Ingrid Bergman from the screens of America *forever*.

The year was 1950 and Ingrid Bergman's career lay in ruins. Estranged from her husband and daughter, rejected by the film industry and scorned by the press, Hollywood's First Lady had thrown away everything to be with the man she loved. No one could have foreseen the tide of hatred that would flow from her decision to leave America and live with the brilliant Italian director Roberto Rossellini.

It all started when the Swedish actress wrote to Rossellini in

1949, congratulating him on the success of his innovative films *Paisan* and *Open City*. Admiring the talented director's cinematic realism, Ingrid offered to star in his next movie.

'If you should ever want a Swedish actress who speaks good English but whose Italian is "I love you" to come and make a film then I am ready if you ask me,' she said.

Delighted at the prospect of the legendary Ingrid Bergman starring in one of his movies, Rossellini immediately dashed off a reply suggesting they meet in California to discuss details. Perhaps if he had been able to gaze into the future at that moment, the Italian director might very well have torn the letter to pieces there and then.

From the instant they saw each other Roberto and Ingrid knew that the attraction between them was not purely professional. When the director dined at the home of the Swedish actress and her husband Petter Lindstrom, he was utterly charmed by Ingrid's manner. She was gracious, lively and warm. In repose her face was beautifully serene but when she smiled Rossellini could not drag his eyes away from the exquisite curve of her mouth. Feeling the warmth of Rossellini's glance, Ingrid knew that here was a man who could change her life if she let him.

Ingrid, who had left her native Sweden at 23 to find stardom in Hollywood, was by 1949 at the height of her career. She wasn't just a celebrity – she was a star the public worshipped. They saw her through rose-tinted glasses as the virginal nun in the movie *Bells of St Mary's*, the sweet young pianist in *Intermezzo*, they thought of her as *Saint Joan of Arc*. But Ingrid needed more from life.

'I was bored,' she later recalled, 'and it didn't look like real life any more ... all those films made on the back lot ... they were too polished, too rehearsed, they were *cardboard*. And then I saw all those real things, those Italian films that Roberto had done ... and they moved me deeply.'

About a month after their first meeting, Ingrid boarded a plane for Italy, where Rossellini was waiting to commence filming *Stromboli*. From the moment of her arrival in Rome, Ingrid found herself being treated like a queen by the gallant director. Rushing up the steps of the plane, Roberto presented her with a huge bouquet of flowers and, laughing, said, 'Welcome to Italy, *cara!*'

Ingrid's stay in Rome was a glamorous round of parties and shows, with Rossellini showering her with loving affection. Her determination to be a good wife and mother started to crumble in the face of Roberto's romantic approach.

'Roberto ... put little gifts everywhere,' she wrote. 'I was simply overwhelmed.'

By the time the cameras were ready to roll on the movie, Ingrid and Roberto were deeply infatuated with each other. During an idyllic drive down the Italian coast to Stromboli, where the film was set, they became lovers, sharing the same room every night. Roberto, all Mediterranean fire, melted Ingrid's Scandinavian reserve – and she gave herself to him completely.

Unlike any man she had known before, the hot-blooded director constantly surprised her with his unorthodox approach to love, life and work. Passing the coastal town of Salerno, Rossellini remembered that he still didn't have a leading man to star opposite Ingrid. He stopped the car opposite a group of fishermen working on their boats and told her: 'You wait here, I just go to find you a leading man.'

Ingrid laughed, thinking he was joking. A short while later the impulsive Roberto returned to the car. 'I got you two,' he remarked casually; 'a tall good-looking young man and a short one. You can take your pick when we get to Stromboli.'

But by now she only had eyes for Rossellini. Drawn by the scent of scandal, reporters and photographers from around the globe descended on the small volcanic island of Stromboli. The illicit honeymoon of Bergman and Rossellini had suddenly become world news, pushing the Cold War, the hydrogen bomb and other trifling matters from the headlines. Ingrid's audiences everywhere were shocked to see their virtuous St Joan playing the role of an adulteress. But Ingrid no longer cared what the public thought – she was in love. Roberto Rossellini had become the most important person in her life.

'Roberto had the same feelings as I did,' she confessed; 'he possessed understanding and knowledge, generosity and love. We lived on the edge of a volcano and we were happy.'

Unfortunately for the two lovers, however, the volcano was soon to erupt. Realising that she could not live without Rossellini, Ingrid wrote to her husband asking for a divorce. Petter immediately flew to Italy to try to change her mind. In a hotel lounge in Messina, Sicily, the beautiful actress and her lover were confronted by Petter Lindstrom in a meeting charged with tension. In fact, Rossellini played the part of a jealous husband far better than the cool Lindstrom, dramatically threatening to shoot himself if Ingrid returned to America.

When the actress and her husband locked themselves in a bedroom to talk privately, Roberto telephoned the local police and told them he had an emergency on his hands. When the police arrived, expecting to find a Mafia feud in progress, the impetuous director demanded that they break down the bedroom door and arrest Lindstrom for kidnapping the woman he adored. The officer in charge took stock of the situation and sensibly refused. Determined not to lose Ingrid back to her husband, Roberto stationed his friends at every exit and circled the hotel repeatedly in his powerful red Ferrari. Eventually Lindstrom admitted defeat and returned to the United States.

The volcano finally erupted when Ingrid found she was pregnant with Rossellini's child. A tremendous crowd of pressmen besieged the nursing home in Rome where she went to have the baby. Still legally married to Lindstrom, with the divorce settlement yet in progress, Ingrid was painted by the media as a scarlet woman. With ironical timing she gave birth to a baby son on the same day as the gala premiere of Anna Magnani's *Volcano*. Magnani was a former mistress of Rossellini's and had been first choice for the lead role in *Stromboli*.

America was outraged. The League of Catholic Mothers picketed Bergman's films and Senator Edwin Johnson ranted that the actress had 'plunged from the pinnacle of respect' to 'the gutter', and that Rossellini was nothing but a 'vile and unspeakable love pirate'. In Hollywood, a town not famous for its high moral standards, Ingrid's stock was at an all-time low. The actress's crime, it seemed, was not so much her infidelity, but her refusal to hide the love she felt for Roberto. With the strange hypocrisy of the

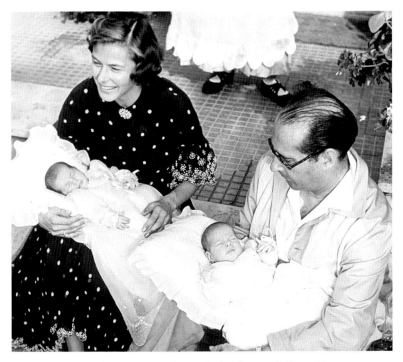

Ingrid Bergman and Roberto Rossellini with daughters Isabella and Isotta

times the public turned its back on Ingrid and her career was effectively finished. In 1952, she gave birth to twins Isotta and Isabella. She continued to act when she could, winning her second Academy Award for her starring role in *Anastasia* (1956), and she also later won an Emmy for her depiction of Israeli Prime Minister Golda Meir in the TV mini-series *A Woman Named Golda*. She died in London in 1982 at the age of 67. To the end, she had no regrets.

The price for her love with Rossellini was high, but Ingrid Bergman showed that she was prepared to pay in full.

ELIZABETH TAYLOR
AND RICHARD BURTON

She has often been called the most beautiful woman in the world, her combination of violet eyes and ebony hair the stuff of poetry. And her life has been as remarkable as her looks: a film star since childhood, fabulously wealthy, many times married. She is Elizabeth Taylor.

He was the impoverished son of a Welsh coal miner, whose brooding good looks and beautiful voice saved him from following his father down the mine. He was Richard Burton. Alone, each was a legend in the acting world. Together, they were dynamite.

They swore – twice – to have and to hold one another until 'death do us part', and finally it was only death that did part them. Neither Liz nor Richard ever seriously claimed to be faithful to the other. But there was no doubt that they were held together through marriage, divorce and remarriage by a love of such intensity that neither could ever fully escape it.

Liz was no virgin when she met Richard. She had already been married four times – to Conrad Hilton, Michael Wilding, Mike Todd and Eddie Fisher. Richard had only been married once before, but he had a reputation for being devastating with women – many, many women.

They met in 1962 on the set of *Cleopatra*. The film was dismissed by the critics, but still they were playing the leads in one of the greatest love stories of all time. The romance was infectious, and the result was inevitable.

'Has anyone ever told you you're a very pretty girl?' were the first words Richard spoke to Liz. A casual piece of underplaying that belied the flame that had sprung into being between them.

'She is everything I want in a woman,' he said shortly afterwards. 'She is quite unlike any woman I have ever known. She makes me not want to know any other woman. I dream of her. She will be my greatest happiness.'

And so she was. She was also his greatest misery. Their love was a strange mixture of passion and antagonism; their passion almost seemed to feed on their antagonism. Almost as soon as they were married in 1963, it seemed they were fighting furiously, in private and in public. But at night they fell into each other's arms and renewed their love.

Their battles were acrimonious, often vicious, and well-recorded by the world's press. 'You know,' Liz told reporters in their home in Hampstead, London, 'in one film he had three girlfriends. He had to keep somebody posted on the dressing room door in case they bumped into each other.'

Richard was just as likely to call Liz 'Fatty' as 'Darling' in front of the paparazzi. Their constant clashes were often embarrassing

Richard Burton and Elizabeth Taylor: an all-consuming passion.

for those around them, but they seemed to revel in the friction. They tore at each other's egos. He played on her fears of her beauty fading, of gaining weight; she taunted him about the series of mediocre films he made, in which all his early promise seemed to have dissipated. Their work together suffered under the strain of their bickering; the films in which they both played – *The VIPs*, *The Sandpiper*, *The Comedians*, *Boom* – were critical if not box-office failures. In only one did the tangled emotions that welded them together shine through – the 1966 masterpiece *Who's Afraid of Virginia Woolf?* It was a film in which they almost seemed to be playing themselves: boozy, brawling, tormenting each other, indissolubly linked together.

They fought and they loved, reflecting the intensity of their strange and passionate natures. 'We slap each other,' said Liz, 'then we become quiet. We embrace. Then we go into the other room and make love.'

But then the fighting stopped. And as peace grew between the tempestuous pair so their passion faded. There came the time when they didn't fight at all. But they didn't make love either. It was time, they decided sadly after ten years of stormy marriage, for divorce. And divorced they were – something that had once seemed impossible.

Nor was it possible for long. 'Our divorce was the most ridiculous in history,' said Burton. It only lasted fourteen months. During this period of estrangement their love flared once more. Legally no longer married, they sought consolation with other lovers but both recognised the inevitable: neither could escape, neither wanted to escape, there was nothing and nobody in the world either wanted more than the other. So they got married again.

And it was exactly the same as before. They fought bitterly, viciously, without mercy, and they made love wildly and tenderly, then started all over again. They were strong people, people who could live on a pinnacle of passion and emotional violence no ordinary human being could sustain. In the end, however, nobody could tolerate the strain of a relationship like theirs. Within a few weeks their second marriage began to crumble. They divorced again. It seemed that Richard and Liz had finally come to the end.

They married other people, once more seeking escape from

each other in different arms. But the love between Richard Burton and Elizabeth Taylor was not a love that could be escaped – except by one road. Richard took that road. They had sworn to have and to hold until death. And finally death parted them forever. In 1984, Richard Burton died of a brain haemorrhage at his Celigny villa in Switzerland. He was 58 years old. The famous and the rich and the powerful attended his funeral. Elizabeth Taylor did not. Burton's widow, Sally, threatened to walk out if Liz attended. So she stayed away.

Shortly after the funeral a sombrely dressed woman was spotted at dawn standing vigil at the new grave. 'I just wanted to say goodbye privately,' whispered Elizabeth Taylor. Perhaps she was thinking of the words that had been spoken over Richard's grave, the words of fellow Welshman Dylan Thomas: 'Do not go gentle into that dark night; rage, rage, against the dying of the light …'

Liz Taylor knew that Richard Burton would not have gone gently; it was not in his nature. He lived hard and fast. The most constant element in his turbulent life was his consuming love for Liz.

She has lived life to the full since losing Richard. A devoted mother, grandmother and great-grandmother, she is a successful businesswoman and has dedicated herself tirelessly to charity work, in particular to the fight against AIDS. 'I've been through it all, baby. I'm Mother Courage,' she says as she reviews her life.

Still beautiful in her early seventies, Liz continues to act. In 2001, she appeared in the made-for-TV movie *These Old Broads*, which showed she still has what it takes. Richard would have approved.

PAUL NEWMAN
AND JOANNE WOODWARD

Why do Paul Newman and Joanne Woodward have a near-perfect marriage?

'We are sex maniacs,' Joanne replies baldly. She is smiling.

'For two people with almost nothing in common, we have an uncommonly good marriage,' says Paul. He is smiling too.

'It lasts because she's marvellous,' he adds. This time he's serious.

The marriage that has been called a beer/champagne union has lasted for almost fifty years. It has weathered the storms of conflicting egos, conflicting interests, the problem of working in the same industry, the many problems of raising a family and the tragedy of the death of Paul's son, Scott.

Paul Newman was born in 1925 in Cleveland, Ohio. He had a burning desire to be an actor from an early age and studied at Yale University Drama school and later at Lee Strasberg's legendary Actors' Studio. After appearing in television dramas and on stage, he made his screen debut in *The Silver Chalice* in 1955, a film that still makes him cringe. But his second film, *Somebody Up There Likes Me*, made him a star in 1956.

The public raved about his classic profile, sensual mouth and dazzling bright blue eyes. One admiring columnist went so far as to write that his eyes looked 'as if they have just finished having a shower'. Paul stood for everything America wanted from a movie idol. He portrayed rebellious characters with charm and cool detachment, and projected enormous sex appeal. He was hailed as the new James Dean and cast in a succession of films that capitalised on his charisma and good looks. During the 1960s, he created his four most memorable characters in *The Hustler* (1961), *Hud* (1963), *Cool Hand Luke* (1967) and *Butch Cassidy and the Sundance Kid* (1969).

Joanne was born in 1930 in Thomasville, Georgia. Like Paul, her main ambition in life was to act. She studied at the Neighborhood Playhouse in New York and soon became known as an intelligent and thoughtful actress. It was while she was understudying the Kim Novak part in the original stage version of *Picnic* that she first met Paul. They were instantly attracted to each other. They were both passionately interested in acting and politics, and they spent hours debating theories of acting and discussing the world's problems. Inevitably, they fell in love. So why didn't they get married?

'Well, for one thing, Paul was married,' says Joanne, 'and although that marriage was over, the decision of getting a divorce was perhaps the greatest in his life. He has that Victorian attitude to such things, you see.'

For the next seven years they threw themselves into their work. In 1957 Joanne won the Best Actress Oscar for her brilliant portrayal of a split personality in *The Three Faces of Eve*. In 1958 they both starred in *The Long Hot Summer*. Whether it was working together or because Paul had finally worked out his problems with his divorce, or simply the fact that seven years was a long time to test a relationship – who knows? – that was when they decided to get married.

'We were married finally in – of all strange places – a hotel in Las Vegas which gave us the bridal suite, the wedding cake, and most of the wedding guests, some of whom I haven't seen again since that day,' recalls Joanne. 'When the preacher had finished the ceremony, instead of kissing one another we surprised our best man by simply falling into one another's arms with a sigh of relief. I suppose Peter Ustinov was right when he said that in our lives together we had "shut out the draughts of difference".'

'Shutting out the draughts of difference' is the phrase that best sums up the Newman/Woodward marriage. They are as alike as chalk and cheese. Paul is very much an outdoors man, whereas Joanne likes books, needlepoint and the theatre. Paul's great passion is car racing; Joanne's is ballet. When she attended one of her husband's races in California, Paul rolled his eyes and grinned, 'This one's gonna cost me ten ballets.'

But they don't let their differences get in the way of their love for each other.

'Certainly we're different,' says Joanne; 'that's what keeps a marriage alive, plus the fact that I adore him. Just that. But think how boring a marriage would be if we were the same.'

Paul Newman and Joanne Woodward: one of Hollywood's greatest and most enduring affairs.

The key to their happiness is compromise. 'I hate flying,' Joanne says, 'but I will fly to be with him when he is working somewhere. I hate skiing, but I go on skiing holidays just to be able to have dinner with him. He hates ballet, but he'll come because I like it and he'll listen when I tell him how a pianist plays at a concert, although he'd prefer to be at a fight or a car race.'

'Actually, there's no more danger in racing a car on the amateur circuit than going up in a helicopter,' Paul says, somewhat defensively. 'When Joanne first watched me race a car she went bananas. She didn't care for it at all. But I wasn't going to stop. You can't live your life totally for other people.'

Although Paul refused to give up his daredevil hobby, he also went out of his way to help Joanne with her passion. As a special favour to her he narrated an hour-long *Dance in America* programme starring the American Ballet Theatre.

One of the main problems that Joanne has had to contend with is Paul's monumental sex appeal. When he walked into restaurants strangers used to rip his dark glasses off to catch a glimpse of those famous blue eyes, on aeroplanes passengers would pluck at his clothes, and everywhere he went fans pestered him for autographs. Joanne, on the other hand, had no such problems. People rarely recognised her. This would have made most women jealous, but Joanne comments simply: 'If the marriage is strong enough, it will probably survive. If there are weaknesses in the marriage that are unbearable, it probably won't. As a female I think that is all the more reason not to be so dependent upon marriage as the total of one's life, because so often break-ups do happen.'

Paul continues to make films, winning a total of eight Academy Award nominations and two Oscars, but he has long found more satisfaction in directing films than in starring in them, frequently casting Joanne as his leading lady. *Rachel, Rachel* (1968) and *The Effects of Gamma Rays on Man-in-the-Moon Marigolds* (1972) were both gentle, richly emotional showcases for her talents.

'She's a brilliant actress,' says Paul.

'And he's a great director,' Joanne smiles.

They sound like a mutual admiration society – which they are, most of the time. There have been problems, mostly for Joanne. When she married Paul she gained a ready-made family of three small children, and went on to have three daughters with him; not so easy when you have a career of your own. 'It doesn't make it any easier for any of us that the kids have a superstar for a father,' she says. 'It gives them a strange sense of values that are very difficult to combat. You somehow grow up with the idea that no matter what, Daddy can fix it. But after a while the time has to come when Daddy can't fix it; you must do it on your own.'

The time came when neither superstar Daddy nor loving stepmother could fix things for Paul's son Scott. In 1978 he died from an accidental overdose of tranquillisers and alcohol. Paul blamed himself for his son's death and refused to talk about the tragedy. He and Joanne founded the Scott Newman Foundation to inform school students about the perils of drug addiction. 'This may sound corny but we just didn't want Scott to have lived in vain,' says Joanne.

Paul and Joanne have continued to combine their acting careers, making *Mr and Mrs Bridge* together in 1990. They have also continued to collaborate closely on charity work, sponsoring a Save the Children foster parent campaign and creating The Hole in the Wall Camp for children with cancer and other life-threatening diseases. Paul has created and marketed his own salad dressing, which has grown into a multi-million-dollar business from which all profits are donated to 80 different charities.

The Newmans seem to have it all – they're great actors, they're great humanitarians and they have a great marriage. And the secret to their happiness?

'We are still lovers,' Joanne smiles. 'However, being married to Paul Newman is a college education. You end up getting a degree in joy and endurance.'

To Paul, the reason why they are still together after almost half a century is simple. 'She's a sexpot,' he says emphatically.